A Summer to Remember

VICTORIA COOKE

ONE PLACE. MANY STORIES

HQ
An imprint of HarperCollins*Publishers* Ltd
1 London Bridge Street
London SE1 9GF

This paperback edition 2019

First published in Great Britain by
HQ, an imprint of HarperCollins*Publishers* Ltd 2019
Copyright © Victoria Cooke 2019

Victoria Cooke asserts the moral right to be
identified as the author of this work.
A catalogue record for this book is
available from the British Library.

ISBN: 978-0-00-833102-3

MIX
Paper from
responsible sources
FSC® C007454

This book is produced from independently certified FSC™ paper
to ensure responsible forest management.

For more information visit: www.harpercollins.co.uk/green

Printed and bound in Great Britain by
CPI Group (UK) Ltd, Croydon, CR0 4YY

For my nanna, Lillian.
For your sense of humour, strength and determination.
xxx

PROLOGUE

2010

The black and white chequered floor whizzes past. Like a psyche-delic trip, it isn't real. I know that I'm running. I can't feel my limbs moving, just the vague sensation of the air resistance caused by the motion. I'm on autopilot, and the only thing tying me to the reality of where I am, is the pungent smell of disinfectant that's been with me at every turn.

I stop abruptly, almost colliding with a person dressed head-to-toe in baggy green scrubs. My heart pounds in my chest. I look down at my hand, the knuckles white, still clutching my phone from when I got the call. It can only have been twenty minutes ago. It's hard to tell because it feels like a lifetime has passed. The surgeon seems to understand that I can't speak; his features are barely displaced, neutral, but there's something lurking in his earthy eyes. Sympathy? 'Mrs Butterfield?' he asks. I nod, my mouth like Velcro, my brain too disengaged to speak.

'Mrs Butterfield, I'm sorry. We did everything we could.'

Did?

You can't have.

The blood pumping in my ears is deafening. Barbed wire is wrenched from the pit of my stomach, right up through my oesophagus. I've never felt pain like it. My legs give way, unable to bear the weight of the surgeon's words and my knees crash to the floor.

I'm vaguely aware of a low, drawn-out wail. It's me. The surgeon crouches down and looks me directly in the eyes. The

1

warmth of his chestnut-brown gaze anchors me, and I'm able to gather tendrils of composure. I take a breath.

'Mrs Butterfield, is there anyone we can call for you?'

I shake my head. I only have one person, and now he's dead.

CHAPTER 1

2018

'Eurgh.' I slam the pearlescent invite down by the kettle. '*Plus one*,' I say in a mocking tone. Coco cocks her head to the side like she's trying to understand me, and I cup her fluffy face.

'I know, I don't get it either.' My cat's emerald eyes are still intent on me so, glad of an audience, I carry on.

'Why Bridget has to assume I need someone by my side is beyond me. As if I'm not capable of going to a wedding without a *plus one*. It's not nineteen blooming twenty. I don't need a chaperone. Perhaps I'll take you, Coco. That'll teach her.' I tickle her under her chin and she stretches out lazily. I'm only half joking.

As I pour my first coffee of the day, my phone rings. 'Someone's ears are burning,' I say on answering.

'Really?' Bridget also ignores the need for pleasantries.

'I got your wedding invite,' I say dryly.

'Well, don't sound too enthusiastic about the happiest day of your best friend's life,' she retorts.

'Aren't we a bit old for best friends?'

'Don't change the subject.'

I rub my temples with my thumb and forefinger. 'I'm sorry, Bridge. I just, well … I'd specifically told you I didn't need a plus one.'

'It's just a formality, Sam. Don't be so sensitive. I just wanted you to know the option is there if you did want to bring someone.'

'Well, I don't,' I say, before feeling a little guilty. 'It just seems

3

so old-fashioned, like, the *lil lady* needs a gentleman to escort her.' I put on my best 'Southern Belle' accent, and Bridget giggles.

'I'm sorry,' she says. 'It wasn't meant to offend you.'

'I did warn you,' I scold. 'Look, I'm not on the lookout for a man, nor am I *resigned* to being alone – I'm *happy* with it. People need to stop assuming I need someone. I got the bloody cat everyone thought I should get, okay!'

'I know, I'm sorry. Everyone else will be coupled up, so I just thought if you wanted to bring a *friend*, then you could, that's all.'

'All of my *friends* will already be there.' I'm aware of my exasperated tone so I soften it a little. 'I was just telling Coco that *she* could be my plus one.'

'You'd better bloody well not.' Bridget's stern tone amuses me. I sense that she wouldn't put it past me.

'Oh, now you've made her sad.' Coco looks far from sad as she rubs her face on my balled-up fist. 'I've seen some gorgeous cat dresses on eBay.'

'Bring her and I'll have you both escorted out,' Bridget replies.

'Then stop assuming I can't be single and happy.'

'Fine!' she sighs. 'But send me a picture of one of those cat dresses, it's been a miserable week.'

I'm happy it's time to drop the subject. It may seem like an overreaction, but Bridget knows as well as my other friends do that my frustrations are the result of a good seven years' worth of do-gooders trying to set me up with brothers, colleagues, friends of friends, and even a sister at one point. I'm happy on my own. It's like the saying goes, 'It's better to have loved and lost than to have never loved at all.' All I need are my memories and my cat.

'How's work?' she asks.

I groan, wondering where to start. 'I'm still working my backside off to make the US team. Seventh time lucky, hey?' Every year five people from our offices are chosen to go to Boston for three months to work on a global marketing project with the American head office team. I've tried for seven years – yes, seven years – to make the cut. It's become my obsession.

'Oh Sam, this year has to be your year,' she says sympathetically.

'It's like no matter how hard I try, someone else shines brighter. This year I've worked my backside off and if I'm not chosen, I might start looking somewhere else.' It sounds like I'm being a drama queen, but I've given everything to Pink Apple Advertising and I've been pretty open about wanting to go to Boston. If they don't choose me this year, I don't think they ever will, and that Boston trip is the only real catalyst to a promotion.

'Well, if they don't pick you this time, they don't deserve you.' Bridget sounds distracted, like most people do when I talk about work.

I stifle a sigh. My friends will never understand how much it means to me. 'The invites are gorgeous, by the way,' I say, stroking the silver ribbon running down the thick, shimmery cream card with embossed dusky pink lettering. She was right when she said it will be the best day of her life.

5

My breath catches in my throat. There he is, chewing the corner of his thumbnail nervously. He looks so vulnerable standing there in his navy suit and tie. When his eyes set upon mine, I can feel their warmth envelop me. His head tilts ever-so-slightly to the side and his watery eyes crinkle when he smiles. I glance down at my simple ivory dress, self-consciously smoothing out non-existent wrinkles. My mum had steamed the thing to death, fussing about invisible creases and generally adding to my overall nervousness.

The music starts, a piano instrumental of Canon in D, and butterflies beat venomously in my stomach when the expectant faces turn towards me. My mum is there, at the front with her new olive-coloured organza hat on. She's clutching a tissue to her face.

'Are you ready, pumpkin?' my dad whispers in my ear. Normally, I'd tell him not to call me that, but today I'm too nervous to care.

I grip my dad's arm tighter in mine, clutch my bouquet of white lilies with the other and take a deep breath before setting off. It's a blur as we walk down the small aisle, past a handful of close friends and family, to where Kev is waiting. When I join him, he gives my hand a gentle squeeze and leans in close and breathes into my ear.

'You … are … beautiful.'

I feel his words.

Suddenly the room is ours and ours alone.

CHAPTER 2

2018

I smooth down the skirt of my Ted Baker dress as I walk into the church, smiling as I take in the beautiful flower displays. Bridget has chosen pageboys and flower girls instead of brides-maids so that she didn't have to choose between her closest friends or fork out for a bazillion extortionately priced dresses. To be honest, I was quite relieved when she told me. Being plucked, waxed and spray-tanned within an inch of my life didn't really appeal, though I have shaved my legs for the occa-sion. I've worn this dress to three recent weddings because it fits my slender five-foot-five frame perfectly. It has a pencil skirt in shades of metallic pink and rose gold, with a plain white chiffon top. My make-up is minimal, and my dark hair hangs in loose waves which look like they dried that way after my morning surf but in actual fact took the hairdresser thirty minutes of wanding, teasing and praying to the hair gods for. I've never surfed in my life. I don't go in the sea ever – too much uncertainty lurking under that strange foamy stuff which floats on the surface.

Viv, Sarah and their husbands are easy to spot as I make my way down the aisle. I slide into the spot they've saved for me next to Viv.

'It could be you next,' Viv gushes as I place my bag on the floor. Seriously, I've just sat down. It's as if she doesn't know better, except for the fact that she bloody well does. I'm about to say something about hell freezing over first but second guess myself. Can you say the word 'hell' in church? The last time I paid any attention to religion was the Harvest festival in 1996, and that was only because the vicar looked a little bit like Mark Owen. Am I about to be struck down by lightning? Maybe I should cross myself.

'So, you didn't bring anyone then?' Sarah leans across to ask. She kind of purses her lips in a sympathetic way. I don't reply, but seriously, it's okay to go to a wedding alone. It's like these people don't even know me, despite the fact we've been friends since Bridget introduced us over seven years ago.

When I first met these women, I'd just moved to London. I couldn't bear to stay in our village after losing Kev. I needed a clean slate. My old life had finished, and I needed something completely different. It was almost a year to the day I'd lost Kev when I bumped into Bridget in the foyer at work. And I mean literally bumped into her, knocking her espresso out of her hand so hard that it flew over her shoulder, luckily without spilling so much as a drop on her cream suit. She worked for a different company in the same building, and being new to London, I was hugely intimidated by her. She laughed off the faux pas and said I looked like I needed a stiff drink. We met up after work, I told her my story, and the rest is history.

Viv and Sarah are Bridget's close friends, but soon became mine too. At first, they took pity on me, listened to my endless stories about Kev and offered sympathy whilst I revelled in my new friendship group. But before long, they started to talk about me 'putting myself back out there'. I've been defending my single-hood ever since.

I give her a tight smile and nod. It's the same old story. Sympathetic glances when people learn you're single in your mid (okay, late) thirties, and the comments are always along the lines of 'you'll meet someone soon.' In some ways, I feel sorry for them, thinking you need a man to make your life better. A man can't make your life better. Only a soulmate can even come close to doing that, and I'd already found mine.

The organ starts to play. The dull sound of pressurised air being forced through the pipes reminds me of death. Why they play this instrument at weddings is beyond me. Everyone turns to catch the first glimpse of the bride. Bridget looks stunning in a simple silk gown with capped lace sleeves and a diamanté-encrusted waistband. Her blonde hair is in a neat chignon with some loose curls framing her face. She smiles at us as she walks past, her rosy cheeks and sparkling eyes radiating happiness. I remember that feeling too, and I cherish it.

***

Thank god. I swipe a welcome Pimm's on arrival at the hotel reception, and it goes down rather too easily. Churches are tinged with the memory of Kev's funeral. Whilst the funeral itself is a blur, I've never felt comfortable in one since.

'Slow down, Sam, it's only noon,' Sarah says, taking mouse-like sips from her own.

'You do you, okay?' I say, before realising I sound harsh. 'Sorry. I love weddings and I love seeing my friends happy, but they do bring back memories.'

Sarah strokes my arm. 'We get it, hon, but if you get sloshed and make a prized tit out of yourself, you'll regret it.'

'That happened one time,' I say with an eye-roll.

'Yes, and I forgave you because everything was still raw and because I wasn't letting anything spoil my big day. You need to be here for Bridget today.' Her eyes bore into me, but their intensity is broken by the waiter offering more Pimm's. I decline and look pointedly at Sarah, who wears a smug expression.

Across the foyer of the hotel, Bridget and her new husband Alex are posing for photographs. The photographer is shepherding miniature humans into a line. It's like a comedy sketch:

9

just as he manages to get one end of the line straight, he loses a child from the other end. His face is starting to redden.

'We should find our table,' Viv says, moving us on.

The tables are not numbered or named like usual. Instead, we have to find ours by working out the punchline of a joke. 'Well, Mrs Killjoy, you'll never find your table,' I whisper to Sarah, who gives me a tight smile and shakes her head. The joke for our table reads: 'What happens when Iron Man takes off his suit?' Viv and Sarah exchange confused glances.

'Oh, come on,' I say. 'Seriously?'

They both shake their heads. I look to John and Mark, their husbands, who are wearing equally blank expressions.

'He's Stark naked! Tony Stark?' I say, chuckling in response to a few groans. I remember Bridget running that one past me and I thought it was hilarious.

We find our table, and sure enough, the centre plaque reads 'He's Stark naked'. As we sit down we watch several bewildered guests wandering around in confusion.

'Are you struggling?' I say to an elderly gentleman hovering by our table.

'Just a little.'

'What's your clue?'

'RIP water.' Puzzlement is etched into his brow. 'It doesn't even sound like a joke.'

I stifle a smirk. 'You will be *mist*,' I say, gesturing to the table to my right. I turn to the others. 'I think this is more fun than the actual wedding.'

'I'm just glad Bridget and Alex found one another, because they're the only two people who get these jokes.' Sarah takes the wine from the centre of the table and fills us up.

'So, I'm allowed to drink now?' I say sarcastically.

Sarah rolls her eyes. 'I was just looking out for you.'

I'm about to retort when Viv's husband, John, interrupts me.

'So, Sam, no handsome prince on the horizon yet?'

'Nope.' I take a long sip of wine in place of a groan.

He tilts his head to the side. 'You'll meet someone soon.' And there it is. I notice Viv giving him 'a look', which I'm grateful for. Maybe Bridget has had a word.

A loud gong interrupts the slightly awkward silence which ensues. 'All rise, for the bride and groom.'

There's a loud cheer and a round of applause as Bridget and Alex enter and take their seats at the top table. The happiness radiates from the pair of them and whilst I'm finding this whole day a little difficult, the smiles they wear are infectious. Not all romances are doomed and the love they have for one another is real, it only takes a quick glance in their direction to see that. They look beautiful together and the solid block of ice in my chest starts to thaw with the warmth that breaks through from just looking at them. I genuinely wish them a long lifetime of happiness.

CHAPTER 3

Pick up, pick up, pick up. I can't contain my excitement and Bridget, who always answers her phone on the first ring, is taking an age to answer today.

'Sam, hi.' She sounds breathless when she does pick up.

'Sorry, I haven't interrupted anything, have I?' It's early evening and her honeymoon was weeks ago so I hope not, but they are still technically newlyweds (eurgh).

'No, not at all. Just had to run downstairs to get my phone. What's up?'

'I did it! I've finally been selected to go to Boston.' I actually dance a little as I say the words.

'Oh my god, Sam, that's great. You've wanted this for so long!' She squeals so loudly I have to hold the phone away from my ear.

'I know! Finally, my boss has seen that I'm capable of bigger things.' God, for the first few years I didn't think I'd get any further than just making coffee and shredding crappy marketing campaigns. But then I got more responsibility, working on my own campaigns for local businesses which went down really well and that led to being part of a team, working on some national campaigns but after that, I got wedged in a giant rut, which I've been trying to claw my way out of for the past two years.

'Oh, Sam, congratulations. I'm so happy for you. When do you go?'

'A week on Sunday.' My insides squeeze with excitement.

'That's too soon! We need to throw you a going away party.'

'It's only three months. It doesn't warrant a leaving party.'

12

'Drinks then?'

If I'm honest, drinks in my honour does sound good. Aside from my wedding, I'm not sure it's ever happened before. 'Okay, drinks. Does Saturday night work?'

***

On my way into the bar, my phone begins to vibrate in my bag. Thinking it's one of the girls ringing to say they're running late, I stand to the side of the door and take it out. The name on the screen knocks the wind out of my sails.

Mum mobile

I watch the screen, willing it to stop. The red and green circles seem to brighten; accept or reject? The name grows bigger on the screen and the vibration becomes more intense.

Then it stops. I exhale and slump against the wall. Why would she ring? I'd sent my dad a birthday card about a week ago and I mentioned the job in Boston. It could be about that. But why would she ring? I stuff my phone back in my bag and head inside.

'Congratulations,' Viv says as the waitress places four mojitos on the table of our booth. 'You finally made the US team!'

Excited butterflies flutter in my stomach. 'I know, I'm hoping to make a good impression so I'll be on future projects. Three months in Boston each summer – yes please!'

After my third cocktail, I turn to my friends. 'So, which one of you is going to look after Coco while I'm away?' I say, feeling a little tipsy.

There are some animated glances around the room, and I swear I see tumbleweed roll past.

'Oh, come on. She's adorable.'

'It's not that, it's the fact you're leaving tomorrow and haven't found somewhere for her yet,' Viv says.

'Oh, come on. You lot convinced me to get a cat, I knew one of you would mind her.'

'She's the Devil incarnate,' Sarah says, to murmurs of agreement.

'You guys told me to get a pet, so she's partly your responsibility.' I put on a mocking voice. 'Get a pet, Sam, so you never have to go home to an empty flat, Sam.'

Bridget rolls her eyes. 'Okay, I'll do it. But if she so much as unsheathes a claw in my general direction, she's going straight to the cattery.'

'Deal.' I raise my glass. Coco will scratch the hell out of her furniture, but Bridget is far too soft to send her away.

'Okay, now that awkwardness is over,' Bridget says, 'I'd like to say a few words.'

'God, she's drunk,' Sarah stage-whispers, earning herself a sideways glance from Bridget, who has actually stood up in readiness for the moment.

'Sam, I know we've given you a hard time about being single, but I want you to know that we've always just wanted the best for you. Getting married is what's expected, but I've come to realise that you are stronger than us.' Her voice wobbles a little, and she takes a sip of her cocktail in what I assume is an attempt to disguise it. 'I guess I thought you were just *saying* you wanted to be single because it was easier than admitting you wanted a partner but couldn't find one, but now I realise that you really are fine on your own. Look at what you've achieved. You're going on a new adventure, and we know you'll be fine. Sam, we love you so much.' She raises her glass. 'To Sam.'

'To Sam,' Viv and Sarah chorus.

'Thank you.' I look at each of them one by one. 'I'm going to miss you, ladies,' I say, suddenly overwhelmed by a stab of emotion. 'I love you three.' Friendships haven't always come easy to me, so the emotion probably chokes me a little more than it would someone else.

'Group hug!' Sarah shouts, wrapping her arms around us all, and we collapse into fits of laughter.

CHAPTER 4

The sky is the most intense blue I've ever seen. Shimmering light bounces off the windows of passing boats and hits the top of the water as I sit looking out across Boston Harbor. The horn of a departing ferry blasts. This place is insane, and I've only been here a few hours. I'm alone, outside a bar watching the boats come and go. The other four members of the team went straight to the company apartment we're staying in, saying they wanted to go to bed, but they've all been here before. It's my first visit, so I'm determined to take everything in and enjoy each second that I'm not in the office. I flick through the pictures I've taken on my phone since I arrived. There's one of the *Cheers* bar. My dad used to watch the TV show religiously when I was a kid, and before I can talk myself out of it, I send the picture to him and my mum with a brief message.

Arrived safely

I feel guilty that I can't write any more but hope they'll see it as me reaching out.

Once I've finished my drink, I walk to the harbour wall and hold my phone up high to try and take a decent selfie to send to the girls. The sun is starting to sink close to the horizon, casting beautiful swaths of pink and orange across the sky which are reflected in the water. It's no use; I'd need Inspector Gadget's arms to be able to capture the beauty and not just a close-up mugshot of myself. As I stretch and twist, I notice a man a few feet away, staring out across the water. 'Excuse me,' I say, flashing my most charming smile. He turns to me with a look of disdain, as though I'd just insulted his dear granny's baking or something.

He doesn't reply but he stands there, continuing to look at me with increased impatience.

'I …' His thunderous face causes me to falter. 'I wondered if you wouldn't mind taking a quick picture of me, please?'

His eyes flick over me then he turns back to the water. I pause, momentarily unsure of what to do next. I could walk on and pretend I'd not asked, but then I wouldn't get the picture and I'm sure he probably just hadn't heard me. Perhaps he thought I was talking on my phone or something.

'Sorry, I was wondering if you'd mind taking a picture of me with the harbour in the background? It's so beautiful.'

'No,' he says, turning away.

'No?' I blurt. I mean, he's well within his rights to say no but it's just a two-second snap and click. Why won't he just do it? 'No, you don't mind?' I ask, hoping some English charm works on him.

'Yes, I mind, and no, I'm not taking the picture.' His words are made harsher by his Boston twang.

He starts to walk away. I stand there embarrassed and dumbfounded for a moment, but his rudeness rubs at me like sandpaper in the seconds that pass and I can't let it go. I call after him before I've taken time to think it through. 'Excuse me?'

'Go away!' He doesn't even turn to look at me.

'No! I shan't. Where I'm from, we don't speak to people like that.' That isn't strictly true, you only have to be out of change when you're passing a panhandler or caught standing on the left-hand side of an escalator at any tube station to encounter much worse in London. Perhaps I'm jet-lagged or something but I'm so flabbergasted by his attitude over something so small that I can't let it go.

'I don't care.' He makes a flappy shooing gesture with his hand.

Heat intensifies in my chest. I jog after him until I'm beside him, matching his pace. 'There's no need to be so rude. I'm a visitor to the States. Do you know how much money tourism

16

brings in to your country each year?' I really am clutching at straws, but I'm in such complete disbelief, it's lucky I can construct a sentence at all. *Why are my legs still moving?*

'Go away, lady.' He continues to walk. I'm incensed.

'What exactly is your problem?' I prod his shoulder – I don't mean to, it just sort of happens, but finally, he stops walking. He turns to face me, and I'm knocked sideways. I hadn't noticed before because I was so taken aback by his attitude but he has the most compelling sapphire eyes I've ever seen and I'm not prepared for them when they bore into me.

'It's not really any of your business.' He clenches his jaw and the muscles twitch beneath his skin. 'And *you* won't leave me alone.' He runs his fingers through his brown hair, and I try to ignore the fact he's incredibly attractive, because beauty comes from within, and there's a gargoyle residing inside him.

'I … I just wanted you to take a quick photo of me, I'm here alone and … Do you know what? You're not a nice person.'

'And do you know what? I don't really care. I'm sure with your pretty doe-eyed routine you're used to guys running around after you, but today, you picked the wrong guy.'

My eyes feel hot and damp. That hurt because he couldn't be further from the truth. I take a breath to steady my voice. He will not see me cry. 'You have no idea how wrong you are. I'm sorry I asked you.' He shakes his head and walks off.

'I hope you're the only arsehole in Boston,' I yell after him. He flips me the middle finger without so much as a backwards glance, and I'm left to simmer. I drag myself back to the idyllic photo spot, but the sun has dipped below the horizon and the sky has gone all murky grey. I've missed my chance, so instead, I key a message to the girls' WhatsApp group telling them about my first encounter with a local. Despite the fact it's midnight at home, they all reply within minutes.

Viv: Americans are just more direct than us. Don't let him get to you hon xx

17

Sarah: Viv is right. You're in Boston, baby! Enjoy xxx
Bridget: Get a lobster dinner and move on, my love xx

I smile. They're right. I'm tired. Things will look better after a good night's sleep.

***

The next morning, I hit the ground running. Yesterday's arsehole is today's motivation to be professional and great at my job. Oh, who am I kidding? Ninety-nine per cent of my confidence was bought from Hobbs in the form of the smart black skirt and burgundy blouse I'm currently wearing. For added oomph, I'm carrying my 'special occasion only' black Marc Jacobs handbag in an attempt to feel every bit the city girl.

As I negotiate the revolving door to the office, my insides are jelly. The receptionist takes me up to the boardroom where I'll meet the team. Four of them are my English colleagues, who left the apartment earlier than me because they wanted to go to Starbucks, and I wasn't ready. They, being mostly bald men, had considerably less hair to dry than I did.

As we approach the glass-walled boardroom, I glance at them all sat around the table. My inner fire dies a little when it registers that they're all dressed casually. The receptionist is smart in her cropped hound's-tooth pants and purple sweater, so it makes no sense, unless we're kicking off with some practical hands-on work.

'Hi,' I say, feeling a little sick. 'So, do you do casual Friday on a Monday here?' I mean it as a joke to laugh off my blunder but soon realise that my British accent and power dressing probably made it sound like more of an underhand dig, a notion affirmed by a few raised eyebrows and a bit of uncomfortable throat clearing.

'We always dress like this. Do you have a problem with that, ma'am?' the man at the top of the table asks. I'm assuming he's Patrick, the boss.

'Er, no. No problem at all. I was j—'

'Good,' he says, before turning back to the rest of the table. I slip into a chair and take out my file. That wasn't a great start, but I'm determined to make a good impression.

'As I was saying before Victoria Beckham over here interrupted—' he jabs his thumb in my direction, as if anyone was in any doubt, and heat rises up the back of my neck '—Rocks need an international campaign for their sneakers, so we really need to get our heads in the game. This isn't a rebrand, this is a new brand so we have to get it just right.'

I glance at my watch and it's only 8.55 a.m. My chest tightens. I can't believe they started without me. How rude! I look around the table. Tony, Dave, Carl and Steve – my British colleagues – are all dressed down and look completely mortified by my intrusion. The other four men are the Americans; I've yet to learn names but they're all equally unimpressed. But *they* started without *me.*

I keep my mouth shut for the rest of the day. Maybe it's first day nerves or perhaps I'm still knocked by that awful man I met yesterday but I can't seem to unravel the knot in my stomach. When the clock strikes five, I almost race out of the door. Tony catches me up. 'Sorry, Sam, I thought you knew it was a casual office – I'd have said this morning if I saw you.' He looks genuinely sorry.

'It's fine.' I brush my hand through the air. 'Nobody mentioned it, that's all.'

'It was in the itinerary email.' He pulls out his phone and begins scrolling through.

'Really, it's fine.' I don't need him to prove it, I need him to drop it. I'm mortified enough as it is.

He looks up. 'Here it is. "And remember, the Boston office is CW." Casualwear.'

'What? Give me that.' I take the phone from his hand and read it for myself. 'I had this email, but how was I supposed to know

19

CW meant casualwear? I thought it was a direction, like "central west" or something.'

He furrows his brow. 'I'm sorry. We all knew. At least you do now, and tomorrow is a new day. We're going for beers; do you want to join us?'

'No, thanks. I have some shopping to do.'

***

The next day, I turn up in my new casual office wear, courtesy of Abercrombie & Fitch: a bright-green logo-emblazoned T-shirt and a pair of stonewashed jeans that both smell amazing, like the shop. Fortunately, my parting gift when I left the office last night was a pair of Rocks trainers. We were all issued a pair to wear and try and connect with the brand. Mine have a purple and pink graffiti design down the sides and glittery silver laces. I feel like a twelve-year-old again, but at least today I'll fit in. And they are bloomin' comfy.

When I enter the boardroom, everyone is already sitting down drinking coffee. 'Morning,' I say with as much cheer as I can muster. I repeat Tony's mantra: *Today is a new day*. There are a few sullen nods, but nobody calls me Victoria Beckham, so I assume I'm already making a better impression. No offence to Victoria, of course – I love her. It just didn't take Uri Geller to read Patrick's mind and determine the remark was intended to be derogatory.

I withhold anything that could be construed as over-zealous and recognise the need for measured, calm and quality input. It's hard because I'm bursting with ideas, and nobody seems to be getting it; they basically just want to rip off the well-known and well-bejazzled little girls' favourite Strides brand which I don't think Rocks will go for. The owners are two rapping megastars who I'd never come across before, but I did my research and apparently they're triple platinum and something of a big deal.

'I think Rocks have more edge than that,' I say as everyone discusses tweens wearing denim skirts with colourful, sparkly ribbons in their pigtailed hair.

Nobody listens. It's the second, no, third most frustrating thing that's happened since I arrived. I speak up and repeat myself and Patrick raises his eyes wearily.

'Is that so?'

I clear my throat. 'I think Rocks are wanting something a little cooler. Perhaps something aimed at older teens too. I don't think they're going to see Strides as their main competitor.'

'What's your name, Beckham?'

My stomach is on a spin-cycle, but I manage to reply. 'Er, Sam.'

'Sam, with all *due* respect, this ain't my first rodeo.' He laughs at his own joke and glances around to rouse a few laughs from around the table. I want to say something, but after that encounter by the harbour the other day, I just can't bring myself to. I hate to admit it, but I'm two days into my dream gig and I already want to go home.

CHAPTER 5

On Thursday, Patrick presents us with some rough visuals based on our discussions from the first few days. They're exactly how I imagined they'd be. They look great, but they have gone with a young girl, aged about ten or eleven, with pigtailed hair and pink ribbons, riding a scooter. I get that a girl like that would love these shoes, but I just can't see Rocks going for this. I look around the table and see nods of approval. Is it really just me that disagrees with this campaign? I can't just sit back and watch them go down this rabbit-hole of failure.

I take a deep breath. 'Okay, Patrick. I respect the work your team has put in here, it looks fantastic, but I still don't think we're pitching the brand to the right market.'

He looks at me with bemusement but gives a tired, one-handed gesture for me to continue.

'I think we need to go older, we need diversity. We're not selling JoJo Siwa bows here, or Strides to little girls. We're selling a rappers' brand to young people. This girl—' I point to the poster mock-up '—will buy the shoes regardless. But boys won't, teens won't, and people who like the rappers won't. We can come up with something different, fresh and powerful if we just think outside the box a little.' I realise I've half risen from my seat with boldness and slide back down into it now I'm finished, my Erin Brockovich confidence draining away.

Patrick raises his eyebrows. 'Thank you for your input, Sam. I appreciate that you're new here, and you're off your leash and it's all very exciting and whatnot—' did he just wave his arms around at me? '—but if you just pipe down a little and let those of us with experience nail this campaign down, we can all knock this ball out of the water and go home on time.'

Knock the ball out of the water? Does he mean ballpark? Or like a fish out of water? *I don't get it.* I glance around the room for other signs of confusion but instead just see several disgruntled faces looking my way. The back of my neck starts to burn and the heat creeps around and up to my cheeks. With nothing left to offer, I nod.

'Why don't you go get us some coffees to see us through the morning, and when you're back we can look at putting you to work with Tony and Dave?'

When I catch Tony's eye, he gives me a sympathetic smile whilst Dave rolls his eyes when he thinks I'm not looking. *Great.*

When I leave the office that evening, Tony catches me up. 'Fancy going for a drink tonight?'

'Who with?' I ask suspiciously. I can't cope with seeing Patrick or Dave, or anyone else from the office for that matter.

'Just me,' Tony says with a smile.

'In that case, yes. I could really do with a drink.'

We find a little bar a few blocks down from the office. It's dingy inside but quiet aside from a few lone drinkers who look like they've been here a while.

'What are you drinking?' Tony asks as we take a seat at the bar.

'Just a beer for me.'

While the bartender gets our drinks, I ask Tony about his wife. 'Pregnant with number three, grumpy as hell. It's one of the reasons I came away when I got the chance.'

'What a catch you are,' I say dryly. 'Husband of the year right here, folks.' I point at him and look animatedly around the bar. The other drinkers look to have fallen asleep.

'She's only in her first trimester so I won't miss anything bar the first scan, and her mother is helping with the boys. I wanted

23

to keep my hand in with the Boston office even though the timing isn't great.'

'Well, if she's okay with it …' I shrug.

Tony turns on his stool to face me. 'You were brave standing up to Patrick today.'

'Well, I don't feel very brave. I feel very stupid.'

The bartender places two beers down and slides a paper receipt over to Tony. I snatch it before he has time to respond. 'I'll get these.'

'Thanks,' he says. 'I don't think you were stupid today. I think you were sticking up for your vision for the project, and that isn't an easy thing to do.'

'Especially when nobody shares that vision.' I lean on the bar to look him properly in the eye. 'Do you really think Rocks are going to go for the campaign as it stands?'

Tony shrugs. 'Maybe, maybe not. Just because Rocks is owned by two rappers, doesn't mean their target audience for these shoes have to reflect that. The Barbie doll was designed by a former missile engineer, but his target market wasn't crazed despots.'

'I thought it was invented by an American businesswoman?'

'Ruth Handler invented Barbie using a doll that already existed. The one the engineer designed. Anyway, with regards to our current campaign, it's what the majority believe will work and I'm happy to go along with it.'

'So, you're a yes man?' Oh god. If I'd have just kept my mouth shut a bit longer, perhaps I wouldn't be the office equivalent of a trolley dolly.

'No, well, sort of. I'm talking about choosing your battles. I don't know if the team got this campaign right, but I do know that the others believe they have. So, if Rocks love it, I share in that glory, and if Rocks hate it, we're all in it together.'

'How the hell did you make the team?' I blurt the words out before I have time to smother them with tact.

Fortunately, he laughs. 'Because I'm bloody good at design.'

'But you agree with me?' I press him.

'I'm saying I don't know, but you didn't exactly have solid counter-ideas. Perhaps if you weren't so vague, Patrick would listen.'

'Or perhaps if I was a man? Maybe you could be my voice in future.' I bat my eyelids acrimoniously before rolling my eyes at the ridiculousness of this truth.

'I'm not saying that. C'mon, you pooh-poohed his idea without anything real to offer in return. I mean, look at the shoes.' He sticks out his right foot and twists it from left to right. 'They aren't your usual teen-buy despite what two rappers think.'

I don't believe for a second that Tony thinks this campaign will work. He's always been so sharp and in tune with clients in the past and Pink Apple are renowned for thinking outside of the box – the current proposal is too easy. We don't change our clients' minds, we change their customers' minds. 'What ideas do you think would work?'

He shrugs. 'I don't know. All my ideas have gone into the current proposal—'

'That you hate?' I interject.

'Well come on, have you seen the state of the shoes?' We both look down at our feet again, as if to clarify they haven't miraculously morphed into something fabulous in the space of a few seconds.

'True.'

'But just because I hate it, doesn't mean it won't work.'

I drain the last of my beer and Tony orders two more.

'Fair enough.'

'I'll get these,' Tony says when the second round arrives.

'Damn right you will. It's your turn.'

When Tony pulls his wallet out, he glances at his phone and groans.

'What is it?'

'Carl, Dave and Steve have decided to join us.'

I can only stomach Tony. The conversation will spiral into a pit of misogynistic crap in no time. 'Great. How long have I got to drink my beer before I need to leave?'

'I missed their call so about—'

'Alright, fella,' Dave says, patting Tony on the back.

'Here she is, black-sheep-Beckham,' Steve says, winking at me like he's made a hilarious in-joke.

'You grab a great coffee, Sam, love,' Carl says. I'm sure it's all just banter and everything, but they're already pissing me off, and it's because I know I'm right about the campaign.

'Yours was the one with the extra-special present?' I wink back and Carl's face pales. 'Oh, come on, I'm joking.' I wink again. 'Or am I?'

The three men take the remaining stools along the bar, engulfing Tony and me. We talk about the campaign, and the main theme of the conversation seems to be that Patrick knows what he's doing, and if we all nod along, we get out of the board-room earlier. I don't even protest. If Tony couldn't see where I was coming from, they never will. We have a few more beers, and talk soon revolves around sport, 'her indoors' and some baseball game they're going to.

'I'm going to crash,' I say.

'Want me to walk you back?' Tony asks.

I need some space and being around these guys is giving me a headache. 'No, I'm fine. It isn't far.'

CHAPTER 6

My second week in Boston is no better. By Wednesday I'm ready to book a flight home. When I get back to the apartment after a day of being practically invisible, I slump on the sofa to ponder my defeat. If nobody is going to pay attention to anything I say, what is the point of me being here? I may as well go back to London and be ignored to a slightly lesser extent there. At least I'd see my friends at the weekend.

Needing to vent, I dial Bridget.

'Sam!' she screams, so loud my ears ring.

'Oh, Bridget.' My voice is filled with desperation.

'That's not the tone of a happy camper. What's up?' Her voice vibrates.

'Are you on the cross trainer?'

'Yes,' she puffs. 'In the words of the great and mighty Elphaba, I want to have my arse defying gravity before I go on holiday.'

'Can you get off? I can't talk to you when you're all breathy. It sounds like you're having sex. And I don't think those are quite the right words to the song.'

She giggles. 'Okay, I'm losing the battle against my saggy arse anyway. So, tell me, what's up?'

I decide to get straight to the point. 'I don't fit in and everyone here is horrible.'

'Oh, Sam. It can't be that bad. It's just settling-in nerves. By next week you'll be fine.'

I shake my head even though she can't see me. 'It's different here. It's so male-dominated. They don't listen to a word I say and they even sent me out for doughnuts. Maybe it's just the men here. They're so arrogant, and the UK team seem to lap it up like it's something to aspire to.'

'Listen to me, Sam.' Bridget adopts a stern tone. 'You've waited so long for this opportunity, and you deserve to be there as much as any one of those men. Don't you dare give up so soon.'

'I know, you're right but …'

'There are no buts about it. You're going to see the three months through, and you're going to make yourself heard. Okay?' I know she'll have one hand on her hip and her eyebrows raised.

'Okay.' I sigh.

'I know it's hard.' She softens her tone. 'Why don't you escape the apartment for the weekend and have some *you* time? You're near the coast – pick a beach and stay a night or two in a hotel.'

Being near the coast hadn't really registered with me. Apart from seeing Boston Harbor on my first day and that wasn't exactly enjoyable. I've not thought about anything other than work since but there isn't really anything to stop me. 'Do you know, that's actually a great idea.'

'I know.' She laughs.

We say our goodbyes and the idea of going away and having some 'me' time makes me feel lighter. Not having to see the four, okay three, buffoons (if I exonerate Tony for being half-alright) from work over the weekend is an added bonus too. When I first arrived, I saw an advertisement for ferries to Provincetown down at the harbour. I don't really know anything about the place, but if there are enough people wanting to go to justify a big ferry, it must be alright. A quick Google search confirms that it's perfect. A beachy little town at the tip of Cape Cod, renowned for its artists, tourism and for being a popular holiday spot for the LGBTQ community, which I'm hoping means there's less room for the Carl, Dave and Steve community. It sounds like the perfect getaway.

I book the ferry for Friday evening.

CHAPTER 7

Boston looks stunning as we sail away from it. The sun glints off the skyscrapers, making the whole city twinkle. There's no sign of the ugliness that lurks there, crawling the streets and seeping into the offices.

Ninety minutes later, we pull into the little harbour of Provincetown, framed by low-rise, wooden-cladded buildings and tree-lined hills beyond. Golden sandy beaches run either side of the pier, and the Pilgrim Monument stands tall and proud above everything else. Perhaps I should take a leaf out of its book and on Monday, march into the office tall and proud and demand to be acknowledged. Or something to that effect.

We disembark onto the pier. A small souvenir shop with a colourful wooden pirate outside catches my eye. Huh, just when I thought I'd escaped all the dreadful blokes of Boston. I drag my case down the pier, which throws me straight into the small yet busy heart of the town. The atmosphere is light and airy; people aren't walking at fifty miles per hour and nobody is grimacing like in the city. My stomach dances a little with excitement. I already know coming here was a great decision.

The no-frills hotel I'd booked is a pleasant surprise. I'd suspected they were over-egging the listing a little when they said all rooms had beach views as standard, but the double doors onto my balcony do, in actual fact, overlook a beautiful sandy beach. I dump my overnight bag on the floral bedspread and step outside, taking a deep breath of the deliciously salty air. This is what makes it all worthwhile.

The air is starting to cool, and my stomach growls, reminding me I haven't eaten since lunchtime, so I take a quick shower and change into a fresh pair of jeans and a strappy vest top before heading back into the town. There's a festival feel to the place which I hadn't expected. Rainbow flags billow outside many of the buildings, and a cacophony of laughter spills from the numerous bars and restaurants. A man ambles past in a gorgeous sarong. He flashes me a smile and it gives me a warm buzz. I feel like I've found the home I never knew I wanted. My eye is caught by two men who are offering body painting by a beautiful church. One of the men, a dark-haired, rotund, cheerful-looking fellow in a crazy patterned linen shirt, beckons me over.

'Come on over and choose a design.' He gestures to a photo board of colourful tattoos in such an animated way it's hard to refuse, even though I want to because I'm far too old for glittery body art. Though I'd estimate him to be about forty so perhaps I shouldn't worry.

'Oh, okay,' I say, hopping into the chair.

I choose a sparkly butterfly that he starts to paint on my right shoulder blade. I've no idea how it will turn out, but I figure it will wash off, and he *is* just trying to earn a living.

'So, how long have you been doing this for?' I ask to relieve the relative awkwardness of a complete stranger touching me.

'Oh my god, you're English,' he gushes. 'Harry, listen to her. Go on, doll, say it again.' He places both hands on my shoulders and forcibly turns me to face a slimmer, blond man in a pale blue short-sleeved shirt who seems distinctly less impressed.

'I, er, I was just asking how long you'd been doing this for?' I ask again. Somehow, the more I speak, the more I seem to sound like my surname should be Windsor.

'Oh my god, your accent is just darling,' Harry says before turning back to his client, a little curly-haired girl who makes me feel more ridiculous.

'Oh, thank you,' I say, forcing a smile.

'And yes, we've been here seven years. We came on vacation

from New York and just fell in love with this place. Gave up our big careers to paint people each evening after lying on the beach all day,' the cuddly one says, gesticulating with his paintbrush.

Wow, I can't imagine just walking away from a career I'd worked hard for. 'So, you escaped the rat race?'

'We sure did. How about you? What do you do?' he asks.

'I'm still fighting my way through the rat race, but I enjoy it.' It's currently a bit of a fib of course, but he doesn't need to know that.

'So, are you here alone?' He must be working closely because I can feel his warm breath on the bare skin of my back.

'Yes. I'm in Boston with some colleagues working for a marketing company, but I needed to get away, so I came here for a weekend of R&R.'

'I hear ya,' he says. 'Actually, I'd love to pick your brain a little, if you wouldn't mind catching up when you're free? We have a great trade here through summer but then autumn comes and we're twiddling our thumbs. We could quite easily do Halloween face painting and things like that but need to reach a wider audience.'

I'm not one for meeting strange men but I'm getting a good vibe from this one, and besides, you don't really hear of many horror stories involving body-paint-slash-glitter artists. 'Of course, I'm here until Sunday so I could come back when you're quieter.'

'That would be wonderful.' He rubs a tiny section of my shoulder blade with his finger. 'You, my dear, are almost done.' He proceeds to spray something cool over the top of the tattoo.

'I'm finished,' he sings, adding vibrato on the last syllable. 'Here, take a look.' He angles a mirror so I can catch a glimpse. I gasp. It's beautifully done, in hues of pink, green, purple and blue. Strategically placed silver glitter adds emphasis to the wings, and shading underneath casts a shadow, making it look like it's floating an inch above my skin.

31

'I love it. It will be a shame to wash it off,' I say honestly.

'Just come back tomorrow and I'll paint you a new one.' He winks. 'That'll be twenty dollars.'

Twenty dollars? No wonder he could give up the rat race to paint people. I take out a green note and hand it over, and he grasps my hand. 'Actually, if you're here all alone, you should come to dinner with us tonight, we can talk about all the marketing stuff then.'

That's a bit forward, isn't it? But I am starving, and it might be nice to speak to someone this side of the Atlantic who doesn't just see me as the doughnut fetcher. Plus, I don't know much about what's available round here and some company would be nice.

'Oh, Barney, you're a plangonologist of living dolls.' Harry glances up from the child's arm he's painting a dolphin on, the curly-haired girl from earlier has gone.

'I am not a people collector, Harry; I'm just friendly.' He turns to me. 'Honestly, he learns a new word and has to toss it into every conversation.'

I smile and look down at the floor, unsure as to whether or not the invitation still applies.

'Come with us?' Barney asks again. 'I could listen to that English accent all day, and Harry over here can sit wallowing in his grumpy pants.'

I look at Harry who gives a casual nod. Barney wraps his arms around Harry and kisses his head. Neither of them look like axe murderers, and I don't think there's an ulterior motive aside from the bit of marketing advice Barney is wanting.

'Okay, I'd love to.'

CHAPTER 8

Double checking the address Barney wrote down, I hover outside what looks like someone's house. There is no indication anywhere that this is even a restaurant, no neon sign or A-frame outside, but I do spot a few people coming and going. How odd. I decide to wait five more minutes. It's already eight and that's what time they said to meet.

I start to feel ridiculous standing here waiting for two strangers. There was a fish restaurant near the pier. I'll go there. As I turn to leave, I spot Harry and Barney walking towards me. Harry takes long casual strides as Barney seems to use all his limbs for propulsion. Relief dilutes the weird cocktail of apprehension in my stomach.

'You're in for a treat,' Barney says, linking my arm like an old friend and frog-marching me up the wooden steps to the veranda. He knocks on the door, and a kindly young woman opens it and gestures him in.

'Your usual table is ready, guys.' Her smile fades as she takes me in. 'Oh, I'm sorry, it's only set for two.' She looks mortified.

'Just pull another chair over and we'll cosy up. We're all friends here,' he says in what I'm coming to realise is his actual voice and not just his 'cheerful' tone.

Once we're seated, I'm handed a paper menu. I'm no expert on the Cape Cod cuisine scene, or any *cuisine scene* to be precise, but this is the most unusual place I've ever been to. 'There's only one choice per course here,' I say, tapping the sheet of paper.

'Oh, honey, this is a *secret* restaurant. It's a surprise menu each day, though we come so often, we know the rotation. Tonight is Harry's favourite.'

'He's right. Butter-poached lobster and wild shrimp.' Harry pats his stomach. The food does sound amazing.

'If it's a secret, why did you bring me here? I've not come across a secret restaurant before but I bet it adds to the exclusivity.'

'It's the worst-kept secret in town but to some extent it keeps the tourists out. No offence.' He pats my hand. 'It just keeps it special for the locals. And as you can see – it's always busy.'

'Well, it's utterly charming,' I say, running a hand over the simple wooden table.

The waitress places some mismatched crockery and a platter of something deep-fried on the table. I'm so hungry I don't care what lies beneath the batter.

'Fried oysters.' Barney hands me the plate. 'Try one, they're to die for.'

I take a bite, and he's right. I don't think I've ever had an oyster before. The thought of them has always made me a bit squeamish. Kev wasn't an adventurous eater and he used to say they were like swallowing a ball of phlegm. The thought makes me heave.

'You don't like them?' Harry says.

'Oh, I do. They're better than I was expecting. I was just … remembering something.'

'Try the hot sauce,' Barney says and I dip one dutifully. It tastes a bit like Dijon mustard and lemon.

'Mmm, delicious,' I say as the flavours and texture alight my senses.

'We think everyone should come here at least once,' says Harry.

'Thank you for inviting me. I don't know where I'd have ended up otherwise.' I dunk another oyster.

'Barney picks up all the waifs and strays,' Harry says. I instantly

34

feel awkward as his tone is more matter-of-fact than Barney who seems to wear his emotions on his sleeve, but when I look at him, the corner of his mouth is lifted. 'I'm just teasing. We *both* love to meet new people.'

'So, I know you're in Boston for work, but why is a pretty girl like you in P-Town alone?' Barney asks as he wipes the last oyster round the dip bowl.

It's a strange feeling to want to spill all to two people you don't know from Adam, but a compelling one, nonetheless. Perhaps it's because they're the first people I've connected with since I arrived in the US, perhaps it's desperation but whatever the reason, I proceed to fill them in.

'Nobody listens to me or values my opinion,' I finish. 'I don't agree with the way the campaign is going and I think the company who hired us will hate it, but apparently, I should just shut up and put up. I guess I just don't fit in with the team.'

Harry points his fork at me. 'You will. You just need to find your place. All groups have roles for people to fill. You'll get there. Like my Barney here is the people collector—'

'I'm intuitive and sociable,' Barney interrupts.

'*I'm* the pragmatic one, my role in a group is the voice of reason. Martha, who owns this place, is the chef. We know most of the people in this town, and they all have their place.'

Barney laughs. 'You are *so* not the voice of reason.'

'Okay, humour me – what am I then?' Harry shakes his head and gives me a 'can you believe this guy?' look.

'The fussy one.' Barney cocks his head to the side as if it proves his point.

Harry looks at me. 'I just like things in order, which in my opinion makes me practical.' He shrugs his shoulders like *that* proves *his* point.

'Well, my place at present seems to be chief doughnut-getter,' I say, breaking up their affectionate bickering.

'Well, there you go – you have a place. But if you want a

better one, you need to play a little game of Snakes and Ladders: work your way up without getting knocked all the way back down. You'll figure it out.' Harry says this so casually. If he's fussy and still thinks it's all just a simple game, then maybe I should too.

The waitress clears our table and I take the opportunity to sip my water then we talk a little more about Harry and Barney's life in New York and how they met. Barney explains how he'd just arrived from New Jersey and got lost in SoHo looking for the library. Harry was passing, and Barney asked him for help. They chatted a little bit and hit it off then Harry drew him a map, only the map led to an Italian restaurant where Harry was sitting outside with champagne and a bow-tie. Barney never did get to the library, and the rest is history. I sometimes forget that my meeting Kev isn't the only romantic story out there, and hearing someone else's makes a surprisingly refreshing change from replaying my own story over in my head.

'What about at home?' Barney asks. 'Is there a Mr or Mrs Sam?'

I knew this was coming, I was braced for it. It isn't Barney's fault – it's never anyone's fault – but I wish a single person could just be so without people questioning it. Is it really so weird to be on your own?

I suck in as much air as I can take and give him the lowdown: I married my true love, he was killed in an accident and nobody else will ever compare. I've made my peace and I'm happy to die alone knowing I was lucky enough to meet my soulmate. Blah, blah, blah.

'Oh, honey.'

I hold my hand up to shush Barney. 'I don't need sympathy. I've moved on.'

'But—'

'Anyway, you wanted to know about marketing?' I say, changing the subject.

'I've told him to use social media but he won't listen. I think he has grand plans of plastering billboards everywhere and going on *Oprah*,' Harry says dryly.

I look at Barney. 'For what you want, Harry is right. Get a Facebook page and start using Instagram to promote your work. A bit of hashtagging and some great photographs should work. If you still need a boost you could have some fliers printed up and do a local door drop.'

'Consider it done,' Barney says, raising his glass.

'I've been telling him this for weeks,' Harry says with a sigh.

The main course is equally delicious, and raspberry-meringue ice cream finishes the meal perfectly. I devour every last bit and I swear my stomach creaks at bursting point.

'How about we go for a cocktail? Sam, you'll come for a bit of Sex on the Beach action, won't you?'

I splutter my water and giggle. 'Maybe another time,' I say before realising how presumptuous I sound. I've had such a good time tonight but it's unlikely I'll ever see these guys again.

'Tomorrow night then? You're still here tomorrow, aren't you, Sam?' Barney reminds me of an excited puppy. This has been the easiest conversation and the most comfortable I've felt since arriving here. Even with Kev cropping up, I've really enjoyed myself.

'I'd love to.'

'What are your plans for tomorrow during the day? We're working until six-ish, but we can give you some pointers for things to do.' Harry talks at a more normal speed compared to Barney's ultrasonic waffle.

'I thought I'd sit by the pool and read for a few hours, then maybe walk down to the beach and perhaps rent a bike in the afternoon.'

'Ahh, we have a bike guy,' Harry says.

'A bike guy?' I ask.

'Yes, Ethan. The bike guy. Go see him, tell him Harry and

Barney sent you, and he'll give you a good deal.' Harry is already scribbling the address on the back of the menu. Fortunately, it's just a printed-off piece of A4 and not some leather-bound affair but I get the distinct impression it wouldn't have mattered to him if it were.

CHAPTER 9

After a morning reading by the pool, I've actually made it down to the beach. There was a bustling little sandwich shop in the centre of town where I picked up lunch – a chicken and pastrami sandwich the size of my arm – and now I'm sitting on the sand eating it whilst watching some kayakers and trying not to ooze sauce all over myself. *This is the life.* It's such a cliché even to say in my own head, but there isn't a phrase more fitting. The sky is blue, punctuated with the odd fluffy white cloud – sky pillows, I used to call clouds like this when I was little. It's such a far cry from my real life, my London life, where I thought lunch in the park or by the docks warranted the phrase 'This is the life'. I think I posted an Instagram picture to that effect once, but here, I can't even be bothered taking out my phone. I just want to enjoy the moment.

And so I realise that being here, despite the woes of work, certainly beats being in the mad rush of London. I can blow my nose and black stuff doesn't come out, for a start. Obviously, there's a lot I miss about London – my friends, the parks, the continuous stream of new places to eat and, of course, the shops, but Boston has plenty of those anyway. I pull the menu from last night out of my bag and look over the address that Harry wrote out. I should be able to find the place easy enough, and a friend of Harry and Barney will likely be as kind and helpful as they are. There were some fliers in the hotel showing a local bike trail which looks great.

I'm pretty sure I can still ride a bike. You never forget how, apparently.

***

The little clapboard shop is only a five-minute walk away from where I sat on the beach. It's painted blue and white, and bikes in their abundance are racked up outside. I feel a little nervous as I walk in and see even more. What if I can't ride? It's been a while. I wonder if they offer incompetence discounts or stabilisers for adults. The place is shockingly quiet, and not a CCTV camera in sight. If this was central London, teenagers would have ransacked the place by now, and these bikes would be accessories to crime as yobs swarmed the city on them, snatching the Rolexes off unsuspecting rich folk. Or at least that's what the press would have you believe. I run my hand along the smooth frame of a red and silver mountain bike.

'Can I help you?' A smooth, deep voice startles me, making me feel like some weird bike voyeur.

'Er ... I ...' I turn in the direction of the speaker and the familiarity of his face has the Medusa effect on me. 'You!' is all I manage to say.

'I beg your pardon?' He narrows those sapphire eyes and tilts his head ever so slightly in a cocky, arrogant way. He doesn't recognise me, but then again, why would he?

'You don't remember me, do you?' But I certainly remember him, because other than Barney and Harry, a bubbly young lady in Abercrombie and, to some extent, my work colleagues, he's the only person I've spoken to since arriving in the States.

'I'm sorry, should I?' His tone isn't completely awful, but considering I'm a potential customer, it isn't great. His eyes make small movements from left to right, searching mine for an answer but still, his face is blank.

'I asked you to take a photo of me in Boston Harbor a fortnight or so ago.' I cross my arms in front of my body defensively.

'Oh, you're *that* person.' He allows his features to drop and begins polishing some bike part.

'Yes. Yes, I am.' My arms are still folded. I'm not quite sure

40

why I'm pressing the issue, but I am, and I'm hoping the arm-folding strengthens my stance.

'Well, are you here for a bike?' His cocky nonchalance is infuriating.

'Actually, yes. Harry and Barney sent me. They recommended you, but obviously you've hidden your arsey side from them, like some weird little anti-hero or something.' I notice the corner of his mouth twitch a little. I can't believe he finds this funny.

'Are all you Brits this uptight?'

'I beg your pardon?' Okay, admittedly, that didn't help my cause.

'Well, you're on another continent, on the sleepy peninsula of Cape Cod, surrounded by beautiful beaches with whales breaching on the horizon, and you're standing there like Mary damn Poppins wanting to correct my behaviour.'

'I'm not uptight, I'm cross. There's a difference.'

'Fine. Do you want a bike or not?'

'Well, of course I do! I didn't hunt you down and come here for the pleasure of your company.' God, I hope he doesn't think that's why I came. Now I've said it, he's definitely going to think that.

'Okay, good.' He exhales noisily and it's irritating. 'Let's get you hooked up with a bike then.'

He looks me up and down. I know it's to size me up for a bike, but I'm still squirming with discomfort. I can feel his eyes on me, and it sends weird tingles down the back of my neck. I can't ever remember being looked up and down before. Suddenly my fairly modest denim shorts feel shorter and my T-shirt much, much tighter.

'I'll get you a medium frame and put the seat up a bit.' He doesn't meet my eyes when he speaks, and it feels more like he's talking to himself or thinking aloud. He disappears outside. The aircon is so cold I have to rub the goose pimples on my arms as I wait.

After a few minutes, he pops his head in. 'You're all set.'

I step outside, and it takes a moment for the warmth of the sun to penetrate my icy skin. He's holding a silver mountain bike out for me, a black helmet hanging from the bars. I take the bike and thank him.

'Do you know where you're going?' he asks as I fasten the clasp on the helmet.

Nope. 'Yes, of course I do.'

'Good.'

'Yes, it is!' I give him a pointed look and push the pedal hard to make my dramatic departure. I wobble a little but correct it instantly. I'm one part smug and two parts relieved.

'If it's the bike trail you're heading for, you're going the wrong way,' he calls after me.

Great.

'I know!' I didn't. 'I need a bottle of water first. Leave me alone!'

'Okay. There's a map in the front basket, you know, for after you've got your water,' he says. I wave him off, and away I ride.

God, I hate that guy.

I keep riding until I hit the safety of the beach where I can sit for a minute and study the map without *arrogant arseface* nit-picking. What are the odds of him being the bike guy? Of all the people in Boston and all the bike rental places in Cape Cod, it's just my luck *he* is 'the guy'. Bridget is going to love this story.

I figure out the route and set off. The breeze blows against me as I ride, taking my frustrations with it, and soon I've forgotten all about work, homesickness and unpleasant bike-rental people. The tarmacadam pathway is a biker's dream. A yellow line down the middle separates the traffic, like a road. I swerve out of the way of an oncoming bicycle and shout 'Sorry' before realising I'm cycling on the left. The lady giggles and cycles on. Everyone seems so friendly here.

Soon, I find my groove. I take in the grassy dunes that line the trail and enjoy the feeling of the sun beating down on my skin. After a while, I find a deserted spot with sea views that is perfect for a rest. I lay the bike down and sit on the sand with my legs stretched out and inhale the briny smell of the air. Kev would have loved it here.

Without fail, if we were ever on a beach somewhere, he'd say we should give up our jobs, move away to the seaside and rent out pedalos for a living. I smile at the memory before sadness frays its edges. Perhaps if we had, he'd still be here today. 'Oh Kev,' I say aloud. I can remember the happy times now, and I no longer have the questions of *Why him*? *Why us?* circling my head, but every now and then a memory bats the wind out of my sails.

A zephyr whips up the sand, and a few grains fly into my watery eyes. I giggle. If we ever watched a sad film and Kev got a bit upset, he'd say, 'I've got a bit of sand in my eye.' *This* right now is what people don't understand. They don't understand the warmth of my memories and how I don't need to meet someone else because the memories and feelings I have in my head and heart are enough. Some people spend decades in loveless marriages. How on earth can that be better than what I had … what I still have?

'I could get used to this.' I'm lounging lazily on a swinging chair under the straw canopy of the hotel's pool bar as Kev hands me a cocktail. Kev had surprised me with a last-minute trip to Mexico. My parents had thought we were mad as we're supposed to be saving up to decorate and I hadn't even had time to get my legs waxed but sitting here now, I know that Kev got it right. It's a beautiful place.

'Don't get too comfy, it's happy hour and you're going up for the next round.' He grins and I throw an ice cube at his bare chest.

'Well, that was just uncalled for.' He puts his drink underneath his chair and gives me a look filled with mischief.

'Kev?' I ask, nervously. I know something is coming, but I'm not sure what.

'Sam?' He mocks before straddling me on the swinging chair. 'I wouldn't do anything mean to you,' he says. Slowly kissing my neck, he prises my drink out of my hand and puts it down on the floor.

Then, all of a sudden, he thrusts an ice cube down the front of my kaftan.

I scream and nearby sunbathers look up from their buy-one-get-one-half-price airport paperbacks and I feel ridiculous.

An almighty roar of thunder rips through the sky. Seconds later, the heavens open and torrential rain pounds the terrace. People scream and dart indoors or under the cover of the bar where we are.

Kev sips his drink and flashes me a mischievous grin.

'What?' I ask.

'Nothing!' He mimics my higher pitched tone. Gently, he scoops me up and lifts me off the safety of my seat.

The rain is like stair rods and I know his plan.

'Fine, take me out in the rain. See if I care,' I say, hoping to suck the fun out of his wicked plan.

He laughs. 'You can try working your little mind game on me, Sam. It's cute, really it is.' He edges towards where the rain sloshes inside the open bar. 'But we both know that today is not a hair wash day and you only have a drizzle of that anti-frizz serum left – you can't afford an unscheduled hair wash.'

Damn! I'm torn between laughing at how well he knows me and the sheer fear of him seeing his plan through. He pretends to swoosh me out in the rain and I scream again, digging my fingers into his back.

'It's so warm,' he says, inching closer to the rain. 'I think I need to cool off.'

'Don't you dare!' As I say it, he runs from under the canopy of the bar and out into the torrential rain. Within seconds we're both drenched through.

I'm furious. 'I hate you!' I shout over the lashing rain, but he just gives me that lopsided grin that melts my insides. Slowly, he slides me down to my feet and pulls me into his body and kisses me as the cool rain beats down on our hot bodies.

Almost as soon as it started, the rain stops and the sun comes back out, burning through my wet kaftan.

'You're an idiot!' I say, whacking him on the arm.

'Sam, it was a joke.'

'You knew I didn't want to wash my hair,' I say, squeezing out the excess water from my ponytail.

'Let me show you something.' He takes my hand and leads me up to our room.

'You're such an oddball, why are we going inside now the sun's out?'

He doesn't answer, instead, he opens the door and puts his hands on my shoulders, positioning me in front of the full-length mirror in the hallway.

Slowly, he peels off my kaftan. 'Look,' is all he says.

'Frizzy hair, bloated all-inclusive belly, red, sunburned chest and freckles.' I fold my arms.

'Gorgeous, natural hair, a beautiful body and cute freckles.' He kisses my neck and my insides flutter, it's amazing he can still do that to me after all this time. 'I'm with you on the sunburn though, but that's your own fault, I told you to wear a higher factor.'

'Oh, shut up!' I bash him playfully.

'My point is; you don't need that hair-frizz gunk. Your hair is stunning as it is, just like the rest of you.'

I turn to face him, and my lips find his. His body feels hot against mine, which is still cold from my soggy kaftan.

'What do you say we have a little siesta?' he says cheekily.

CHAPTER 10

When I arrive back at the bike rental place, the Grinch is messing with the wheel of a large black and red mountain bike outside. The anger I felt towards him earlier has dissipated a little, in light of such a wonderful afternoon. I'm ready to return the bike and go back to my hotel, freshen up and perhaps find a new bike rental place should I ever need one.

He gives the wheel a little shake to make sure it's fastened on tightly and then glances up at me, his hair falling into his eyes. 'You found your way back then?'

'Oh, ha-ha.' I sound very British, like the British people in American films do. It's odd to hear myself this way and it isn't as though I'm speaking any differently; I just sound different because of the thick American accents around me.

He stands up, wiping a streak of black grease on his jeans. He's intimidatingly close, almost a full head-height taller than me and a good six inches too close. Scratch that, he's six feet too close. I swallow hard, unsure as to whether I'm going to get another earful. I'm braced and ready. He's only a foot away, and I can feel something between us. An energy of some sort which binds itself into a hard knot in my chest. I don't step back. I put my hands on my hips and stand my ground.

'Do you want to pay cash or card?' he says eventually, slicing through the tension. The breath I was holding escapes. *Was that it?*

'Er, cash … no, card.'

'Do you need a moment to think about it?' There's a frustrating sarcasm in his tone.

47

'You do know there are customer service courses available, don't you? I bet repeat custom isn't the foundation of your business model.' I jab the air in front of his chest. 'It's a good job you're based in a tourist town where you have a constant flow of new and unsuspecting victims to rent bikes to. You could be the Bates Motel of the bike rental world.' *Too far?*

The corner of his mouth curls up in a bemused smirk that makes me all the more cross. 'If you're finished, and I really hope you are, closing time was fifteen minutes ago and I'm starving so I'd like to wrap this up. I open up again at 9 a.m. tomorrow though, if you'd like to carry on.'

'Oh.' Okay, so maybe I'm in the wrong this time but that just makes us even. 'Well, here.' I hand over my card, and he heads inside without a word. I follow because, well, he has my card.

'You could have just said you were closing,' I say when I reach the counter.

'Well, you know … customer service.'

Touché.

He runs off a piece of paper and presents a slip for me to sign. I haven't paid this way in ages. I look at him to check it's right, and he gives me an impatient look, so I scribble my signature and slide the paper back across the counter.

'All done then?' I ask, and he nods. 'Okay, well thank you and goodbye.' Eurgh, why did I thank him? I just can't help myself. He raises a hand, and I walk out with the strange feeling of unfinished business.

CHAPTER 11

'There you are!' I spot Barney and Harry at a long wooden table in the outdoor bar. The decking offers views across the bay and the calm ocean, which appears to be resting after a busy day of throwing kayakers from their vessels. The bar is bustling, and I had to fight my way over to their corner. I plonk my handbag on the table and slump down on the bench.

'Well, you're not a happy camper,' Barney says.

'Is it that obvious?' I ask dryly.

'What happened to the perfect day you had planned out?' Harry said. 'Actually, hold that. You need a drink first.' He holds three fingers in the air. The bartender nods and I assume three 'somethings' will arrive soon.

I give a wistful sigh. 'It *was* perfect – I read by the pool and had lunch on the beach. Then I found the bike hire place—'

Barney gushes. 'So, you met Ethan?'

I frown, unsure why anyone would react that way. 'Yes. And why on earth are you friends with such an arrogant—'

Barney gasps, clutching both hands to his face. I glare at him.

'If you keep reacting so dramatically, I'm not telling the story.'

'Sorry, but I've never met anyone who hates Ethan before. We adore him and thought you would too. All the women in this town are head-over-heels besotted with him. I don't know how he manages to stay single.' The barman places three elaborately adorned cocktails down, breaking Barney's trail of thought, so I seize the opportunity to fill them in on our encounter in Boston and his lack of regret today.

'That doesn't sound like Ethan at all,' Barney says.

49

'I don't know; he can be a bit of a brooder,' Harry adds.

'I kinda like that,' Barney says.

'When was it you say it happened?' Harry says, ignoring Barney.

'A few weeks ago.'

Harry and Barney exchange glances and when they don't elaborate, I sit confused for a minute. Then it hits me. All that talk about head-over-heels women and whatnot. They're matchmakers, I bet he'd had a bad date that day and took his hatred of womankind out on me.

'I do hope you only sent me there for the bikes.' I give them a warning look.

'Well, of course,' Barney says, and in fairness he does look quite horrified at the thought.

Harry shakes his head. 'Ethan is a great guy. You just have to get to know him.'

Barney rests his chin on his hands and smiles. 'It's as though his mother went to the gene-pool buffet when she was making him and had first dibs on all the good stuff.' He puts on what I assume is supposed to be a female voice. 'I'll have a couple o' those blue eyes, some sun-kissed skin and a chiselled jaw for this one.' Harry giggles at Barney's impression and it shows a side to him I hadn't witnessed before. I swear, if these two were emojis, they'd have hearty eyes.

'Looks aren't everything.'

'Well, I've never met a woman, or a man of that inclination, who didn't swoon over Ethan before. You, Sam, are a tough nut to crack.'

'I swear, if you were trying to play matchmaker …' The thought still horrifies me.

Barney and Harry shake their heads a little too quickly and I resist the urge to discreetly check my breath doesn't smell.

'Good. I would hate for our friendship to be over before it's even started.' I punctuate my stern words with a sip of my cocktail. 'Mmm. This is nice. What is it?'

<50>50</50>

'It's a ginger Cosmo. Aren't they yummy?' Barney sounds excited. Like Dory the fish, it seems he's already forgotten about my warning.

'Sam ...' Barney suddenly sounds serious, and he glances at Harry warily. Harry shakes his head and tries to brush away whatever it is Barney wants to say.

'What?' I ask.

Harry looks at Barney. 'Do we need more drinks? I think we need more drinks.' He stands up to walk to the bar.

'What on earth is going on?'

If the ocean was guilt, a huge wave has just slapped Barney in the face and drenched him. 'We've invited some friends to join us tonight, that's all.' He sips his drink, but the slight rise to his eyebrows suggests it's not a simple case of friends getting together.

'Oh, okay. What friends?' I hadn't anticipated there would be people joining us and try my best to avoid giving any hint of the disappointment I feel at having to share company and make small talk with strangers.

'There's, Susie the cake girl, Blair the gift-store owner, Marty the coffee-shop guy, who we just invited because he overheard us talking about drinks, and then ... Ethan the bike guy.' He says the last bit even quicker than usual.

'What?' I groan. This is all I need. I suppose I could always talk to the others. I don't have to speak to him.

Harry returns with three more cocktails, different this time, and catches the disappointment on my face. 'Ahh good, you told her Blair and Susie can't make it. Don't worry about being the only girl in our gang.' Barney makes a cut-throat gesture at Harry to shut him up.

I guess I can talk to Marty.

He looks at Barney. 'Oh, and I already told you Marty couldn't make it.' Barney's face is a picture. 'Oh, I didn't.'

'You know what, Ethan is your friend, and I am someone

you've just met and kindly invited out. You've every right to invite your friend for drinks.' I can be civilised.

Barney seems to get a sudden whoosh of positive energy and sits upright. 'Oh good, because he's here.'

My insides wither as he approaches our table. He's smiling at Barney. It makes his face look weird, completely different in fact, like a light has come on. When he catches sight of me the light goes out. '*You* again,' he says with disbelief.

'Nice to see you too,' I retort as he slides on to the bench opposite me.

'Ethan, I got you a cocktail.' Harry pushes his own glass over to Ethan, but Ethan's eyes remain fixed on mine, even as he moves his hand to the drink and takes a sip. The golden light of the setting sun casts a glow across his face, illuminating him like an exhibit in a museum and his eyes shine like jewels.

'Phew-ee, you could cut this tension with a knife,' says Barney, flapping his hands around wildly. Ethan looks away, but his jaw is tense and the muscles twitch beneath his skin. My insides turn to lead. If he's purposely trying to make me feel uncomfortable, it's working and I can't bear it. I'll finish my drink and go.

'Sorry, guys.' Ethan's face relaxes again. 'I've just suffered an earful from *her* today.' He nods at me as Barney and Harry, who are now flanking Ethan, each place a consoling hand on his shoulder and give him 'there, there' looks. Ethan's solid frame doesn't flinch, even though I suspect Harry and Barney (but mostly Barney) are enjoying the contact more than they should be.

'Why don't we clear the air?' Harry suggests. I tilt my head to the side expectantly and Ethan sips his drink like he hasn't got a care in the world. He's infuriating.

'For the sake of enjoying a few drinks in peace, I'm sorry,' Ethan says, but there's no feeling in it. He's doing it purely for the benefit of his friends, and since I'm an outsider, I'm hardly going to make a big deal out of it. I'm going back to Boston tomorrow anyway.

'For the sake of enjoying the rest of the evening, I accept.' I hold out my glass and he clinks it.

'Great,' says Barney with an excited clap. 'We just knew you two would get along.' For someone who professes to be intuitive, he really isn't.

The next few hours pass amicably. Harry and Barney flirt ostentatiously and without shame, both with each other and with Ethan. I pretend not to notice, but I get the feeling that Ethan actually doesn't notice at all. He's so sure of himself.

Harry slurps the last dregs of his cocktail and frowns, realising it's all gone. 'So, are you heading back to Boston tomorrow?'

'Yes, let's see if I can find my place.' I wink.

'You will. Think Meryl Streep in *The Devil Wears Prada*,' he says with a wink.

'At this point, I'd settle for Anne Hathaway's role. I'll just be happy if someone acknowledges my presence,' I say.

Ethan snorts. 'Huh! You're definitely more of a Streep.'

'Excuse me?' I ask. He hasn't spoken to me directly in over an hour, and when he does, he basically calls me a bitch.

'Oh, come on. I was joking. That's what we do, isn't it?'

I'm a little bit lost for words. I wouldn't exactly call it joking, it's more of a strange bitterness between us. Whatever it is, it feels weird to address it, we don't even know one another.

Ethan drains the last of his cocktail. 'Anyway, *Hathaway*, tell me what's happened?' I look at him, shocked he even cares enough to ask and also slightly surprised he knows so much about the film. I assume he's just making polite conversation for Barney and Harry's benefit but explain regardless.

'Well, that sucks. If you've been sent here, your boss back in England must think you're up to the job.'

'My thoughts exactly. You know, my impression of American men hasn't been great. Present company excluded.' I gesture to

Barney and Harry. 'You're *not* excluded,' I say to Ethan, but light-heartedly, since he's making an effort and all.

'Okay, okay. Look, I shouldn't have spoken to you the way I did back in Boston. I was … having a bad day.' The alcohol has obviously infused his system because he's more relaxed now. He's speaking to me like a human being, which I believe is progress.

'It's fine. It really doesn't matter. I was perhaps a tad sensitive because I'd just arrived in the city all excited and you smothered my excitement with a huge wet blanket.'

'Well. On that note …' He claps his hands together. 'I'm going to call it a night. Some of us need our beauty sleep.' Ethan stands with one hand on Barney's shoulder and the other on Harry's. They both look delighted. On the other hand, I'm left feeling a little deflated. I opened up to Ethan to try and move on from our little spat and he basically ignored me. Just when I thought he might be decent too.

'We'll see you soon, honey,' Barney says as Ethan walks off, taking away a strange feeling of tension with him. Now I can relax.

'So how do you know Ethan?' I ask, interested by the strange dynamic. I wonder if Ethan knows that these two fancy the pants off him. Maybe he's gay, and he thought I was trying to flirt with him when I asked him to take the photo. Maybe he's sick of women trying to come on to him. Not that I was, but he's definitely cock-sure enough to have assumed so.

Barney wiggles into position to fill me in. 'Ethan was one of the first people we met when we came here. His family own a lot of the local businesses, and he's such a nice guy, he made us feel right at home.'

Really? 'He doesn't strike me as much of a talker.'

'Granted, he's a man of few words, but what he does say is kind and generous.' Barney presses his palms to his cheeks. 'He's a manly man. A real alpha-male.'

I stifle a giggle.

'He's the best of the best.' Harry smiles with warmth.

'I'll take your word for it.' I drain the last of my drink. 'I suppose I'd better go to bed too.'

Harry's and Barney's faces drop. 'Oh, Sam, are you going to come back? We're not going to lose you forever, are we?' I giggle at Barney's theatrics.

I'm sure Boston is great, but it's lonely and I haven't really felt at home there. Provincetown is beautiful, and even when I've been alone here, I haven't felt lonely. The sound of the ocean, the friendly hellos from passers-by and the feeling of the warm sun together make for one big snuggly blanket of comfort. I would like to come back.

'I hadn't thought about it,' I lie.

'You must come back next weekend. We're having a cookout on the beach, and *everyone* is invited,' Barney says.

Next week will probably be as horrendous as the last and escaping to this beautiful, quaint little town will be a healthier equivalent of taking a few Xanax. Plus, these two let me vent.

'That sounds fabulous. Are you sure I wouldn't be imposing?' I chew the side of my lip self-consciously.

'Not at all. We'd love you to come,' says Harry with sincerity.

CHAPTER 12

The following week is just as horrible as I'd imagined it would be. I'm sent for coffee on Monday, Tuesday and Wednesday, and not one of my English colleagues speaks up or offers to go on my behalf, though I did think I caught a very subtle flash of sympathy from Tony. This lunchtime, I was sent on a sandwich run while the men were actually fleshing out key components of the media campaign. It was almost the final straw. I was going to stand up for myself and say something – part of me is still reeling that I didn't – but throwing away the seven years of hard work it took to get here seemed too big a trade-off. Harry was right: I've got my place, but I need to work on getting a better one. I'll bide my time and be smart about it.

When I'm tucked away in my room away from the others, I call Bridget for a catch-up.

She answers on the third ring. 'Hello, you.'

'Hello,' I say, exhaling loudly for effect.

'Oh no. Are things still terrible?'

'Yes! When I speak it's like nobody at all has heard me. Honestly, I'm not exaggerating. It's bizarre. There are moments where I sit there wondering if I've actually spoken at all, or if I just thought the words in my head. I honestly think I could strip naked in the centre of the boardroom and nobody would notice.'

'Oh, honey. Please don't strip naked in the boardroom. Have you spoken to any of the UK team about it?'

'I tried to after the first couple of days. It just sounded so petty and whiney when I said it aloud. I asked Tony if he'd heard my idea today, and he just paused for a moment until I reminded him what it was, then he said, "Oh yeah, I think so" but that was it. Nobody is interested in what I have to say. It wouldn't be so bad if they were interested enough to say, "Your ideas are rubbish", but they don't even do that. I might as well be invisible.' My voice falters on the last word as emotion hits me from nowhere. Even my own body is choosing to ignore me. I'm not even emotional, I'm angry.

'Oh, Sam,' she says. 'Keep at it, hon.'

'I know. I've just never felt so small and insignificant before.' Or at least not in a very long time. I suck up a lungful of air. 'At least I'm in a wonderful place and I can go to the beach at the weekends.'

'Definitely. How was Cape Cod?'

'Amazing.' I fill her in on my escapades and Harry and Barney and Ethan.

'So, let me get this straight; *Ethan* is the arse from Boston? And he was *there*?'

'Yes, and yes. What are the odds of that? He has now apologised, at least. He was having a bad day apparently.'

'Well, we all have those but jeez. At least you can put it behind you now.'

'Yes,' I agree. Except I can't. Not the incident as such, but Ethan. Over the past few days, I've caught myself randomly thinking of him. When I'm walking to the office, eating lunch, even brushing my teeth, for goodness' sake, I see his face and hear his voice. He's got under my skin and I don't know why. I've encountered rude people before, but something about the dark look in his eyes that day, the tense muscles in his face, were different to how he was on Saturday night at the bar. Even when he was being all cocky in the bike place, the vacant, disengaged look I saw at the harbour was nowhere to be seen. I can't shake the feeling that he was having more than just a bad day.

'I'm going back to Provincetown at the weekend for a cookout – a barbecue, as far as I can tell – with Harry and Barney.'

'Ooh, lovely. Don't forget your real friends here in miserable and grey London, will you?'

I giggle. 'As much as I love the sunshine and gorgeous beaches of Massachusetts, you can't beat a bit of drizzle and a bitch-fest with you lot.'

'My sentiments exactly. Anyway, I have to go. I need to be in bed before midnight at least one day this week.'

'Oops. I'd forgotten about the time difference,' I say, feeling bad for calling so late.

'It's fine, I'll catch a few mid-morning zeds when I'm at my desk tomorrow.'

'I hope you're joking, I can never tell.'

'Unfortunately, the truth is in the eyebags,' she cackles.

'Okay, give the others my love.' We exchange goodbyes, and I hang up feeling a little lighter. Just one more day of work to survive before I'm back in my happy place.

***

The ferry journey to Provincetown passes pleasantly. It's a great way to blow away the office cobwebs on a Friday afternoon. I shall definitely be making it a thing. I while away the time switching between reading and looking out across the ocean, watching the city fade away until it's clouded by the rugged little islands that surround it and the deep blue of the water and sky all around.

I get a warm welcome back at the hotel as the lady on reception recognises me, and once I've dumped my bags, I head to the main street to find Barney and Harry, who are just packing away their body paints.

'Knocking off early?' I say.

'I need to go and see my meat guy for the cookout tomorrow.'

'Your meat guy?' I ask.

'He means the butcher,' Barney says. 'Everyone has to be "a guy".'

'Oh, okay,' I say, trying to sound upbeat at the discovery of my being at a loose end.

'You should come,' Barney says. 'We're going to cocktail afterwards.' He does a little wiggly finger dance, whilst I amuse myself, imagining the Collins Dictionary entry for his new use of cocktail:

Cocktail (**verb**)

Kok-teyl

to sip mixed alcoholic drinks in the company of friends.

Unless *to cocktail* is like the US version of peacocking or something. I hope it isn't. I hate drawing attention to myself, and besides, I don't have my good shoes. 'That sounds great. Are you sure you don't mind me tagging along?'

'We invited you. Of course not.'

I relax a little. 'Okay, but this time, cocktails are on me.'

Harry winks. 'I knew we liked you.'

***

'So, have you climbed a rung of the ladder yet?' Harry leans on the wooden table, sipping a blue cocktail which he says is called 'The Harry'. It tastes like a Blue Lagoon to me, with perhaps a hint of something cherry-flavoured if I'm being optimistic. Barney has gone to back to their apartment to put the meat in the fridge and said he'll catch us up.

I shake my head. 'I almost gave a big Jerry-Maguire-cum-Erin-Brockovich speech, but I didn't think it would get me anywhere.'

'Good. It wouldn't have. What you need to do is show, not tell.' Harry's tongue is blue. It's hard to take serious advice from him when he looks like he's eaten a Smurf.

'How do I do that then?'

'Well, you've said their campaign ideas are unoriginal and that you've tried telling them how to be different, yes?'

I nod. 'The problem is, I'm dealing with an international

59

company who've been running campaigns for some of the biggest global brands for years. What if I'm wrong? All my other projects have been for much smaller, local businesses in London.'

'Are those things on your feet the trainers you're marketing?'

'Uhm, yes.' I'd forgotten I was wearing them. As hideous as Rocks are on a woman of my age, they are bloody comfortable.

'Okay, so I'm assuming your target market is tweens to teens?' he says.

'How did you guess?' I say dryly. 'They don't seem to have the target audience in mind, though. They've gone too young with the pitch, and I think that kind of campaign will alienate the older kids. Young kids will want them anyway if the older ones are wearing them, so targeting them seems redundant.'

'I agree with you, not that I know anything about the field of marketing, but I definitely think the image needs to be cool.'

'I think they're trying to go head to head with Strides, and to me that seems like a bit of a cop-out. They can piggyback off the brand strength of Strides and undercut the prices or throw in some tacky gimmick like a free keyring or something, but that won't build the Rocks brand, which is I'm sure what the client will want.'

Harry nods. 'Agreed.'

I sigh. 'So, what are teens into? I could sell sand to a desert-dweller normally, but when it comes to kids, I'm not really *au fait.*'

'Pop concerts, smartphones, skateboarding …' Harry tails off.

'They have a pigtailed girl holding a doll at the centre of their campaign idea. Rocks are going to hate it. I just don't know how to get them to listen to me so we can actually work on something worthwhile.'

'You can't. But you can show them. Put a mood board together or something, and you can storm in there on Monday with something real to show them.'

Could I do that? Usually, we discuss our ideas first and then put the concepts down on paper, but I don't want to bore Harry with that fact. I'm not sure how I'll be perceived if I go rogue. Still, I can't exactly sink any lower in any of their estimations and there's no obvious Spice Girl Patrick could call me in that scenario, so what do I have to lose?

'I'll have a think,' I say. 'You're good at this. Why on earth did Barney want advertising advice from me when he already has you?'

'He doesn't think I know what I'm talking about.'

'Well, he's wrong.'

'It was Barney's way of befriending you. I don't like to massage his ego too much, but he *is* intuitive. He just has this knack for knowing when he meets a great person.'

Heat floods my cheeks. 'Well, I'm glad you think so.'

'You know, maybe tomorrow night I can help you out a little with your project.'

That sounds promising. Before I can reply, Barney comes bounding over. 'I've worked up a thirst.' He presses the back of his hand to his forehead dramatically. Harry moves a blue cocktail over, and Barney takes a huge gulp.

***

The next day, the cookout starts at six, and Harry and Barney have refused my offer of help – despite getting all frazzled when discussing the planning – so I've decided to rent a car for the day and explore a little. They recommend a 'car rental guy' just off the main street. When I arrive, I see a few different types of cars on the small forecourt, but it's the shiny red soft-top Jeep on the road outside that catches my eye.

I go inside and ring the bell on the counter as instructed by a little pink sticky note beside it. The small office smells of oil and rubber, and a sports car calendar hangs on the grubby wall behind the desk.

'Hello there, what can I do you for?' a cheerful older man asks as he comes in from a side room marked 'Private'.

'I'd like to rent a car for a few hours, please.'

'Well, you've come to the right place.' He laughs and then coughs with the dryness of it.

I choose one of the very cool Wrangler Jeeps and ask for the top off. I can't wait to go beach-hopping. While we're sorting out paperwork, the old man calls out 'Son!' to someone in the back and asks them to prepare the car. I get a little rush of excitement at the thought of driving down some beautiful American roads with my hair blowing in the wind like Thelma or Louise.

'You—' a male voice travels from the entrance behind me '—are all set.'

'Fantast—'

'You have got to be kidding me.' As I turn, the recognition hits us both at the same time.

'Is there a problem?' The kindly man's tone has become much more formal.

'No!' Ethan and I say in unison.

'Good,' says the older man, but his single, raised eyebrow suggests he's humouring us. 'Then Ethan can show you the controls,' he says before heading into the private room.

'Why are you *everywhere*?' I whisper bitterly as we walk outside.

'Why are *you* everywhere?' he repeats childishly. 'I thought you worked in Boston.'

'You were in Boston when I first met you, so what does that matter?'

'I was there for the day. You're here all the time.'

'It's my second weekend here. That's not all the time.' I realise I'm pouting, but I keep it going because I'm committed to it now. 'Anyway, I thought you were the bike guy, not the car hire guy.'

'I am the bike guy. My father owns most of the rental places in Provincetown, and occasionally I move around when we're short-staffed. Your turn – why are you here?'

'Barney and Harry invited me to the beach later for the cookout, so I have today free to explore.'

Ethan groans. 'So you'll be there too?'

'Yes, but apparently everyone from the town is invited, so I'm sure we can keep our distance.'

'Good.'

'Yes. Brilliant,' I huff. 'So, are you going to show me the controls so I can leave or what?'

He explains how it all works, which is pretty much how any car works, but I do listen carefully to how to put the hood on, just in case. I adjust the seat and get ready to drive off. 'So, is there anywhere else I should avoid if I don't want to see you?'

'I wouldn't rent a kayak,' he says. 'And I go over to Boston Harbor once a month to take our promotional fliers to the tourist information booth.'

'Noted,' I say.

'Would you like any maps or anything?' he asks.

'Yes, please.'

'Here you go.' He hands me a thick pile of folded maps.

'Why are you being so civil all of a sudden?' I ask, taking them. It's unnerving, like dealing with a Jekyll and Hyde.

'It's my job,' he says dryly. 'And I'd like you to try and find your way back before closing time.'

'Oh.' I should have known.

Once I'm on the open road, I forget all about Ethan and enjoy driving down the beachfront road. It's not like the beachfront drives in the UK, all built up and busy with fried doughnut stalls and amusement arcades; it's largely natural and unspoilt. There are some clapboard beach houses and small motels dotted around, but mostly it's sand and grassy dunes stretching out into blue water and salty air. I find myself in North Truro, looking up at the tall white Highland Light lighthouse and park up. A few summer tourists have already begun to gather in a queue, and with nothing better to do, I join them.

I climb the winding steps of the red brick cylinder until I reach the top. It's not as high as I imagined, but the view still reaches far across the grasslands and ocean. I walk around the large bulb in the centre, moving aside so that a couple can pass me. Then I rest my hands on the rusted sills and just gaze, enjoying the tranquillity of the moment.

The reality of where I am hits me, and I pinch myself discreetly, making sure the couple don't see. I'm in one of the most beautiful places I've ever seen, and no amount of arrogant men will take that away from me.

64

CHAPTER 13

'So, where did you get to today?' Harry asks me. It's 6 p.m. and the sun sits low in the sky, casting a pinky-orange filter across the wide, sandy Herring Cove beach, as though it wasn't already beautiful enough.

'After the lighthouse, I walked down the beach and just sat for a while. Drove a little more and then spent two hours back at the hotel detangling my hair. Convertibles, sea breezes and long hair do not mixeth well.'

Harry is busy building a fire but acknowledges me with a smile. I realised before I got here that by turning up on time, I'd probably be one of the first people to arrive, but I wanted to offer a helping hand. Everything seems to be under control, though, and Harry won't hear of me helping when I offer.

I notice Ethan walking through the sand and with nowhere to turn or task to busy myself with, my stomach sinks. He's wearing cargo shorts, and he's shirtless, his T-shirt tucked into the back of the shorts, flapping behind him. I try not to look at his tanned, toned chest, whilst Barney, even from a good fifteen metres away, is less discreet. His jaw is practically in the sand.

'I come bearing gifts.' Ethan places a cooler in the sand with a thump. 'Steaks and beers,' he says when we glance at it quizzically.

'Hi. Again.' He runs his hand through his hair, and the few golden strands mixed in with the brown ones reflect the sunlight. His eyes catch mine and I realise he's talking to me.

'Hi,' I say back. Other than Harry and Barney, we're the only two people here.

'I'm just going to double check Barney got a beach-fire permit before I light this thing.' Harry stands up and makes a beeline for Barney, who is setting up a foldaway table and some deckchairs and my heart starts to beat rapidly. I've never been in Ethan's company and lacked a snarky comment before, but he's brought steaks and beers, what could I possibly snipe about? He's a delightful guest.

'How was your drive out?' Ethan asks after a few moments of uncomfortable silent shuffling. This new dynamic between us feels weird.

'Fine,' I say, not wanting to speak any more than I have to, but the silence is so awkward that I add, 'I loved the car.'

He takes his T-shirt from the back of his shorts and lays it out on the sand and sits on it, his movement casting a fresh, lemony scent. 'They're fun in the summer.'

I nod and glance over to Harry and Barney for a reason to go over. They're having a heated discussion about napkin positioning that I'm ill-equipped to get involved with. I'll have to wait.

'Your customer service has improved,' I say and add a smile so he knows I'm teasing. To my surprise, he smiles back.

'I figured I should work on it if I want to keep taking your money.'

Hesitantly, I untie my hoodie from around my waist and look at Ethan, who gestures for me to sit. I lay it down a couple of feet away from him before sitting down on it. 'So, it seems that you like to be on time for a party too.' I'm scrambling for conversation.

'I thought these guys could use a hand, but they've got it under control.' He leans back to rest on his hands. 'Actually, that's a lie, I thought they said five-thirty, so technically, I'm an hour late.'

I laugh softly, though I can't tell if he is late or he really did want to help. Something inside of me thinks it's the latter.

'Do you want a beer?'

66

I'm a little taken aback, small talk is one thing but having a drink together is another. Some alcohol would be brilliant though.

'I'd love one.' I feel guilty when I catch how full Ethan's cool box is. All I'd brought along was a bag of giant marshmallows, and that was only because I'd never seen them before and got excited by them in the shop.

There's a hiss as Ethan pops the lid off the cold bottle before handing it to me.

He tilts his head to take a sip of his beer, and his Adam's apple glides up and down. 'This has got to be one of my favourite places to sit and enjoy a beer.'

'It's beautiful,' I agree, without taking my eyes off Ethan, who is staring out across the water. Whilst he has a near perfect record of driving me mad, something about him is so compelling. I can't put my finger on what it is and it's hard not to look at him when I know I won't get caught. He almost seems lost.

'So where do you live when you're in England?' he asks, and I'm grateful for his help with the conversation. A woman arrives with two children, a girl and a boy, who both look around twelve. Ethan waves, and she shouts 'Hey Ethan' before heading to place a bag by the table which Barney has almost finished setting up. When Ethan doesn't move to go and talk to her, I fill him in briefly on my past seven years in London.

'Where did you live before London?'

I swallow a lump in my throat. 'The Cotswolds.'

'The Cotswolds?' The words sound funny in his gravelly American voice. 'Sounds quaint.' He smiles before taking a pull of his beer.

'How about you? Have you always lived here in Provincetown?' I ask, mostly to make polite conversation but also because I find myself intrigued, both by Ethan, and by growing up in such a place.

'I was born here, but I went to the University of Massachusetts

Boston and ended up living over there for about ten years …'
He trails off and stares out across the ocean.

'What did you study at university?'

'Environmental Sciences. I was on the marine science track there. I've always been interested in marine ecology – living here it's hard not to be.' He lets out a small laugh.

Marine ecology to bike rental? I sense there's much more to his story, but I don't probe any further. I know only too well how an innocent question, intended to scratch the surface, can open quite a deep wound.

'The ocean fascinates me. It's like a whole other world,' I say. 'It terrifies me too though.'

'You have to respect the water. I've always surfed and kayaked. It's a given, living so close to the ocean. But even now, I'm still on my guard when I'm out there.'

'I get scared if I'm ankle deep and something brushes past me,' I confess, and he smiles an easy smile that warms his features.

'You'll have to stop by our kayak rental place, face your fears and all that.'

'Well, I suppose it isn't worth trying to avoid you anymore, is it? You're literally everywhere.' I laugh softly at my own joke and whilst it would be a bit strong to say I'm enjoying talking to him, I don't hate it either.

He pulls a pretend-hurt expression. 'The bike rental is my usual haunt, so unless Harry and Barney poison everyone tonight, there should be no need for me to cover. You'll be safe if you go tomorrow.'

'Thanks, but I'm not sure I'd know how to kayak. I'm happy with a book and a sun lounger,' I say, suddenly aware of how dull I sound. How odd it is that I care. When I look around to see Barney and Harry, I'm surprised to see quite a large crowd has gathered around the now-crackling fire. Barney is talking and animating with his hands and everyone is laughing.

'We should go over there and be sociable,' I say, not really wanting to move from this quiet, beautiful spot on the sand that seems to have embraced the shape of my bottom like memory foam. The sun has disappeared and the sky above the water has turned a soft grey-blue. It's the perfect companion for the gentle lapping sound of the water.

'Yeah, I should get these steaks on the grill too.' He stands up and dusts the sand from his toned calves.

Harry runs over panting. 'Guys, there are some burgers ready. Come get one.'

Ethan and I exchange glances. He holds out his hand in an 'after you' gesture, so I follow Harry.

'You two seem to be getting along now,' Harry whispers as Ethan goes over to where he dumped his cooler.

'We're being civil, but I do hope you didn't leave us together on purpose earlier? Your two single friends ...' I raise my eyebrows in anticipation of a confession.

'Listen, I'm a sucker for a real-life romance, and I'm not completely above matchmaking, but not this time. You're being paranoid. Ethan is off limits, and I know you are too, so believe me when I say it was nothing more than a coincidence that you two ended up sitting together.'

I eye him suspiciously, but he says no more. I wonder why Ethan is so off limits. At least I can chat to Ethan tonight knowing that it will be a simple, face-value conversation. That fact helps me relax a little more.

Barney is by the large charcoal barbecue, flipping burgers with an exuberance rarely seen outside of the Pineapple Dance Studios. I've no idea how they got that thing here, but I'm glad they did because I'm starving and the food smells delicious. 'Here you go, my dear,' he says with his hallmarked cheer, sliding a chargrilled patty onto my paper plate. 'Buns and ketchup are on the table.' I thank him and head over to where everything is. People have each brought a little something; noodle salad, guacamole and potato salad sit temptingly in mismatched bowls from different homes, and I love the community spirit of it all.

I take a spoonful of everything and head towards the fire, where Harry has just sat down on a deckchair with teeny legs that allow him to stretch his own out in the sand. There are about twenty people of all ages and walks of life gathered nearby. A family of four sit on a picnic blanket, a nomadic-looking man sits strumming an acoustic guitar in a world of his own, and Harry chats animatedly to the woman I saw arrive earlier. I eat and enter into polite chitchat with some of the local people, but I don't feel as comfortable as I did when I was sitting with Ethan. I suppose large groups intimidate me a little because I'm not used to them. Maybe that's why I'm getting nowhere in the boardroom.

'This is Sam, who I was telling you about.' The sound of my name jolts me out of my thoughts. Harry smiles at me then back at the lady. For a second, I wonder what's going on. 'Macy here has two children. Perhaps one of them could help with our little project?'

I tilt my head slightly, wondering what project he means, and then it dawns on me. 'The Rocks campaign?' Macy turns to call her children over, and I take the opportunity to give him a quizzical look.

'Give me the shoes and trust me,' he mouths. I dutifully pull off the trainers and hand them over. Harry disappears, so I pinch his chair, then slip off my trainer socks and pop them into my beach bag before digging my toes into the cool, damp sand. It feels heavenly.

'Is the burger no good?' Ethan sits down beside me, and I realise I've only taken a bite.

'It's great. I just got lost in my own little world for a while.' It's dark now, and little red-orange sparks spew from the fire and float down to the sand.

Ethan is cutting a steak with wooden utensils. He glances up, and the glow from the fire catches the side of his face. 'Wooden party utensils are more eco-friendly. It's irresponsible to bring single-use plastic to the beach,' he says, apparently anticipating a question I'm not sure I'd have asked.

'We need more people like you who care about the environment. Though I'm not sure how eco-friendly those Jeeps you rent out are,' I joke.

'I know! But I think you'll find I'm the bicycle guy. And I'm on kayak duty way more than I'm on Jeep duty.'

'Fair enough,' I say, taking a bite of my burger.

'Hey, Zac.' Ethan waves his arm in the air before turning to me. 'My little brother.'

A huge guy comes over accompanied by a petite blonde lady in a plain red slip dress and thong sandals. She has that stunningly effortless beachy look going on that I've never managed to pull off.

'Hey, bro,' he says, slapping Ethan on the back. Zac, I notice, appears to be made of one hundred per cent pure muscle. He makes Ethan look short and slim, even though I've always thought him quite tall and beefy.

Ethan introduces us, and Zac takes my hand and kisses it. When I see my tiny pale hand in his gigantic sun-kissed one, it reminds me of a scene from *Beauty and the Beast*. 'It's a pleasure to meet you. Sorry to rush off but I need to eat,' he says. His voice is deep but affable.

The blonde lady smiles and gives a shy wave. 'Nice to meet you, Sam. I'm Cindy. Hope we'll get to chat once the big guy has been fed.' She smiles again, and they walk over to Barney, who is still taking his chef role ever-so-seriously.

'My brother and Cindy are married, and Cindy has just found out she's pregnant,' Ethan says casually. I glance over and get a pang of something that I try not to acknowledge as jealousy, but I'm kidding nobody. It was the path Kev and I had been destined for. We would have made great parents. He was so patient and young at heart, playful too. My eyes moisten, and I use the sleeve of my hoodie to pat them before anyone notices.

'That's great. Have they been married long?'

'Two years.' He stands up. 'I'm going to get another beer. Do you want one?' I nod and he walks away. It seems a little strange that he'd start a conversation and then disappear, but then I see him chatting to Zac and Cindy. I guess he wanted an excuse to go and catch up.

When he returns, I've finished my food, and the beverage couldn't have come at a better time.

We chat some more, about work and our school lives, and it seems we're a similar age. We went through all the same phases, and I have to laugh when it turns out we were both addicted to *Eerie Indiana* when we were tweens, despite living thousands of miles apart and whilst I fancied the pants off the main character, he wanted to be him. He talks about how he did lab research in marine biology after he'd graduated and then came back to Cape Cod after a few years. He doesn't say why and I don't ask. I do notice that he doesn't ask me if I'm married or have a partner. I don't know why it seems so odd, he probably couldn't care less, but it's such a go-to question that I'm always ready for it. It's refreshing that it doesn't come up. The level of respect I have for him rises a little more.

Perhaps he's suffered something terrible like I have. It's plausible and I realise now that the reason he was so off with me in Boston could be connected and my stomach knots at the thought that it was me who was so out of order. Some of the things I said to him were awful.

'Ethan, I'm sorry for the way I've treated you.'

He frowns but then relaxes his face almost immediately. 'It's fine, I was a jerk.'

'I was a cow and all this time I've thought it was you who was the arse, but I think I share a big chunk of the blame. I should have left you alone—'

'I should have just taken the picture.'

'No, you weren't obliged to do anything. You're actually a really nice guy. Harry and Barney were right about that. I'm glad I've gotten to know you a little better.'

'There you are.' Harry collapses just behind us. 'Come on, we're all ready for you.'

'Someone's ears were burning,' I whisper to Ethan, who laughs and waves me off as Harry pulls my hand and leads me over to another fire further down the beach.

'Move away, people, private area,' Harry says to two men walking hand in hand, obviously spoiling their moment.

Macy's daughter, who I think is called Kayla, is sitting cross-legged by the fire, messing about on her phone. She's wearing my Rocks.

'It was a case of whoever the shoes fit,' Harry says. As I take in the scene, the initial ideas I'd had for the campaign start to develop. She's definitely the right age and seeing her playing on her phone looks so right. 'Harry, you are brilliant.' I jump up and kiss him on the cheek.

'Why thanks, Sam, I'm not one to turn down a compliment but I'm hoping you'll be quite brilliant too. So, what are you thinking?'

I'm already making my way around the fire, taking in the angles, the lighting. 'This is perfect.' The girl tears her eyes away from the phone for a second. She's beautiful. Caramel skin, braided black hair, and dressed in denim cut-offs and a baggy white T-shirt. She has an effortless flair about her that's perfect.

'Are you sure you're happy to do this, Kayla?' Harry asks. She shrugs and looks back at her phone. 'Perfect.' He smiles.

'Okay, I'll get to work.' I move to Kayla's right, where the light from the fire catches her silhouette perfectly. She's now lying back, head propped on a huge hooded sweater, legs crossed with one foot in the air. I pull out my phone and start filming in reportage fashion, taking candid footage of her scrolling away through Instagram, making sure to get the shoes in. I capture her facial expressions as she scrolls. They range from smiles to grimaces, and the way she lounges in the sand with one leg flung over her opposite knee is so very teen-like.

When I've taken enough footage, I walk back over to Harry. 'This is exactly what I needed, thank you.'

'Not a problem. I'm happy to help.'

I spot a skateboard near Kayla. 'Can you ride this?' I ask, picking it up.

'Uh-huh,' she says, her face glowing in the bluish-white light of her screen. *Brilliant*. I have another idea.

After thanking Kayla and letting her get back to her digital world, I sit with Harry as I crop bits of the video and play it back. It needs some dancey-pop music, but as a prototype idea, I think it will work. The second part of the video plays. Kayla is in the carpark. She jumps off a skateboard, flicking the back so it leaps up into her hand. The lighting isn't great – in the absence of lighting technicians, Harry had to shine his phone torch on her – but you can get the gist. It's so much more than pigtails and teeny-boppers. This is the Rocks brand; I can feel it.

'Harry, I think this is going to work.' I can hear the giddy excitement in my voice.

'I think it gets your message across perfectly. You go in there on Monday and knock their socks off.' He nudges me playfully.

'You'd better get back to your party,' I say, feeling more than a little guilty for dragging him away.

'I guess so.' He stands up and dusts his shorts down. When I don't move, he says, 'You're not coming?'

'I might just sit here for a while and check the video again. Maybe see if I can figure out a way to add music.'

'Okay. Don't be too long though. I've heard Mrs Penny the baker has made her signature salted caramel chocolate brownies, and you do not want to miss those.'

74

'Definitely not.' I smile at him warmly and when he's satisfied I'm okay, he heads back to the party.

I get nowhere with the video, but I'm sure there will be an app I can download when my phone is connected to Wi-Fi again. And to be honest, I quite enjoy the quiet time. When I look over to the barbecue, the crowds have dwindled, and people have broken off into small groups. Harry is nestled in Barney's arms, and I don't want to spoil their moment. Cindy is between Zac's legs, wrapped up in his arms, gazing at the fire. I catch Macy walking Kayla and her brother off the beach. I scan the group for Ethan. He's chatting to an attractive brunette woman who is laughing and flicking her mane around wildly. His body language suggests he's at ease, his arm resting lazily on his bent knee with one leg outstretched in front. I smile at the scene but then get a twinge of something uncomfortable and unfamiliar. Not wanting to break anyone's special moment, I slip off back to my hotel room.

My Lara Croft costume is small, and I mean small. I'm a size ten, but this costume is more of an eight – I knew I should have tried it on before I bought it. I know some of my old school friends are going to be in the pub later, because there is nowhere else in the village to go and it's the millennium eve for crying out loud, so I wanted to look good because I haven't seen them since going away to uni. I don't really have any proper friends here, so I've made a point of staying away from the village. Nobody has really seen the new me without the 'puppy fat' as my mum used to call it. This outfit is certainly going to make sure they do tonight. It's sad really, that I still care what they think of me, but once they see I'm not some loser anymore it will give me closure.

I take the plastic guns out of their holsters and stand outside for a minute debating whether or not I should walk in holding them to frighten the life out of everyone before deciding it would be too much.

'Woah. Don't shoot.' A brown-haired guy around my age is standing outside the pub with his hands in the air. 'I swear I did not help myself to a vol-au-vent from the buffet.'

I glance down at the guns and laugh. 'Oh, sorry. I was just sorting my costume out. I didn't mean to frighten you.'

He points his thumb to the door. 'You do know it's not a costume party in there, don't you?' My heart pounds and my eyes widen.

'Relax, I'm pulling your leg.' He flashes a cheeky grin and I get a weird fluttery feeling below my bellybutton. 'It is dull in there though.'

'Who are you?' I ask. I'd have noticed someone as good-looking as him around. 'I've not seen you in the village before.'

'I'm Kev.' He holds out a hand which I go to shake, but instead, he takes my hand and kisses it. 'Love your costume by the way.

76

I was a bit of a *Tomb Raider* addict back in the day. I think I even wore out the buttons of my PlayStation joy pad.'

'I hope that's not a euphemism.'

He raises both eyebrows and I giggle.

'And why are you at this New Year's Eve party if it's so dull?' I ask, trying to get the conversation back on track.

He leans his head in towards me a little and whispers, 'I'm sort of on a mission.'

'Is that right?' I say, placing one hand on my hip.

'Top secret.' His eyes twinkle with mirth under the orange glow of the streetlight.

'Hmm. And what does this mission entail?'

He glances upwards then rests his eyes on mine. 'I don't know if I should be telling you this.'

'You might have to. You've seen I'm armed.'

'Okay. I'm here to rescue all the pretty girls from the party. I can't begin to describe the horrifying scenes of carnage in there. There's an eighty-eight-year-old Elvis dancing with a ninety-year-old Madonna. Every under twenty-five is a St Trinian, and there's a Catwoman whose costume is made entirely of bin bags. The cheap kind – you know, the ones that tear easily and spill your rubbish out everywhere.' His brow puckers, and his mouth twists. 'And they have torn.'

'Oh dear,' I say, feeling giddiness rise in my chest. 'And this rescue mission … where would you have to take the evacuees?'

'I understand there may be some trust issues here, me being a stranger and all, so I'm happy to sit on that bench there.' I'm impressed he avoided the more obvious 'Back to my place' answer.

'It's freezing.'

'I know, but when I'm undercover, I pose as a beer delivery guy. See.' He gestures to a Transit van parked next to the pub. 'I have beer and coats.'

'Coats plural?'

'Hey, I have to be two people every day, an undercover agent

77

and a beer delivery guy. I can't be expected to remember where I've left all my coats too.'

I giggle. 'What about all the other pretty girls who you need to rescue?'

He leans forward so his lips brush my earlobe. It tickles. 'I've only seen one.' The feel of his warm breath makes me shiver. I should go inside but I don't want to.

'Okay, I'll have a beer.'

My parents are in the pub expecting me to join them, but they'll be three sheets to the wind by now and unlikely to notice that I haven't arrived. Still, they'll have something to say about it tomorrow, no doubt. I sit on the bench and snuggle into the parka jacket that Kev gives me, and we sit and chat. He's so easy to talk to, I find myself telling him about my school years and how I had no friends, and he can't believe the other kids could be so cruel. He wasn't a cool kid either, because he was into playing the guitar and the cool kids played football, but he had friends at least. I've never spoken about my school life before, I've never met anyone who understood, but with Kev, I find myself wanting to talk.

'God, it's almost midnight,' he says, standing up and pulling me up to face him. 'My work here is almost done.'

Our eyes meet, and frissons of electricity surge through my chest.

'Ten, nine, eight …' He brushes the two Lara Croft hair strands behind my ears. 'Six, five, four, three, two …' I swallow hard. 'One.' He kisses me tenderly on the lips. His are warm and soft, whereas mine are like ice from the beer bottle. 'Happy New Year.'

'Happy New Year,' I say. People start to tumble out of the pub, and I realise I never actually set a foot in there. I got so lost in Kev's upbeat personality I just didn't care about seeing any of them. Proving myself seems so irrelevant now.

I knew this night was the night that was going to change everything.

This night was supposed to be the start of a new me, and it is. I just didn't have the right plan.

CHAPTER 14

'Hey, you disappeared last night.'

I turn to see Ethan jogging up the main street behind me when I come out of the coffee shop on the street near the pier. Is that disappointment I sense in his tone?

'Oh, I got tired and left.'

He raises his eyebrows. 'That's a shame – the guitars came out and we had an acoustic Red Hot Chili Peppers set, courtesy of Billy the Biker.'

Billy the Biker? 'Sounds like fun.'

'What are you doing for the rest of the day?' he asks.

I point my reusable coffee cup towards my wheelie case behind me. 'Early ferry back to Boston.' I booked it thinking I should spend some time there, maybe do some shopping. Now I've been paid, some more clothes would come in handy.

'Oh.' His eyes flick to the floor and back to meet mine. 'I was going to see if you fancied kayaking.'

'Kayaking?'

A wide smile erupts on his face. 'Don't look so worried. It's just because we were talking about it last night. I was going to ask you if you wanted to come down to try it, but you'd vanished. Another time maybe?'

I look at the solid outline of his jaw. The left side of his mouth curves upwards, decorated with light brown scruff, and I have a compelling urge to reach out and trace a line down it with my finger. I clench my cup tighter. I'm not sure whether it's to guarantee that I won't or the frustration of wanting to.

'Okay. I'm probably going to be back next weekend, if that

79

works?' The thought of spending the weekend in the apartment with the blokes is far from appealing. I'd most likely be holed up in my room as I have been for the past two weeks.

'Saturday morning?'

I pause for a moment and can't think of a reason to say no. 'Saturday morning it is,' I reply, not quite sure what I've signed up for.

'Okay. It will be fun, I promise,' he says and my stomach dances.

The ferry has pulled into the dock, and Ethan notices too. 'I'd better let you go, but come down to the boat rental place on the beach about nine next week.'

I nod. 'See you next week.' I turn to leave.

'Oh, and wear something you don't mind getting wet,' he says, and I catch myself smiling.

***

The next morning I'm filled with optimism as I stroll into the office, coffee in hand. There's an unusual buzz about the place, and everyone, even the janitor, looks frazzled. 'What's going on?' I ask the receptionist as I scan my ID badge.

'The chief execs from Rocks have turned up unannounced for a progress meeting.'

I give her a look of horror and she just shrugs but then, she doesn't have to deal with the situation. I make my way to the boardroom. Through the glass, I see Patrick is already sitting around the table with two men I haven't seen before. One of the men is black and wearing a red T-shirt with indigo jeans. He has chin-length braided hair and on his wrist is a diamond-encrusted watch that looks like it cost the same as a three-bed detached on the outskirts of London. The other man is white with fair hair, dressed similarly but with a green T-shirt and the addition of a huge blingy gold necklace. As the rest of the team filter in, I reel with horror at the fact I haven't had time to show Patrick my new ideas for the campaign. This is going to be a disaster. I feel like I've swallowed a lead weight as I clutch the handle, but because they spot me hovering outside, I walk in holding my head high.

'Good morning,' Patrick says tersely as I slip into the only vacant chair.

'Morning.' I mimic his dry tone and begin to shuffle the papers that have been set out.

'Okay.' Red-T-shirt-Rocks-guy clasps his hands together. 'I'm just gonna come right out and say it. We ain't feelin' this project, man.'

Patrick's jaw slackens, and I can practically see the bravado oozing out of the black cavernous hole.

Green-T-shirt-Rocks-guy slams his right foot on the desk, and several of us jump. 'Look at my feet. I am wearing Rocks. Do I look like a sweet little girl to you?'

'No, sir,' Patrick says.

'My man Karma over there is wearing Rocks too. Does *he* look like a sweet little girl?' He gestures to red-T-shirt guy.

Patrick shakes his head vehemently. 'No, sir.'

'Good, cos that ain't the look I was going for when I got dressed and put my kicks on this morning and that image ain't Rocks.'

'We just felt that for the teen line—'

Green T-shirt guy holds a hand up. 'Just show us what else you got?'

A sheen has formed on Patrick's brow, and the rest of the team members' behaviour ranges from staring at the papers on the desk in front of themselves to glancing blankly at one another. The silence is thick, almost tangible, and I know for a fact they have nothing else. Patrick was so sure he had this nailed that the team put everything into this one idea.

It's now or never. My pulse races, pounding in my ears. Should I play them my video? It could save the day, and I could be hailed as a heroine. Or it could be career suicide and a one-way ticket back to Blighty?

My hand trembles as I take out my phone. I clear my throat. The sound cuts through the air, and everyone turns to face me.

'The ... er ... other idea is in its very early stages,' I say, trying and failing to sound confident. I glare pointedly at Patrick and the others, willing them to stay quiet. Nobody speaks, so I continue. 'It's just a prototype video, nothing flashy. Think of it as a mood board or brainstorm.'

I hand my phone to red T-shirt guy, or Karma, as I now know he's called. His blank expression gives nothing away, whereas Patrick's fixed glare speaks volumes. I ignore him.

The bass from the music I added last night starts pumping, and I sit on eggshells watching Karma. Green T-shirt guy is leaning over too. Soon, both of their heads start nodding with the beat. I'm hoping that's a good sign. A few of the guys around the table start nodding along too and I have to fight the urge not to slap them round their heads.

Patrick's fixed glare has softened to a look of hope as he takes in the scene.

When the music finishes, Karma slams the phone on the desk, and I wince – it's new and uninsured and if I'm fired, I won't be able to afford a replacement. 'Now that is more like it. What you thinkin', Peace?'

'I get why they tried two different approaches, it makes sense, but *you* get us,' Peace says, pointing at me.

They both stand. 'We'll be back next week to see the ideas for this campaign in full.'

As they leave, the palpable tension wafts out with them, and there are sighs of relief from around the table.

'What the hell was that?' Patrick asks as the door closes. His face is red.

'Me saving your arse,' I say sharply, though my English accent alone would have added the necessary edge.

82

'Not exactly a team player, are you, missy?' His jaw is hard-set. 'What, did you sit on this waiting to undermine us and make us look stupid in front of our clients?'

In for a penny … 'Patrick,' I reason, 'I've been trying to be part of this team since I arrived here, but you keep sending me on pointless errands and ignoring my suggestions. I tried to tell you on day one that the ideas weren't in keeping with the brand, and you dressed me down and sent me for coffee and doughnuts.'

He stares at me for a moment. I'm painfully aware that all eyes in the room are on me.

Then he exhales and throws his hands up in the air. 'Show me what you've got.'

***

A few days later, Patrick and I have come up with a whole campaign of ideas together, using my video as the basis. We've talked about activities, style, fashion and using a diverse range of models and actors to represent real people. My voice and body are jittery with excitement, and I'm not ashamed of myself for smirking when Carl is sent out for coffee and doughnuts on Tuesday and Wednesday. They taste so much better when someone else fetches them for you.

On Friday, the mock-ups come back from the art department.

'Wow' is the general consensus when we present the finished prototype adverts to the team.

We have a range of online ads, including stills and snippets of my video for Facebook and YouTube, thumbnails and stills for online remarketing and a range of glossy, printed stills for in-store displays and magazine adverts. A still shot of Kayla's trainer-clad foot in the air with the fire glowing behind it has provided the basis. If the people from Rocks are happy, we can go ahead and start organising shoots with actors and models.

'Let's grab a celebratory drink.' Patrick is addressing the boardroom but looks at me pointedly. I chew on my lip for a second. I have a ferry booked to Provincetown tonight and Ethan had mentioned that kayaking trip, but this is my career. Ethan will understand, it was only a casual invite anyway, nothing was set in stone.

I smile. 'Sounds good.'

I tap out an email to cancel the hotel for the weekend and book it for next weekend instead. The mood these guys are in makes me think I'll be in no fit state for a boat trip tomorrow either.

CHAPTER 15

Karma and Peace from Rocks loved the designs, and now our people are working with their people to get the project off the ground and I'm enveloped in dreams of attending the Grammys with Peace and Karma as their 'good friend'. They haven't invited me yet, but Patrick has bumped me up to project leader, much to the dismay of the previous leader, Frank, who, as far as I could tell, didn't have anything to contribute anyway. Patrick took us to a baseball match on Thursday night to celebrate the success of the project. I'm not usually a sports fan, but something about eating a hotdog in that electric environment gave me a huge buzz, even though I didn't have a clue about what was going on. I've come to realise, Patrick isn't as bad as I first thought. He can even be quite funny at times, though not always intentionally; he has a knack for muddling up his sayings when he's trying to make a point and sometimes his body language doesn't fit what he's trying to say. Since things are going so well, I haven't confronted him about his attitude when I first arrived. I will, but I want to make sure that this project gets the attention it deserves, and that means us both working together at our best.

By the following Friday evening, I'm very much looking forward to my weekend slice of R&R in Provincetown. Harry and Barney have invited me to their house for a small friendly gathering tomorrow, and I can't wait to tell them all about work.

When I arrive at the hotel, I'm worn out from the week. I grab a snack from the bar and eat it by the pool, watching the sunset, then have an early night. The following morning, I head to Ethan's boat hire place to apologise for not showing up last week.

'If you're here to go kayaking you're about a week too late.' He's racking up some kayaks and doesn't even turn around to acknowledge me. He must be able to sense my guilt.

'Ahh, about that. I'm so sorry. A work thing came up. I was so wrapped up in the project I didn't think.'

Silence.

'I'm here this weekend though, if you want to take one out?' I try to ignore the building tension. I hadn't expected him to be so frosty about it. I thought it was just a polite invite. We hadn't even set a time. Ethan is just being, well, Ethan, I suppose – ninety-five per cent grouch.

'I'm working, but you can go out.' He points to a kayak on the sand.

'Oh, I …' I think for a minute. Perhaps I could try it out. I don't need Ethan to go out in a one-man boat anyway, and how hard can it be? Besides that, I can hardly come marching down here saying I'm free to go out kayaking and then turn down the opportunity.

'Okay,' I say defiantly.

'Okay?' His eyebrows shoot up.

I jut out my chin. 'Yes. How long is it for? An hour?'

He rubs his jaw and looks amused. 'Go for it. I tell you what – no charge.'

'I don't need your charity.'

'Oh, I know, it's just that I wasn't going to charge you last week because it was, you know …'

What? What do I know?

'A friends hanging out thing, I guess,' he finishes, glancing away.

'Friends, yes, I see. Okay, thank you.' Is that what we are? I hadn't given much thought to it, and now having a label feels a little weird.

I take the oar from his hand and march towards the boat. He jogs to catch me up. 'You need one of these.' A life jacket is hooked over his index finger.

'Thank you,' I say politely, taking it and putting it on and zipping it all the way up for extra life-saving ability.

I push the kayak into the shallow water at the shore and get in, wriggling into position. My exposed legs are a magnet for the sun and I want to kick myself for forgetting to apply sun lotion.

'Okay, I have to give you a little safety briefing but first, do you have any idea what you're doing?' He pushes the back of the vessel far enough into the water that it's no longer touching the sand. It bobs about in the waves and already feels unstable.

'Left, right, left, right.' I mimic rowing. 'I think I've got it.'

He rests his hands on his hips but doesn't speak. He thinks I can't do this and that makes me more determined to show him.

He shrugs. 'Okay then. There's a whistle on your life jacket if you get into any danger. Stay between the buoys and don't go too far out.'

When I'm about two feet deep, I try the oars properly. The boat rocks side to side precariously and I have to wrestle with the oars to try and steady myself.

'You know what? It's pretty quiet. I'll come out with you,' he shouts over the sound of the surf.

'It's fine. I just need to get the hang of it,' I shout back. Frustration builds inside me at the fact he thinks I'm incapable.

'Nobody's going to come and rent a kayak today, the place is dead, and I haven't been out this week. Let me come with you.'

'Fine,' I shout. At least I'll get the opportunity to show him how capable I am.

Moments later, he pulls another kayak over to the water. 'I made a picnic last week, you know.'

My stomach aches with guilt. I hadn't expected him to go to any trouble. 'I'm sorry.'

'Don't worry about it. I make a mean chicken sandwich and I got to eat two of them, so really, you did me a favour.' He pats his flat stomach, which doesn't so much as twitch under the impact. When he's not looking, I can't resist patting my own out

87

of curiosity. Beneath the life jacket, the soft squashy skin jiggles. Maybe one day I'll do a sit-up or something.

'Why don't you have to wear one of these?' I yank the strap on my life jacket.

'Because I'm really good at this. And I was in a hurry. Plus, if anything goes wrong, I'm not going to sue myself.'

He slides into the kayak with the ease and grace I suspect I lacked. 'Okay, first of all, find your centre of gravity, and just rock your hips a little to get used to how the boat moves.'

He demonstrates, and I copy. As the boat moves, I instinctively grab the side, but once it starts to feel natural, I slacken my grip, riding each gentle wave that knocks the side of the boat.

'Good. Now, the trick is to keep the strokes light. Dance with the oars; don't just jab them into the water. Next, engage your core.'

'My core hasn't been engaged in a long while,' I say, recoiling at the memory of a bootcamp Bridget tortured me with before a trip to Marbs with the girls a few years ago.

'Try it.'

I tense the muscles underneath the remnants of my winter blubber (which I'm totally saving for next winter by the way) and discreetly jab a finger into my stomach. This time, I can almost feel my abs beneath the soft flesh.

'I'm engaged,' I say. 'I mean, my core is. I'm not engaged.' I'm babbling.

'Good. About your core, I mean.' Our boats bob up and down in the gentle surf as Ethan surveys the water ahead. 'We'll head out that way.' He points towards the horizon. I hope he doesn't mean too far that way because if I lose sight of land there's a good chance I'll panic and that will ruin the whole 'showing him I can do this' vibe.

'After you.' I watch his biceps tense with each stroke as he glides the oars through the water with ease. I try my own. *They need to dance.* Lightly touching the surface does nothing but splash me, so I dig them deeper and I start to move, but it's hard work. One big pull to the right and the boat turns sharply left.

'Are you okay?' he shouts. His boat is side on to mine and stopped in the water.

'Yes,' I wave flippantly. 'Just dancing with these oars. One step at a time, yadda, yadda.'

'You're going in too deep. Watch.' He sets off. I try to determine the correct depth of oar stabbage, or whatever the technical term is, but the few ocean droplets dotted around his chest are reflecting the rays of the sun, and it makes for quite compelling viewing. What has gotten into me?

I try again and manage to gain some momentum and balance, and once I find my groove it's quite easy. I follow Ethan as we head out further. Each wave knocks me a little, so I focus on them, anticipating what the next one will do and what I need to do to correct it. After a while, we stop for a break, and I start to feel a bit queasy with the relentless rocking to and fro.

'Look. A bluefish.' Ethan points to a large dark thing that darts beneath us.

'Wow,' I say, rather quite glad of the boat. As we bob up and down my nausea increases, and my skin starts to feel warm and clammy with the churning in my stomach.

'Are you okay?' Ethan asks. 'You've gone pale.'

'Um.' I nod. My mouth has become too watery and tingly to speak. I know it's coming.

My stomach lurches. I lean to the right to avoid throwing up down myself, forgetting the precarious centre of gravity I was keeping with my core. Instinctively, I reach out to grab the side with my left hand, but all that does is tip the kayak over even faster. The very moment the bile reaches my lips, my head hits the water and I'm in. I flail my arms about, trying to reach the surface and gasp for breath, but it's too soon, I haven't fully emerged and instead get a lungful of saltwater.

I cough and splutter in the confusion. I'm aware of rough

hands on me, yanking me out of the water and laying me over the fronts of the two kayaks. I lie there for a moment, still coughing. Ethan swims around and clamps his hands on the side of the boat.

'Shit, Sam, are you okay?'

'Why? Don't I look it?' I joke once I've caught my breath. I'm pretty sure I snorted some mucus out through my nostrils, and there's a good chance the sea hasn't rinsed all the chunks of vomit away.

'Not really.' He laughs, running a hand through his hair. 'What happened?'

'I think I got seasick.'

'Seasick? But you've been travelling here by ferry.'

'I know. It hasn't happened before. Maybe it's the small boat.' I let my head flop down to rest on my arm as my stomach continues to waver. My body starts shaking violently. I'm not out of the woods yet.

'I don't think I can paddle back,' I say, quickly, because I'm not quite sure what else will accompany the words.

'It's okay, I'll push us in.' He tethers the kayaks together and pulls himself back into his. I get back in mine and rest the oar across my lap and my head in my hands. The quickest route back to the shore means we land a little way down the beach from the rental place. The ground feels so solid beneath my feet, and I feel so heavy and cumbersome being out of the water that I fall to my knees straight away, taking a few deep breaths to calm me.

'Are you okay?' He kneels down beside and puts his hand on my shoulder. The heat from it makes it hard to think of anything else.

I swallow hard. 'I'm fine. I just wasn't expecting to fall in. Or throw up.'

'Well, there's a story to tell Harry and Barney at the party later.' He pats my back and takes his hand away, but I can still feel it. 'You are going, aren't you?'

'Yes, definitely.' The thought of going gives me a tightness in my chest and all I really want to do is curl up in a ball and hide.

We walk back to the rental hut, leaving the kayaks. Ethan says he'll sort them and instructs me to go in the cabin and get something to eat or drink. All I want is for one of the nearby whales to swallow me whole like Geppetto in *Pinocchio* but since going back out to sea will make me vomit again, the opportunity to hide in the hotel would do. 'You're not leaving until I see some colour back in those cheeks,' Ethan says as he starts closing up the shop.

'I'm fine, honestly,' I say. I'm surprised I don't have a lovely crimson colour in my cheeks to be fair.

'You swallowed a lot of water back there, I want to make sure you don't start coughing, there's a risk of secondary drowning.'

I frown.

'It's true.' He reaches up to hang my life jacket and I watch his arm muscles ripple beneath his skin. 'I was a lifeguard in my younger years. The job helped put me through college, or beer, if you want the absolute truth.'

I laugh. 'I don't think I'm secondary drowning. I'm suffering with nothing more than a good old-fashioned bout of primary embarrassment.'

'It happens all the time,' he says.

'I'm sure it doesn't.' I raise my eyebrows and he flashes me a grin.

'Maybe not.' He hands me a blanket. 'Put this on.' He must have noticed me shivering. I look at him with intrigue but he carries on tidying up the shop as though it was nothing.

'I had you all wrong,' I say, 'you aren't a bad person at all.'

'Well, *I* knew that all along.' He winks at me with good humour and it makes my stomach flip.

'I'd better go,' I say before anything else flips. My stomach has had enough exercise for one day.

Once in front of the mirror in the privacy of my hotel room,

I assess the damage. It's worse than expected. How is it that some people have runny mascara and manage to make it look sexy, whilst I, on the other hand, didn't even put any on but somehow have yesterday's smeared all around my eyes and look like I've gone ten rounds with Mike Tyson? Or one round. I can't honestly say I'd last much longer than that and I'd only last one round if he took pity on me and didn't actually fight back. I make a mental note to invest in a better eye make-up remover.

I can't believe another person saw me like this. Somehow, it feels worse that it was Ethan who did. And I threw up too. I let out a groan and hit the shower. Under the heat of the water, I start to feel human again, and that comes with some uncomfortable thoughts. Why am I so bothered about Ethan seeing me in such a state? He's just a guy. So what if he's good-looking, or he intrigues me a little? Why can I still feel his hand on my shoulder? He's 'off limits', whatever that means. I pinch myself on the back of my arm as I'm washing it with my pouf. It doesn't matter that he's off limits. *I'm off limits!* I don't even know why I'm thinking about this stuff.

After a power nap and a can of Coke, I'm able to drag myself to Harry and Barney's house. Heading into a room full of people I don't know isn't exactly at the top of my list of 'things to do' on a good day, but on a day like today, it's more akin to hell.

'Hi Barney.' I beam as he opens the door and pulls me into a warm, cuddly hug.

'Oh, honey, I heard all about kayaking. Are you feeling any better?' he asks, holding me at arm's length to look me over animatedly.

'I'm fine, but if the story has already done the rounds, I'm probably going to need a drink.'

He holds his own out to me. 'Here, take this. It's a Harney.'

I raise my eyebrow.

'Delicious, exotic and fun, just like your two Provincetown

92

BFFs. Drink that and you'll be fine.' I'm not sure being American counts as being exotic to a Brit, but I take it gratefully. He shepherds me through to the open plan kitchen-dining area, which opens out onto a large wooden balcony overlooking a small, well-stocked garden.

'Hey Sam!' Harry calls as he heads outside carrying a tray of shrimp.

I give him a wave and down my Harney. The house is already quite full. It's not exactly what I'd call 'intimate' with about twenty-five people all squashed in, but I suppose these guys are so open and welcoming they're just a magnet for people. Ethan is out on the balcony chatting to the brunette I recognise from the beach. She's laughing and twirling her long hair with her fingers. Going over to say hello seems a little intrusive, so when I can't catch his eye, I wander to the kitchen area and pour myself another Harney from the jug of green liquid, all the while feeling a little bit disappointed that Ethan has some woman fawning over him. It must be homesickness that's tampered with my chi or something.

A few people I recognise from the barbecue say hi, and some make polite conversation before heading over to talk to their actual friends. The moments I stand there alone, my skin prickles and I'm tensely aware of myself. I shuffle about, trying to find a way to stand that looks casual, but every position feels uncomfortable, unnatural. Harry and Barney are working the room, scattering their smiles, gesticulation and warmth around flamboyantly like confetti. Ethan is still chatting away to the brunette. I watch the clock, wondering what would be an acceptable length of time to stay before making my excuses and heading back to my hotel.

After polishing off a salmon blini, I finish my drink and prepare to say my goodbyes when I feel a warm hand on the small of my back.

'Sam?'

'Ethan.' He's smiling, and it's genuine, broad and natural. I wonder how many 'Harneys' he's had.

'How are you feeling?'

'Oh, you know … I'm fine now. Nothing some full-fat Coke couldn't fix.'

'Maybe next time we should stick to dry land.' His eyes glint. Next time?

'I don't think you can kayak on dry land,' I say in a playful tone, easing into the different feel of the conversation.

'You don't get as far, but it's much harder to capsize so, y'know …' He makes a balancing-scales gesture with his hands.

'Thank you, but I think my kayaking days are over.' Though the thought of not having an excuse to see Ethan next time I'm here gives me a sludgy feeling in my stomach that I'm not entirely comfortable with.

'Sam!' Barney makes a beeline for us. 'Ethan told us how he saved your life! I've visions of the Hoff in his *Baywatch* days.'

'I didn't say I saved her life.' Ethan's cheeks flush.

'Manhandled me more like,' I laugh. 'It wasn't quite as glamourous as *Baywatch*.'

'Hey! I was just making sure you got out of the water quickly. It's cold in there and it can disorientate you.'

'Hmm.' In all honesty, vomit and drowning aside, I quite enjoyed being rescued.

'You, Ethan, are far too modest,' Barney says, before heading towards his next target.

'Are you coming over next weekend?' Ethan asks when Barney is gone. 'I have Saturday off and was wondering if you wanted to go for a bike ride? I'll pack some of my signature chicken sandwiches.'

Instinctively, I want to yell 'yes' because I can't think of a better way to spend my Saturday. But at the same time, I'm turning into someone I don't recognise, and experiencing sensations that I shouldn't be. I don't like it at all and now all I can think about is Kev and my throat is thick.

I've met good-looking, kind men before, but I've always managed to remain unaffected. Whatever this weird feeling is I feel between us is new and it's ruining everything.

'I'm sorry, Ethan, I don't think I'll make it next weekend. Since this project took off at work, the guys want me around. It's a work hard, play hard thing.' I bite my lip before I can say, 'Maybe some other time', because there will not be some other time.

He glances down at his shoes before his eyes come up to meet mine.

'Maybe some other time?' he asks with a hopeful look.

'I'm sure I'll be back again,' I say, but it's a thin response which I don't thicken with feeling. 'I'm still not feeling great. Can you thank the guys for me? I need to go.'

'Wait!' He takes my elbow gently. 'It's late. Let me walk you.'

'Don't be silly, you'll miss the party and I've just seen Harry making a new jug of Harneys.'

'I'll come back. C'mon, I've probably had too many Harneys as it is. The air will do me good.'

Without reason to argue, I agree and once we say our goodbyes and step outside, everything feels different. The warmth of their small house is replaced by a fresh, salty breeze and the background chatter is now silence punctuated with the odd squawk of a seagull.

'It can get a bit much can't it?' Ethan says after a few moments of walking in silence.

'What?'

'The party scene. Especially if you don't know many people. I love those two but sometimes I just want to sit back and watch TV rather than make conversation.'

'Yet here you are having to make conversation with me through choice.' I make sure my tone is light and I glance at him, catching the hint of a grin.

'It doesn't feel like so much of an effort with you.' His words

95

linger, and little bubbles pop in my chest. 'You don't ask the same old questions about how business is going and if I'm heading off anywhere for winter.'

That makes sense.

'So, are you?'

'What?'

'Heading off anywhere for winter?' I tease. He nudges into me playfully as a few tipsy revellers spill out from a bar across the street singing a Lady Gaga song I can't quite place.

'I actually like it here in the winter. It's quiet, like the tide has gone out leaving just a special few …'

'Crustaceans?' I giggle. 'I'll be sure to let Barney know you called him a crab.'

'Yeah, I'm not quite sure where I was going with that.'

'Well, here we are,' I say, coming to a stop outside my hotel.

'Great views.' Ethan nods his head towards the building, which is bathed in the warm glow of the external lighting.

For a moment, we stand, staring at one another, like the awkward end to a first date or something. I know I should say goodnight and walk inside but for some reason I can't pull myself together. All of a sudden, Ethan leans forward and kisses my cheek.

'Goodnight, Sam.'

'Goodnight,' I mutter before turning around and speed-walking into the hotel lobby. I don't look back and I don't stop until I'm in the safety of my room. Ethan's kiss lingers on my cheek.

When I'm in the comfort of my hotel bed I can't help but play snippets of our conversation over. 'It's a work hard, play hard thing.' 'I'm sure I'll be back again'. 'It's different with *you*.' I flip over, burying my head in my pillow. I've always been fine with the way I live my life. Thinking about Ethan is disrespectful to Kev and that notion sits at the bottom of my stomach like an out-of-date cheesecake. I give my head a shake, but Ethan won't fall out of there.

Why does doing the right thing feel so wrong?

I wake up with a start. 'What is it?'

I realise Kev is shaking me. My heart pounds in my chest as my eyes dart around the room. Slowly, they adjust to the navy light.

'Kev? What is it?' I clutch the covers tight to my chest as I sit up to look at him.

'Shh, relax.' He strokes my arm. 'I've been awake all night, thinking about stuff and I couldn't wait until morning.'

'Jesus, you scared the crap out of me! I thought we were being robbed.' I shuffle backwards to lean against the headboard. He does the same.

'We are.'

Panic rises again. 'What?'

'We're being robbed of our happiness.'

'What are you talking about?'

'You're not happy at the printer's and this isn't the life we signed up for. When I married you, I promised you I'd make you happy and you're not happy.'

'Kev, I am happy.' I yawn. 'I'm tired but I'm happy.'

'You're not, you're miserable, I can tell.'

'It's not my dream job, but it's fine, we don't need to talk about this now, it's two in the morning and I will be miserable come 7 a.m. when I have to drag myself out of bed.'

'Things are going well at the brewery, I've managed to get our craft beers line into loads of bars in Gloucester and Cheltenham and we're already a recognised brand in the Cotswolds. I think you could give up work and focus on finding something you really want to do.'

'My boss asked my opinion on a font style the other day,' I say with as much optimism as I can force at this time.

'Sam.' He turns me to face him and places both hands on my

98

shoulders. 'Don't go back there. The world is our oyster, we can live off my wage for a bit until you find something you enjoy. Take some time to put a portfolio together and show off what you can do and put yourself out there.'

I think about what he's saying. The printing company I work for mostly designs logos and prints branded workwear for the building industry – it isn't exactly going to propel my career in the way I want but the money is handy. On the other hand, I could spend some time putting some dummy campaigns together and try to get in at some local businesses.

'We'd have to cut back, it wouldn't be fair to you.'

'Sam, you supported us when I was just the delivery driver. Let me support us for a bit now.' He runs his hand up the inside of my thigh and it tinges beneath his touch. 'You never know, we might start a family in the future and it will be financially impossible then.'

The thought of quitting the printer's fizzes through me, igniting little sparks of passion that I'd long forgotten about. 'You really don't mind?'

'Mind? No! Sam, you're wasted there.'

'Jimmy doesn't really need me there anymore anyway and his dog Mabel could probably fill in for me if he got a bit behind.' I look Kev in the eye. 'Okay, I'll do it. I'll quit my job.'

He cups my face with his hands and I get a shiver down my spine. 'You're going to shine.'

I pull him close and press my lips against his as his hands run down my back and under my nightshirt. 'Kev, it's like half two,' I say, breaking off for air.

His kissing becomes more passionate and breathy before he pulls away. 'It's not like you have to be up for work.'

CHAPTER 16

The next morning, I stay by the hotel pool to be sure not to bump into anyone. It's for the best to not come back to Provincetown for a while. I need to give these feelings a chance to simmer down. There are loads of other places with beaches I can go where I can relax by myself without drama.

'It's self-preservation,' I say to Bridget when she calls me whilst I'm on the ferry back to Boston.

'From what?' she demands.

'I know you don't understand, but the way I live my life works for me. It keeps the memory of Kev alive, and it keeps me sane.'

'But what you're saying is *insane*. It's normal to like someone. It's normal to move on'

'You know what, the signal is really bad. I'll call you back.' I make a crackling sound from the back of my throat and hang up on her. I know people don't understand me, and that's okay because I don't know how to explain it to them.

Later that night when I'm in my bed back at the apartment, I take out a photo of Kev and study it. The man who made me smile, who never said a cross word to me, the man whose face could lift my spirits in an instant, the man who made me feel invincible. Nobody knew him like I did. Nobody knows what they're asking me to replace when they make flippant remarks about my single status.

The rest of the week passes fine. At work we're in the throes of progress. The planning is done, and we're overseeing different ads as they materialise. The guys from Rocks are happy with everything so far and it now feels as though the campaign is coming together.

'There's my star player,' Patrick says as he enters the boardroom on Wednesday. I still can't quite get used to the complete personality transplant he appears to have had and one day I will tell him how his initial rudeness was unacceptable. Right now, I'm just enjoying the job and loving the headway we're making, and I still have my heart set on attending showbiz parties with Karma and Peace. 'Fancy a working dinner tonight? Sushi?' Patrick asks, barely lifting his eyes from the new mock-ups which just came in. I agree before I have a chance to mull over any potential awkwardness.

***

'Am I early?' I ask, sitting down at the bar next to Patrick. I'd told him to go on ahead whilst I freshened up at the office.

'You're right on time.' He smiles and there's a lazy warmth to it that I don't understand.

I glance around to see if there's any sign of Tony or the others, but there isn't and they left work when Patrick did.

'Is everything okay?' Patrick notices I'm distracted.

'Yes. Sorry. I was just wondering where the others were.'

Patrick fiddles with the cuff of a shirt in a way that makes him seem vulnerable. 'Actually, I only invited you.'

'Oh.' A million questions race around my head but not one of them presents themselves coherently.

He glances at the cuff he's still fiddling with before looking me in the eye. 'I just felt like we were starting to get somewhere at work and thought it would be good to get to know each other a little better.'

'Of course, that makes sense.' I let out a little sigh of relief as the waitress approaches us to let us know our table is ready.

I let Patrick lead the way and when I'm behind him, let the

101

air in my lungs puff out my cheeks until it's all expelled. By the time I sit down in the small booth opposite him, I feel reset and ready.

'You mentioned a working dinner. Have you brought something along you'd like to focus on?' I ask, but unless he has some paperwork and an iPad stuffed down his pants, I can't see how.

He bats his hand through the air. 'Oh, yeah. I just meant chatting through the ideas and building our relationship a little more.'

This is a new side to Patrick. The question I've been dying to ask is bubbling to the surface, but I swallow it down. At least let's get through the appetisers.

Patrick and I discuss the campaign as the waitress brings us two steaming bowls of miso soup and a couple of Sapporo beers.

'Okay, enough about work,' Patrick says, after we've chatted non-stop for a good half an hour and we've munched through several tempura rolls. 'Tell me about you.'

'There's not much to tell, I suppose I'm one of those types who lives to work. I go out with my close friends when I'm in London and I have a cat, Coco.'

'Oh, come on.' He gives me a playful nudge. 'I'm sure there's more to you than that.'

He's grinning and for the first time, I notice that he's actually quite attractive when he's not belittling me in front of the team. He smells quite good too and I can't help but wonder if he's made some special kind of effort for this dinner.

'I'm serious.' My voice comes out all high-pitched and it doesn't sound like mine. 'I live alone, I'm single—'

He gasps, in an over-the-top way. '*You* are single?'

'Uh-huh. And …' I lean in to whisper and I realise I've had a beer too many. 'I'm happy about it.'

I take a sip of water. 'Anyway, Mr!'

His eyebrows shoot upwards.

'I have a bone to pick with you.'

He groans and throws his face into his hands. 'I know.'

'You know! So why were you so rude to me when I first arrived?'

He sighs. 'I misjudged you. For years the same guys came over from the UK and we had a rhythm, then you waltzed in like some power-dressed super-bitch with new ideas and I thought you were there to ruffle feathers.'

I splutter my beer. 'What? I was trying to make a good impression and if you didn't assume everyone was up-to-date with your abbreviations and wrote the dress code out properly, you could have saved me some embarrassment.'

'I know. I'm sorry, I really am. I shouldn't have said that, nor should I have put you on coffee duty. I guess us dinosaurs just don't like change. You've certainly showed me what you can do now and I'll eat my words, all of them. Just not right now because I'm going in for another salmon tempura roll.'

'I forgive you. But only if you promise not to judge a book by its cover in future.'

He holds his hand to his heart. 'I do solemnly promise.'

The waitress places two sake shots down with the bill.

'Oh, come on. This calls for a selfie. Take out your phone and we'll mark our fresh start,' Patrick says, pulling me into the crevice of his armpit. Without the capacity to protest, I do as he says and snap a picture.

'See, now I'm your fun boss and not your asshat boss.' He laughs and I smile a little uneasily. This new side of Patrick is a little hard to get used to.

The waitress comes over and begins clearing our plates away. 'If you post that picture on your Instagram account and use the hashtag "Harborsushi" we'll give you a free cocktail of your choice,' she says cheerfully.

'Post it,' Patrick says and being a sucker for a free cocktail, I oblige.

'Okay. Done,' I say before glancing at the cocktail list. 'Two Boston Sidecars please.'

The waitress nods and disappears.

'I'm having a really good time with you tonight,' Patrick says.

'Me too,' I say, realising I haven't thought about Ethan once.

'Here you go.' The waitress grins as she places two rather potent looking brown cocktails down in front of us and two more shots of sake. 'These are on the house too.'

I have a niggling feeling that I shouldn't drink any more.

'Cheers,' Patrick says holding up his shot glass.

'Cheers.' I down my shot. 'Yuck!'

'So,' Patrick says after his shot, 'we make a great team huh?'

'Yes.' I smile politely. The room is dark and some kind of jazz singer has set up in the corner and started playing. It seems strangely out of context but I like it.

'Two potatoes in a pie,' he says. I glance at him sideways, unsure as to whether he means something different to the original saying or whether he does that muddling up thing on purpose. He's watching the singer and there's no hint of humour there.

He shuffles closer to me in the booth for a better view of the singer. He's so close that I can feel the heat radiating from his body. In the woozy haze of brandy and rum, I'm surprised at how comfortable I feel and so I watch the singer without shuffling away. I sip a bit more of my cocktail and start to feel an exciting electricity in the air. Patrick turns to face me. His profile is illuminated by the candle on the table. He looks warm and appealing. He glances at my lips and for a moment, I wonder what it would be like to kiss someone who wasn't Kev. My feelings are all confused with the buzz of alcohol and when he leans forward and his lips meet mine, I don't stop him. The reflex that normally kicks in doesn't, and for a second I kiss him back, out of curiosity not attraction. A second or two later, I pull away.

'I need to go.' I feel sick. It could be the alcohol but it could be the fact I kissed someone. I did something I vowed never to do again and my heart is pounding. I feel clammy.

'Sorry,' Patrick says, 'I don't know what happened.'

'It's fine. It's those free cocktails. I'll see you on Monday.' I grab my bag and bolt for the door.

***

On Saturday I take the ferry to the Boston islands and explore. During our bonding evening, Patrick recommended some places to visit, so I decide to see more of the areas around Boston. He texted me after the night at the sushi place and apologised. He said he won't mention it again and it won't affect our working together which I'm grateful for. I'm still riddled with guilt but it cements the fact that I'm better off alone. In some ways, I'm glad I kissed Patrick and not Ethan. Kissing Ethan feels messier somehow and it might have meant the end of our friendship.

On Sunday I head to Revere Beach, a vast sandy beach north of the city. I walk the boardwalk past the hotels and restaurants before setting up camp on the golden sand. There's an old-fashioned 'seaside' feel about the resort, and I love it. I snuggle into my towel and take out a book when my phone buzzes. I glance at the screen.

Where are you? BnH xx

My chest tightens. Part of me wants to ignore it because I don't want to have to explain myself, but that would be rude, so I tap out a quick reply.

Stayed in Boston this weekend. Hope you guys are well xx

I roll over and open my book, and my phone buzzes again.

We miss you. Are you coming next weekend? xx

I'm really not sure how to break it to them.

I think I already have plans. Sorry xx

Chapter One, I read. My phone buzzes again. This time I huff.

Is everything okay?

Since I got back from Provincetown, I haven't been able to stop thinking about Ethan. He's got under my skin and ever since the night he walked me home, I haven't been thinking of Kev in the same way. I've not felt comfort in my memories and it's almost like I've had to force them. The brain can only hold so much I suppose. I need to hit reset and get things back to normal because that's the way I know how to carry on. It pains me to do this, especially since they've been so good to me, but there's no other option. I have to tell them.

Guys, I don't think I'm going to come over for a while. You've both been great and I love spending time with you, but I have so much on at work and I want to see a little bit more around Boston before I go back to the UK. You should come for a night out in the city before I leave, and I'd love you to come over to London when I'm back there – it will be so much fun. xx

My phone goes quiet and, tentatively, I start reading again.

CHAPTER 17

'As project leader, you need to sort this out now.' Patrick's words are stern and final and the fact he's the same guy who kissed me just a few days ago is hard to believe. He marches out of the boardroom, leaving everyone gawping at me. Apparently, the people from Rocks don't think we've expanded the campaign enough. We've based everything around the footage I shot on the beach, only we used a range of models instead of Kayla, and professional film crews and photographers. We even hired some local skateboarders for the out-of-focus shots, and it was all done at one of the local beaches. We had, or so I thought, plenty of material. Patrick is right to be cross. This entire project has my name on it and if it fails and Pink Apple lose this contract, my career could be over and then what will I have? The thought gives me palpitations.

'What are you looking at? Get brainstorming,' I yell to the seven sets of eyes still on me.

Carl raises his hand. 'I'm not sure where we go from here. Do we look at other sports? These people are hard to read.'

I shake my head. 'I think we need to branch out further than that. We're covering the teen age-range. The material we have so far is still at the lower end of that. I say we think about incorporating some older models and have a wider range of activities. Let's take the afternoon to get some ideas down and report back tomorrow.'

It's a miserable week and by Friday, we have some ideas but nothing mind-blowing, and what the internet has taught me about the men who own Rocks, is that anything less than mind-blowing simply won't do. We've added basketball, track, cheerleading and dancing to the original mix and Patrick thinks a big gig scene might crank the campaign up a notch. With a few older models, it could work, but I'm hardly feeling excited about it. There really is only one thing I can do if I'm going to save this project. I need to go back to the place that inspired me the first time and talk to the person who inspired me.

***

It's been two weeks since I last spoke to Harry and Barney. I didn't hear back after I texted them from the beach but they have liked a few of my Instagram posts and things since. I can't wait to see them but I'm a little worried that they might feel like I ditched them when I stayed in Boston for the last couple of weekends, so as I stand here on the doorstep with my hand hovering over the knocker, my apprehension is palpable.

'Sam?' Barney opens the door before I've worked up the courage to knock.

'Hi.' I smile meekly, but Barney's mouth doesn't so much as twitch. Harry appears next to Barney and purses his lips when his eyes land on me.

'We thought you'd ditched us for the big city folk.' Barney crosses his arms over his chest.

'Oh, Barney, please don't be like that. Things have blown up at work, that's all.'

'Blown up socially, you mean. We saw your Instagram. Sushi, baseball and drinking with your office friends. It seems like you've found your way up the ladder and Harry and I were just the first rung you had to step on,' Barney says coldly.

'Barney.' Harry speaks gently and puts his hand on Barney's arm but Barney doesn't react. 'It did look like you were getting up close and personal with that guy in the last picture. It kind of felt a bit like you'd taken us for a ride after all your protesting about dating. Then you seem to hit it off with Ethan one minute and the next, you're off with some other guy.'

I plead with my eyes. 'You have it all wrong. If you let me in or let me take you for a cocktail, I'll explain.'

They look at each other for a few moments, and I wonder if they can communicate telepathically.

'We were just heading out,' Barney says, picking up his man-bag for effect.

'Can I join you, or is it a date?'

They look at each other. Harry looks like he's about to nod, but Barney's expression is more steadfast.

'She could come, I guess,' Barney says to Harry as though I'm not standing pathetically in front of them.

Harry shrugs. 'We're going to the beach bar.'

When we arrive, I tell Harry and Barney to sit in the back corner, overlooking the beach, and I go to the bar. The least I can do is get the fruitiest, most glitzy cocktails I can to make up for not being in touch.

'Here you go.' I place down three shimmery pink Cherry Sunsets. They have sparklers in and everything. Barney can't help but let the corner of his mouth lift with joy. I knew I could crack him.

'Thanks, Sam,' he says. Harry echoes it with forty per cent less cheer.

'I've missed you guys. It's just, well, I've been …' My throat becomes so dry it sticks together when I try to force out the words. It turns out admitting you fancy the pants off someone never gets any easier.

'You've been what?' Harry says impatiently.

'I've been … god, this is hard to say.' I draw a huge mouthful of cocktail and gulp it back.

Barney sighs. 'She's been falling in love with Ethan.'

Nobody speaks.

'What? No!' I protest when his words register. 'Not falling in

109

love. I hardly know him. I've started to like him more than I want to, that's all, and I wanted to put some distance between us before I did something I might regret. I don't mean physically,' I add. 'I know he's off limits. I mean that I just don't want to start to like him any more than I do already, so I stayed away, that's all.'

Harry looks at Barney. 'How did you know this?'

'He didn't. I'm not in love, remember?' I butt in, but nobody is looking at me. I don't think they're listening.

'It's obvious. The way she was looking at him when he was talking to Kimberley at our house. The way they were together at the cookout too. I've never seen Ethan like that either, even though Kimberley is always flirting with him. He spends most of his time trying to ease away from her.' Barney is far more perceptive than I've given him credit for.

'Oh.' Harry nods. 'I'd never noticed.'

'What is it about Ethan that makes him so off limits?' I ask gently, hoping that the truth will help me put to bed any feelings I may have developed.

'Oh, honey, it isn't our place to say. Maybe he'll tell you himself if you do get to know him a little better, but that's up to him,' Barney says.

'So, if you're avoiding Ethan, what brought you back here?' Harry asks.

'I missed *you* guys, but I also came for inspiration.' I fill them in on the backtracking that Rocks have done, and how I wanted to come back to the place that inspired me in a desperate bid to come up with a ground-breaking idea that really knocks their Rocks off. God, even in my head my pun game is shocking.

Barney throws his arms in the air, almost taking Harry's eye out. 'These showbiz types are divas, then they go into the business world and take their divaness with them.'

'I don't disagree with you there, but I still have to fix the problem. It's a big project, and if they strop off somewhere else,

I'll probably get the sack, so I need to put my kid-gloves on to handle them and fix this.'

'But they liked the stuff you shot on the beach, right?' Harry says.

'Yes, they just want more of it.'

'And they want to appeal to older teens too?'

I nod. 'They used the phrase "Generation Z".'

'I think I have an idea, but I'm afraid it's going to involve Ethan.'

I know where Harry is going with this. If I'm completely honest with myself, it's the reason I came here.

'I know – cycling, kayaking, riding an open-top Jeep down to the beach, maybe with a surfboard thrown in the back?'

'Woman, you don't need me.'

'I guess not.' My chest tingles with excitement. 'I suppose my confidence was knocked a little and I panicked. I think I'm going to head back to the hotel and outline some ideas for tomorrow. Then I can shoot some footage.'

'It sounds like you have yourself a plan.' Harry smiles, and I stand to leave. 'Sam? Will we see you again?' he asks.

One thing this evening has proven to me is that I really do belong here. I have to come back. I love the place so much and being without Harry and Barney left me feeling a little empty. I grin. 'Yes, I'll deal with my issues. I meant it when I said I'd missed you guys. I'll take you out to dinner next Saturday. How does that sound?'

'We could be tempted,' Barney teases.

I walk back to my hotel feeling lighter than I have in the past two weeks.

CHAPTER 18

I wake up early to the comforting sound of the surf and seagulls. The sun streams through the wispy curtains covering the balcony doors, and its effect on me is better than caffeine. My notebook lies open on the bedside table, and the pages of scribbled notes I wrote last night fill me with excitement. I'm raring to go.

It's not until I'm about to leave that the reality of seeing Ethan sets in. I have to convince myself that any thoughts or feelings I have on that matter are one-sided. He doesn't know why I haven't been back to Provincetown; he probably hasn't even noticed. Harry texted to say that Ethan is working at the kayak place this morning, so I make my way there. The initial sight of him stops me in my tracks a little. He's wearing a loose black vest, arm muscles rippling as he kneels in the sand to clean down one of the boats. It takes me a second to work up the courage to go over to him.

'Hi,' I say when I'm close enough. His eyes widen in surprise.

'Oh, hi Sam.' He stands, and I'd forgotten how imposing his full height was. 'I wasn't sure I'd see you again.' His tone is unreadable.

'I know. I've had a lot of work drama to deal with, and I haven't had the chance to come back. I've missed this place though.'

He nods, and his hair falls into his eyes.

A kaleidoscope of butterflies is disturbed in my stomach. 'I actually wanted to ask you a favour.' I explain all about the marketing project and my ideas.

'I'd be happy to help. Do you want me to model?' He strikes an Arnie-inspired pose, and I giggle, not because the joke was particularly funny, but because seeing him act the goat is so unusual. It adds another dimension to him. I'm suddenly aware of my own heartbeat.

Aesthetics aside, I am short of a model. 'Actually, I've been so wrapped up in the location and activity planning that I'd not arranged for a model. Not that I need a proper model, just someone to demonstrate how the actual shots would work.'

'I'm serious, I don't mind helping you out. This weekend has been pretty quiet so far, so I have the time.' He dabs his forehead with the hem of his vest, and I catch a glimpse of his toned abs. Testosterone is practically oozing from him.

I catch the yes before it explodes from my mouth, and mould it into something less eager. 'That would be really helpful.'

Using Ethan for the model would be okay if I had a pair of Rocks to fit him. His black-and-camouflage Havaianas are not going to work. If I don't have the product in the demo, the directors are going to be so pissed off they won't see past it. Then it dawns on me.

'Seeing as though I'm the only one of us wearing Rocks, I might have to realise my teenaged dream of being the next Kate Moss and do the modelling part myself.' I pull a face to emphasise how uncomfortable this makes me. 'Is there a mirror anywhere that I can use to knock a good twenty-odd years off myself?'

He laughs gently and points inside the office. 'In the staff bathroom.'

I return five minutes later with my hair in a high ponytail, hoping the Croydon Facelift is as miraculous as the tabloids would have had you believe. My denim shorts and white vest work in an ageless sort of way, and the fact I don't have any make-up on other than a slick of mascara also works in my favour. 'I don't think I'm fooling anyone into believing I'm Generation Z, but I think I could pass for a millennial.' Ethan stares at me for a moment then shakes his head slightly.

'I definitely wouldn't serve you any alcohol.'

I feel my cheeks prickle and turn my back to Ethan so that

113

I'm facing the cobalt water. 'I don't think I want to be out there kayaking.'

'Not after last time.' Ethan's tone is light, teasing.

'Funny, smart-arse. I meant that you won't really see the shoes.'

'Especially not if you vomit all over them.' He rubs the stubble on his chin and studies them. 'Although, it wouldn't make them any worse.'

I give him a faux glare, and he laughs easily. 'Can I use that kayak there?' I point to a turquoise and white one that I think will look nice in the shot.

'Sure. I'll pull it to the water.'

'Actually, I'll do it. A shot of me dragging it to the water might work well.'

He shrugs and takes the phone I proffer. He indicates when he's started filming, and I take the fabric handle that's attached to the nose of the boat and pull it through the powdery sand to the water. I wipe my brow and look out to the ocean.

'That looks pretty good,' Ethan says, handing me the phone.

I play back the footage, prickling with the discomfort of seeing myself on screen, but at the same time relieved that it does what I want it to. Motivated by that shot, I sit on the nose of the vessel with one foot in the sand and the other resting on top. I wrap an arm around my elevated knee and look out across the water. 'Okay, can you just pan around, making sure you have the whole of me in the shot, including the shoes?'

'You're really bossy when you get going,' he says. I ignore him. When he's done, he hands me the oar. 'Rest this on your lap and let me try it again.'

Bemused by his enthusiasm, I do it.

'That's a wrap,' he says.

'And still only 10 a.m.,' I say smugly.

The footage looks great. I have to admit, the oar was a nice touch. The whole thing suggests a nonchalance that lets the shoes speak out. It's perfect.

'Now then.' I pull my sweetest smile and kink my knee coquettishly. 'I was hoping to ask for another favour.'

An hour later we're in my favourite red Jeep, heading to Herring Cove. Ethan's brother, Zac, kindly drove the Jeep over to the kayak place and said he'd hold the fort for the day while Cindy manned the bike shop. I knew we wouldn't need the full day, but for some reason, I didn't protest. I can't seem to give up on wanting to spend time with Ethan.

'Okay, how do you want to do this?' Ethan asks when we've pulled up overlooking the bay. I jump out of the car and walk around it, surveying the vantage points. Ethan gets out to follow me.

'You stand here.' Absentmindedly, I place my hands on his shoulders to manoeuvre him, and the shock of their firmness and sheer size jolts me and I almost recoil. Touching a man is such uncharted territory for me. It's been such a long time that I feel like I've reached out and grabbed a forbidden sculpture at the Louvre or something.

Trying to act casual, I jump in the passenger seat of the car and put my feet up on the dash. 'Okay, if you can pan around from the back of the car to the front, keeping the camera on me and the shoes, that should work.' I make an arc with my arm. 'Oh, get the car and the ocean in the shot too.'

He does as requested, and I ask him to do it again after I've taken out my ponytail and let my hair blow in the breeze. I rest my head on my arm, and the orange glow of the sunlight flows through the gap it makes.

'This is looking fantastic,' he says. We take a few more shots of me running and skipping in the sand, and we sit on the bonnet (or hood, as Ethan calls it) of the car to play it all back. In the final scene, I run through the sand and turn around. The wind catches my hair, sending it in a dark stream behind me, and because I don't realise he's still filming, I smile. I was being silly, I felt silly, but I play back the footage and it looks almost flirtatious. I'm horrified with myself. The camera zooms in on my face, my smile. It takes me a second to realise that Ethan had to have done that on purpose. A tingling sensation runs up the back of my neck and I lock my phone and stuff it into my pocket.

'You mentioned bikes. We have time to take a walk on the beach or something first if you want to.'

That same feeling of unease I got when Ethan walked me home starts to creep up on me again. I want to run back to my hotel room, as far away from Ethan as possible, but I need this footage. I must pull myself together for the sake of my job. It isn't like Ethan has come on to me, and there is the whole 'off limits' thing. I'm just being ridiculous.

'It would be best to do the bike ride, I think.'

We call at the kayak place on the way to the bike place because Ethan wants to collect his backpack or something. Whilst he's inside, Zac comes out to say hello.

'Hey, Sam.' He smiles and leans on the side of the car. His size once again surprises me; he's built like Aquaman, but, strangely, he doesn't intimidate me like Ethan does.

'Hi,' I say.

'Thanks for getting Ethan out there.'

'What do you mean?' I'm confused. Ethan is 'out there' all the time. In fact, that's always been my problem with him. He's everywhere.

He rubs the back of his neck. 'I shouldn't really say. It's just that, other than work and family stuff, Ethan doesn't have much else going on in his life. Helping you out will do him good. I haven't seen him as enthusiastic about anything in a long while.'

'Oh. Yeah.' I'm not sure how to react. I'm not even sure what Zac is implying, but before I can ask, Ethan returns with his backpack, which he slings onto the back seat.

'Okay, Hulk Hogan, I'll see you later.'

His brother laughs, clearly proud of his size.

As we drive over to the bike place, I take a short video of the main street. The atmosphere is so carefree and happy that I hope

116

I can use it in the footage. We abandon the Jeep and Ethan kits us out with some bikes, puts on his backpack and turns to face me. 'I have a few ideas of where we can go if you're happy for me to take the lead?'

I let my arms fall to my sides. 'I have nothing.'

'Just down the bike track, there's this beautiful spot. I haven't been in a while …' His jaw tenses and he swallows. 'I'd really like to show you.'

Our eyes are locked on each other's and I realise I've not blinked in what seems like a long time. It's probably just a few seconds. When I do blink, it breaks the moment.

I force a smile. 'Great, let's go.'

'You go on in and help your mum, you know she'll be flapping. I'll unload the car,' Kev says, kissing me on my cheek.

'Are you sure? You'll be there ages. I think you've completely emptied Waitrose out today,' I laugh. Kev never does things by halves. 'In fact, leave a couple of bottles of white in the boot, oh, and one of the tubes of Pringles – we'll take some of it home. It'll never get eaten today.'

He laughs and shakes his head a little but doesn't argue.

'I'll see you in a min.' I kiss him, and inhale his scent. He smells of the fancy aftershave I bought him last Christmas; oud, bergamot and lemon. I don't want to be apart from him for a second.

Tearing myself away, I leave him repacking all the shopping that has spewed from his over-filled carrier bags and scattered across the boot, and make my way down the side of my mum and dad's house. As I unlatch the gate, the sound of my name jars me, stopping me from walking around the corner of the house.

'She's still young,' I hear my mum say.

'They're so besotted with one another though,' my dad says.

'I love Kev, I really do. But he's just so reckless. The way he drives that bike around ...' My mum tails off.

'I know,' my dad mutters. 'I thought he'd calm down after a year or two. Booking a holiday to Mexico with two days' notice is one thing – it's exciting, I get it – but then he gets her to quit her job and then he talks about wanting to move abroad every time they come back off holiday. I think he's getting worse.'

'And she wants children now too, she's said as much,' my mum butts in. 'God, we'll never see our grandkids if Kev has his way and they go gallivanting abroad.'

118

'I just thought she'd get fed up of him after a few years. You're right, he's a lovely guy but so unstable. She needs someone more … dependable.'

'What can we do about it?' my mum says. I can't listen anymore. All the weekends we've spent together eating Sunday lunches and going for walks in the countryside together, I thought they loved Kev. Was it all a lie? My blood burns with rage as I slam the gate shut and march around the corner.

'Oh, hi, Sam.' My mum's face already has red blotches of guilt smattered across it.

'Don't worry. I'm not staying. I know exactly what you think of Kev and our marriage now.' My voice is trembling. 'The good news is, you won't have to worry about us anymore because what you don't know won't hurt you. I never want to speak to you again.'

'Sam?' My dad's voice is thick with culpability.

'Save it.' As I turn to leave, I see Kev standing behind me wearing a puzzled expression as he balances a top-heavy carrier bag in both arms.

'What's going on?' he says, wide-eyed, almost scared-like.

'Oh Kev.' His innocent face makes me want to cry. 'We're going home.'

CHAPTER 19

We head out to the cycle route, Ethan ahead, carrying the rucksack. The sun glints off the shiny metal of his bike. I follow, admiring the view, which admittedly has Ethan in it. The long grass sprouting from the dunes that line the path blows in the breeze, and the ocean crashes against the shore beyond. Once we're on the smooth tarmac trail and have found a rhythm, Ethan slows and waits until I'm cycling beside him.

'You can't beat this view,' he says, looking out over the bay as we reach Race Point Beach.

'It's so unspoilt.' I'm more used to the commercial beaches of Southend-on-Sea and Brighton. 'I can't believe we could cycle here in less than half an hour.'

'It's one of the many reasons I love living here.' He looks wistful for a moment. 'I think a few shots of you riding up and down this stretch will do it.'

I look around. I love the rugged natural aspect of it. 'It's perfect,' I say, and we film the last bit of footage for the day. Being busy helps my consciousness of Ethan subside a little.

'It's a great spot for a picnic,' he says, gesturing to his backpack.

'Ahh, that's why it was so important. Food.'

He pats his stomach. 'I'm a growing boy.' He's joking, obviously, but for some reason, it sets me off thinking about those muscles again, and the thought of them getting even bigger is a bit too much. I swallow hard.

'Let's eat,' I manage.

We leave our bikes, and Ethan carries the bag to the water's edge and unpacks a picnic blanket. He gestures for me to sit.

'My finest culinary creation,' he says, unwrapping a sub roll sandwich before handing me half. I force my eyes towards the ocean because I can't help but watch him.

'Sorry, it's not actually a picnic, it's just my lunch, but if I'd known you were coming I'd have at least made you a full sandwich of your own.'

'Your generosity is astounding.' I nudge him playfully. 'So, how did you come to know Harry and Barney so well?' I ask after a few mouthfuls of sandwich, which is, as he promised, delicious.

He purses his lips and shifts position, shoving his hair out of his eyes. I'm sensing some tension. 'They helped me through something a few years ago,' he says, and I nod.

'You sure know who your friends are when you're going through something awful.' I let out a dry, humourless laugh.

'You've had that experience too? Though I'm sensing not quite the positive one I had with Barney and Harry.'

Damn it. I didn't really want to get into the whole Kev thing, but for some reason, I needed Ethan to know I could be there for him if he wanted to talk. In hindsight, mentioning it was a dumb move, and now I have no choice but to see this conversation through. Otherwise, I'll just look like I was fishing for attention.

I can remember it so vividly, the still, darkness of the house. The fact none of our so-called friends came in the weeks that followed his death. I saw them at the funeral, when they scrambled for words to say and came up with a few tired clichés. Having Barney and Harry around would have been a huge help, I'm sure.

I draw a deep breath of my own and begin. 'I was married. A long time ago, that is. Kev found me on the eve of the millennium and sort of changed my perspective on life.' As my mind wanders back to first meeting Kev, I realise I'm smiling. I feel Ethan's eyes on me, so I compose myself and continue. 'I was quiet at school, a bit of a loner I suppose, and I never felt good enough for anyone, and no matter how hard I tried, I never quite cracked it. I was always under the radar at best and I wanted to go back to my home village and make an impression to a bunch of people who probably couldn't have cared less. That is until Kev came along and properly saw me.' I rub my upper arms and smile. 'We were inseparable, and naturally we got married. Lived happily ever after blah blah blah. We were this sickeningly sweet pair. He was spontaneous and I was the planner but we worked well together; the strength to each other's weakness. People sometimes thought we were putting on our affection because it was so rare to see it, I suppose, especially after so many years together. But the truth was, we couldn't take our hands off one another.' I stop before the moisture in my eyes becomes too hard to conceal.

'What happened?' he asks softly. 'If you want to tell me, that is.'

I dab my eyes with the sleeves of my hoodie and study the damp patch the action leaves. Surprisingly, I do want to tell him. 'We'd stayed up all night, chatting about starting a family. We were both so excited we talked about names, nursery colours, childcare. Everything. Then the next day we dragged ourselves out of bed, bleary-eyed after just a few hours' sleep, kissed, and went to work in a happy daze. Bang on seven o'clock that evening, I got a call from his mobile.' I stop as my voice starts to tremor, but a warm hand on my arm gives me the strength to continue. 'It was the police.' I pull in a lungful of air.

'You don't have to say any more,' Ethan says, stroking my arm, but I'm committed; I can't pull back from the story. It's been trapped inside of me for so long, it needs to come out.

'He'd been to the chemist on the way home from work, to get ovulation strips. We hadn't even talked about using them, but he was just so excited about us trying. That's what he was like. He'd do anything to help his cause, or anyone else's for that matter. The hospital gave me the little pink gift bag he'd been carrying them in when …' My shoulders judder and loud sobs begin to escape. Reliving the moment never gets easier. 'He crashed his motorbike into the back of a car that had stopped suddenly because some drunk had stumbled into the road. His reactions were probably a bit slower because he was so tired ... The impact broke his neck. I got to the hospital as soon as I could, but it was too late.' The last two words are fractured by the wrecking ball in my throat.

'Oh, Sam. I'm so sorry,' Ethan says, and I notice his jaw tense as he stares out across the water.

The hollowness I felt that day, when everything inside me was ripped out and shoved back in, is still as raw as it was eight years ago. That's the first time I've ever told anyone the story. Everyone just sort of knew, and since I moved to London I've told people I lost my husband and how wonderful he was, but that's as far as I've ever gone. Even Bridget doesn't know the full story. She asked once and I practically bit her head off and she's not mentioned it since. I wipe my nose and eyes. I must look a real state.

'It was a long time ago, and I've come to realise that not everyone gets to experience what we had. I'm lucky to have that to hold on to.'

He nods. 'I get it. I had it too.'

I look at him, still staring across the water, his strong, tanned profile twitching ever so slightly in the shadow of the sun, and remember what Harry and Barney said about Ethan being off limits to women.

'Want to talk about it?'

'Nope.' He wraps up the last bite of his sandwich and stands, dusting down his shorts. 'Shall we make a move?'

'But what about lunch? We just got here.'

He rubs the scruff on his chin and shakes his head as though he's trying to rid himself of something. 'Sorry, you're right. Do you want a beer?'

I study him, confused, as he sits back down and pops the lid off a bottle of Budweiser. He takes a long slug before passing me the bottle.

'I don't normally drink at lunchtime. This one was left in the bag from a fishing trip I took with Zac a few weeks ago.'

'You don't have to explain,' I say, thankful for the taste of the warm beer. 'I didn't mean to pry. I just wanted you to know that I'm, y'know, here if you wanted to talk.'

'I know. I'm sorry, I don't *do* this. People have been on at me to *share* or talk ever since it happened, and I suppose I'm a bit like you in that I want to keep my private memories … sacred or something.'

'That's completely okay.'

'My wife, Nicole, was my high school sweetheart. In a small town like this, you meet someone you like, you keep them.' He smiles. 'She was killed too. Car accident. Six years ago …' He pauses and rubs his face. 'Six years to the day I met you in Boston.'

Cogs start to whirl and click into place. 'God, I'm so sorry. So, when you said you were having a bad day, you really were having an awful day.' I feel like a narcissistic idiot looking back on my behaviour that day. Why the hell didn't I just leave him alone? All because I couldn't get a decent selfie.

'It's no excuse for being so rude to you, but I'd just been to the Public Garden in Boston to see the swan boats there. They're these cheesy boat things with huge plastic swans on that Nicole used to love. Every time we were in the city she'd drag me on them. Anyway, they'd brought back a few memories, and you caught me in the middle of them.'

My stomach turns. 'I bet the last thing you needed was a giddy Brit with a camera and bags of enthusiasm.'

'You deserved some good manners at least.'

'That's true,' I say. He smiles, and its brightness makes me smile too.

'Anyway, Barney and Harry knew me from the bike place – would you believe that they used to cycle a lot? They were so

124

supportive and helpful when they heard the news, especially with Lexi.' He casts me a sideways look, waiting, I think, for a reaction.

'Lexi?'

He clamps his lips together and breathes out through his nose. 'My daughter.'

Daughter? Wow. I nod encouragingly, trying to remain impartial to this huge bombshell.

'She was only six months old at the time, so you can imagine how difficult it was. Nicole had always done everything for Lexi – I was in Boston a lot, working at the university. I knew come summer, it would ease off and I'd be home to care for that little baby and give Nicole a break. She was finding it tough, but …' His voice cracks, and I flex my fingers, resisting the temptation to wrap my arms around him. 'Well, we didn't make it to summer.'

I swallow back my emotion, but it feels like my heart is breaking all over again. 'I'm sorry.'

'That's what everyone says. "I'm sorry", like it was their fault, like they can take away a chunk of your pain with those words.'

'I know,' I whisper as I'm catapulted back to 2010, when I wanted to scream at people, *You're not sorry, you're sorry you have to deal with me and feel awkward, you're sorry you don't know what to say to me.* I can't believe I've just used those words.

'It's an instinctive reaction, I guess. People know it's a tried and tested "safe" response. They don't have to worry about saying the wrong thing.'

'What would you have wanted to hear?' I ask gently, not sure if I would even have an answer to that.

He hugs his knees to his chest and reaches down to rub a scuff mark on his trainer. 'Our families told me how much she loved me, how her memory will live on in Lexi and so on, but it was all just words; they couldn't quite cut through the pain I was in. I guess I wanted people to let me know that whatever I was feeling was okay. Even the anger, y'know? I needed someone to tell me to pull myself together because I needed to be there for Lexi. It was Barney and Harry who actually said those things in the end. It must have taken a lot of balls for them to do that, because I'll admit I wasn't particularly nice to be around during that time.'

'I didn't have anyone like that around me. Our friends didn't even visit, they just sent texts to say they were giving me space but they were "there for me". I let out a dry laugh. 'But I had pity by the bucketload from our relatives, neighbours and random villagers. Everyone buzzed around me, wanting to know what they could do. Could they get me some shopping in? Make me a meal? Drive me anywhere? I wanted to shout at them that it wasn't *my* neck broken in the accident, I was fully able-bodied, and that a broken heart didn't render you completely useless.' Even though it did.

'People mean well.'

'I know. I guess I just wanted someone to sit with and reminisce, someone who didn't react with awkward aversion if I cried or yelled about how unfair it was that Kev was gone, not space or pity.'

We sit in silence for a while, listening to the waves crash against the shore, sipping the beer, lost in our own memories.

'How's your daughter now?' I can't imagine how a child copes with losing a parent.

'Great; full of energy, very cheeky and far too big for her boots.' He laughs. 'Obviously, she doesn't remember her mother. She knows her mom died when she was a baby, and we talk about Nicole and look at pictures, but she's fine. She has the whole family doting on her, though. She spends far too much time at my mother's place and has the sass to prove it.'

I smile. 'It sounds like you've done an amazing job.'

'Believe me, it was a team effort.' He glances at me and our eyes meet, freezing me for a moment. 'I blamed myself for so long that I couldn't even look after Lexi at first.'

'I know how that feels. I wished I hadn't kept Kev up all night. I blamed myself for the fact he was tired, and if he hadn't gone for that ovulation kit … But we mustn't. Sometimes things are out of our control, and sometimes all we can do is remember the good times.' I smile and rub his back instinctively.

'The best times were the simple times. Her painting Lexi's room when she was seven months' pregnant and splashing me when I teased that I hated the colour.'

'Pizza in bed for breakfast the morning after a night out. Pretending we'd got our extravagant wedding favours from a posh department store when really we'd spent all the money we'd saved for them on a posh meal that we couldn't afford and bought them from the pound shop.' I smile.

Ethan's arms loosen around his legs and he lets his shoulders drop. 'I haven't spoken like this in a long time. It's nice to have someone to talk to who understands what it's like.' He glances at me. 'I wish you didn't have to go through what you did to understand.'

'I know. I get it. Me too.' I offer the last of the beer to Ethan who shakes his head, so I drink it and take the bottle to a bin near where we left our bikes. When I get back, Ethan stands up and stretches his long limbs.

'Do you want to meet Lexi? She's at Barney and Harry's, modelling for some face paint pictures for their Facebook business page.'

I freeze. Meeting his daughter feels like it would be crossing another line, taking one step further towards the unknown and crossing into a territory that I'd vowed never to enter again. But it's his little girl, and if I had a little girl, it would break my heart if someone refused to meet her.

'I'd love to.'

We cycle back to the shop then walk the short distance to

Harry and Barney's place. I start to get butterflies as we near the house, which is a strange reaction to meeting a six-year-old, but it isn't just any six-year-old – it's Ethan's six-year-old.

'Hi, Ethan,' Barney coos as he swings the door open. He spots me. 'And Sam.' He elongates my name, and a small smile dances on his lips.

'Daddy!' A little girl with sandy brown hair comes running down the hallway before leaping at Ethan, who catches her and wraps her in his strong arms. 'These guys can do mermaids, and pandas, but their attempts at Paddington Bear are actually dial-a-bolical.' Her voice is sweet, thickened with a confidence I've never encountered in a young child before.

'That's great, pumpkin, but you know, if these guys can't even do Paddington Bear, they can't be that good,' he stage-whispers.

She giggles. 'If you want something doing, do it yourself,' she says before sliding herself down and running back to the kitchen.

'I warned you about the sass, didn't I?' Ethan says.

'She's adorable.'

'For the record,' Barney says, 'Paddington is very difficult to do as a face paint. She wouldn't sit still for the fine detail, and if she'd have just let me put a red hat on her …' Harry puts a hand on Barney's shoulder, which he rightfully takes as a signal to stop talking.

When we walk into the kitchen/dining area, Lexi is perched on a stool at the breakfast bar and has managed to cover herself in brown paint. She looks pointedly at Barney. 'Okay, it's harder than it looks.'

'Thank you,' Barney says, visibly relieved.

'Although, I'm only six and three-quarters, not a grown-up like you. And I'm not charging twenty bucks for my services. You should really keep practising.'

I clasp my hand to my mouth to stifle a giggle as Barney's face reddens. He looks like he's gearing up to argue back but thinks better of it.

'Anyway, Lexi, I'd like you to meet my friend, Sam,' Ethan says, lifting her off the stool.

She looks up at me with big hazel eyes and tilts her head slightly. 'You're very pretty.'

'Oh, I, er … Thank you.' I smile. 'It's nice to meet you, Lexi.' I hold out my hand, not knowing what the correct protocol is for meeting a child like this one. She takes it and shakes it hard whilst studying me. Her eyes are deep, soulful even. It's hard to tell through the brown paint and whiskers, but she almost looks as though she wants to ask me something, but I can't tell what.

Suddenly, she glances to her left. 'Barney, can I borrow a washcloth?'

'Sure, honey,' he says, taking her from Ethan. 'I'll take you up and you can borrow Harry's good soap. The one from the fancy shop.' He giggles as he helps her down from the stool.

'Sometimes it's like living with my mother,' Ethan says, but his words are laced with warmth and pride.

'She's a little character, alright,' I say.

She returns with Barney a short while later, her face all pink and shiny. 'Harry, when did you last wash your washcloth?' She pulls a disgusted face. 'A dirty washcloth! Grams would say, "Oh, the ironary."' She giggles and shrugs. 'I don't know what ironary is, but I think she means you should wash the cloth.'

Ethan and I laugh as Harry shifts uncomfortably. 'Anyway.' Ethan clasps his hands together before Lexi runs any more rings around Harry or Barney. 'Shall we get pizza, or do you guys want us out of your hair?'

'Pizza sounds good. And anyway, Barney doesn't have much hair,' Lexi teases.

'Okay, but I'm on a juice cleanse,' says Barney, allowing Lexi's comment to slide. 'Just order me half-fat cheese.'

We all look at him in bemusement, and he throws his arms up and sighs. 'It's tough, okay?'

Whilst we wait for the pizzas, Lexi asks if she can paint my face.

'I don't see why not.' I'm not wearing any make-up anyway so she can't do too much damage. I sit on a stool, and she climbs up to sit on the breakfast bar.

'What characters do you like?' She cocks her head to the side and lightly sweeps the make-up brush across my eyelid.

'I like Minnie Mouse,' I say, realising I have no idea about what's 'cool' anymore.

'I like Princess Jasmine.'

'I do too. I used to love *Aladdin*,' I say as she moves on to my head. I catch a flash of blue on the paintbrush and suspect I'll be using Harry's ironically manky washcloth sometime soon.

'Oh my, you'll be working with us in a few years.' Barney leans over for a nosey.

'Thanks, but I think I'd make more money working for myself.' She shrugs, and I can't help but smirk. I like this girl.

After a few more minutes she announces that she's finished, causing Ethan, Harry and Barney to look my way. 'Ta-da,' I say to a chorus of oohs and ahs.

'Fantastic work, Lexi,' Harry says.

'I know. Maybe I'll train people when I'm older.'

'That's a great idea,' Ethan says, kissing her on the head.

'Daddy, I'll do you next!'

He laughs and sits on the stool opposite me.

'I need to see this fine artwork,' I say, standing up and walking over to the mirror on the wall by the dining table.

'Wow. Blue is really my colour.' I take in my entirely blue face. There is a smudge of black around my chin, which I'm guessing is my beard. 'So, I'm the genie? I thought I was going to be Jasmine.'

'I'm always Jasmine.' Lexi smiles sweetly as she paints Ethan's face green. The little monkey.

'Well, it's very good.'

The doorbell rings and Harry goes to answer it.

'You could get some tips off this girl,' I say to Barney.

'Oh, come on,' he whispers. 'You look like a bad *Avatar* cosplayer.'

I laugh. 'You can't be jealous of a six-year-old.'

'It's not so much her artwork I'm jealous of, it's her management skills. If she worked with us we could expand our empire.'

'Pizzas are here.' Harry dumps the grease-splodged boxes on the table.

'Daddy is finished. Guess who he is,' Lexi asks excitedly.

Ethan turns to us and hunches his shoulders. 'Well?'

'Shrek,' we all say in unison, and Lexi claps.

Soon, we're all sitting around the table eating sloppy pizza slices and sipping Coke. Harry and Barney share funny stories of their past, like when they got a supposedly male cat called Frank who gave birth to a litter of five kittens after disappearing for a few days of no-strings-attached fun. The kittens were homed, and Frank died a peaceful death a few years ago.

By the time we've finished eating, Lexi has curled up in a ball on Ethan's lap and fallen asleep. 'It's time we made a move,' he says. 'Sam, I'll drop you back at the hotel.'

I'm about to protest, but the bike ride and sea air have pushed me to a point where I could happily curl up and fall asleep. We thank the guys for the pizza since they'd insisted on paying and say our goodbyes.

'She's wonderful,' I say.

'She gets me through,' Ethan replies as he jumps into the driving seat. I climb in and buckle my seatbelt.

'I'd really like to thank you for today,' I say as we drive the short distance to the hotel.

'Really, there's no need. I enjoyed helping.'

'Let me take you out to dinner next week,' I blurt before regretting it instantly. It was so natural to make the offer to Harry and Barney, but asking Ethan sounded so presumptuous, and the ring of it sounds uncomfortable in my ears. My stomach churns, and I wish to all the gods that Ethan didn't hear me.

'Sure, okay.'

I swallow hard. 'Well, okay. It's a date!' I want to punch myself in the mouth. 'A dinner date, in the diary, I mean.'

'A dinner-date-in-the-diary it is then!' he echoes with amusement.

I've already told Barney and Harry I'll take them out on Saturday, so I agree to take Ethan out on Friday. At this rate, I'll be skint by the end of this campaign.

'Goodnight, Ethan,' I say.

'Goodnight, Sam.'

When I'm through the door of the small reception I slump against the wall. Even though I've spent the whole day with him, and we've really bonded, dinner with Ethan seems like a massive step out of my little familiar puddle of comfort, into a wide reservoir of uncertainty.

'It's just a thank you,' I whisper.

CHAPTER 21

'Kev?' I sit bolt upright, sweat covers my body. It takes me a second before I recognise the small room of the apartment that I've come to call home. I blink and rub my eyes. *A dream. But it felt so real.* He was right there. I lift my hand to touch my face, where seconds ago, Kev's hand rested. He was looking at me, smiling as he stroked my cheek. Then he started to float and I grabbed his hand, trying desperately to pull him back to me but I couldn't make a fist tight enough. Then I woke up and he was gone. I put my face in my hands and heave out tears. This whole Ethan thing seems to be going down a dangerous path. It needs to end. I know I'm attracted to him because I can't stop thinking about him. I don't know if it's because he's wounded like I am, or because he understands me in a way nobody else does, or if it's simply because he's gorgeous, yet honest and down-to-earth. I don't know if it's because he strikes me as a wonderful father, or because he's helped me despite me being no more than an annoyance to him most of the time, or if it's the fact I can just be myself around him and talk to him in a way I haven't talked to anyone since Kev. Whatever it is, it's dangerous and I need to stop. I'll stand by my offers of dinner next weekend because they're owed but that's it. No more Provincetown.

***

Patrick taps his pen nervously on the table, and the sounds of fingers tapping, and papers shuffling can be heard around the room, but nobody speaks.

134

Macy, the receptionist, pops her head around the door. 'They're here.'

Patrick springs to life, testing the projector connection by jabbing keys on his laptop to wake it up. I walk to the front of the room, clutching my hands together to stop them trembling. 'It will be great,' Patrick whispers, but I'm not sure if it's me or himself he's trying to convince.

Karma and Peace walk in. Their size dominates the double-doored entryway, so if any of us wanted to escape, we couldn't, but believe me when I say the urge is strong.

'Show us what you got,' Karma says, slapping his hands together.

Patrick takes a deep breath. 'We're just going to roll the footage for now, and we can talk through it afterwards, if that's okay?' Karma and Peace nod, and Patrick hits play.

Seeing it on the big screen is impressive – I look like a professional. Dare I say, I even look good. Is that how Ethan saw me when he was filming? Tony and Dave have edited little dust motes and sparkles into the sunbeams that glow around me as I dance on the beach. The shot of the main street cuts in, and one of the rainbow flags billows in the wind. The cycling and kayak scenes have been edited to look like dusk, then the film cuts into the older footage with Kayla. It looks like a day-to-night film, which was unintentional but looks great.

'Alright. Now we're talking.' Peace points at me. 'You have really pulled something special off here. You got talent … damn girl!' he says, looking at me. I giggle stupidly before composing myself.

Inside I'm screaming with excitement. I'm definitely one step closer to the Grammys. 'We're so glad you like the ideas. If you're happy we'll get on with the shoot.'

'We—' Karma puts a hand on his chest '—at Rocks prefer to say, "We see all colour".'

'Oh.' I tense, wondering if I've done something wrong.

'Girl, I'm loving the rainbow flag. That's what Rocks are all about, embracing everyone, from all walks of life, be they black, white, gay, trans ...' He bangs his hand on the desk enthusiastically and I'm sure there's a small reading on a Seismograph somewhere in the Southern hemisphere. 'Nice touch.' He winks, and they leave.

Patrick exhales. 'Well, that went pretty well.'

'Apparently so,' I say, relieved. 'I guess we're back on track.'

'Well done, Sam. You've pulled it out of the hat again. Alright, everyone, let's get to work.' As I smirk at his jumbled phrasing, he punches the air and shouts a loud 'Yeah!' A few people jump.

Planning is put in place; more models and actors are recruited, and locations are sourced. We've decided to go with a more diverse group of models at the request of Karma, and we couldn't be further from the original campaign. There is a buzz in the office that reignites my passion for the job – even the Pink Apple Instagram account is awash with pictures of our team out 'bonding' (or getting sloshed in fancy places as I call it when I'm filling Bridge, Viv and Sarah in on WhatsApp) in place of the usual business posts and meaningful quotes. I'm not ashamed to say I'm proud of everything I've done so far with this campaign. Once all the footage and stills are done, we can start working on the full campaign, social media, TV, magazine and so on. It's going to be great. By Friday, I'm on a high as I head to Provincetown.

***

Ethan suggested a little seafood restaurant on the seafront not far from the Macmillan Pier. It's nothing fancy, he said, but has great views and great food. When I arrive, he's already sitting at one of the outside tables with a beer. The sight of him takes my breath a little. His medium-length hair has been styled off his face, and he's wearing a white shirt with a few buttons undone, showing off his caramel tan. I feel a little underdressed in my blue jeans and red camisole top and to be honest, seeing that he's made an effort, throws me. Does he think this is a date? I give my head a little shake before walking over.

'Hi, Ethan,' I say, taking the seat opposite him.

His features lift as he smiles. 'Hi. How's your week been? Please tell me our efforts last weekend paid off?' He raises his hand to catch the eye of the waiter, who comes immediately over and takes my drink order.

'Ethan, it was perfect. They loved the entire thing, so we're back on track. I can't thank you enough for helping to save my bottom.'

He looks amused. 'I enjoyed saving your bottom.' The word 'bottom' sounds funny when he says it, and I giggle, which is a great distraction from the blushing I feel coming on. The waiter brings my glass of rosé. I take a sip, allowing the crisp, cool liquid to surge through my chest and ease the tightness. Sitting opposite Ethan is weird. Somehow, we've always sat side by side before, and looking into his deep blue eyes is hard. It's like our eyes are magnets with opposite poles. But some kid has hold of them and is desperately trying to force them together anyway.

'What do you think of Boston?' he asks, filling the silence.

'I love it. I know I'm always here at the weekend, but after work I see a lot of the city. It's much more laidback than London. Still busy though, which is why I like to come and get away from it all.'

'How much longer do you have here in the US?'

'Just short of four weeks.'

His Adam's apple bobs beneath his skin. 'It's going to go fast.' He sounds disappointed.

'Yeah.' I pull a sad face. I'd not really given much thought to going back to London, but now I'm thinking about leaving here to go back to my life there, it depresses me.

'Barney was showing me the Pink Apple Instagram account. It looks like you guys have fun.'

'I guess so.' If you ignore the first few weeks.

'It must be hard thinking about going to London and leaving that behind.'

'Yes. It's a very different environment.' I'm not sure where he's going with this.

'That guy, the boss …' He sips his beer. 'He seems to like you. Do you get along?'

'Er, yes, I guess. Though he hated me at first, remember?'

Recognition registers on his face and he nods.

'Have you got any more places you want to see, things you want to do?' His tone picks up a little.

'If I had the chance, I'd be here every weekend.' I really would. I feel so at home here. 'But since I only have the weekends free to explore, I might have to try new places. I'd love to see Salem and Rockport and Manchester-by-the-Sea.'

He smiles, but it doesn't reach his eyes. Giving up on spending time together is going to be hard and I wonder if he's feeling that too. Thankfully, he's 'off limits' because that makes my decision to stay away easier and all the more sensible.

I sip my wine. 'So, other than Provincetown, what are your favourite places?'

He sits back in his chair casually and the warm light of the setting sun illuminates his features. 'There's Martha's Vineyard and Nantucket too but I like being out at sea. I love the whale-watching trips.'

I want to kick myself for not doing the whale-watching trip, I'd seen the sandwich boards advertising them but not got around to booking. It was on my hitlist. 'I'd love to go to whale-watching.'

'If you don't mind an early start, I could take you tomorrow?'

I want to say yes so badly because I really want to do the trip and I love Ethan's company. 'I can't do tomorrow. I'm still doing my rounds of thanking people and it's Barney and Harry's turn tomorrow. Anyway, if you have any more days off work because of me your father will start invoicing me for cover.'

The corner of his mouth lifts. 'I'm a grown adult. I can arrange time off if I want to.'

I smile. 'Like I say, another time.' Something feels different. This feels easy and agreeing to go whale-watching with Ethan feels natural. It's the lie that I'm telling that feels wrong. My chest tightens, and my throat feels dry. I take a huge gulp of wine.

'So, tell me about growing up in England. I don't think our stereotypes do you guys any justice.'

'Likewise,' I say, thankful for the change of subject. 'My school years were not my best, to be fair. Have you ever heard of the story, *The Ugly Duckling*?'

Ethan narrows his eyes. 'No, I don't believe that.'

'It's true. I was a chubby kid, with terrible fashion sense, and I was good at maths. I really had very little going for me.' I add a small, dry laugh.

'I bet it was all in your head.'

'I wish. I used to get called all sorts of names, Big Bird, The Purple People Eater, Sloth … Kids are so cruel.'

'Well, if I was at school with you, I'd have stood up for you.' He reaches across the table and puts his hand on mine. Electric heat bounces between our skin, and the back of my neck tingles.

'Thank you, but you'd have definitely been in the cooler kids' gang.'

'Oh, I was a nerd at school.'

'No!' My eyes goggle.

'It's true. See, I was interested in marine life back then too. I loved dolphins. Everything I owned had a dolphin on. The other kids used to call me Eaphin.'

'They did not.'

'They did, and what's worse, I liked it.'

I burst out laughing. 'Ahh, that's cute though.'

'Cute is not what a teenage boy wants to be. Not in the British sense anyhow.'

'So how far did this dolphin obsession stretch? I'm intrigued.'

I rest my face in my hands, and in the light-heartedness of the moment I find I can look directly into his eyes.

'All my clothes. My schoolbag. My pencil cases and their contents, my ring binders …' He looks up.

'Well, that's not too bad,' I say. 'My Take That obsession was worse.'

He holds up a finger to let me know there's more. 'My underwear.'

'Okay, I stopped short of Take That knickers.'

'I told you I was a nerd, and that's not even the whole of it. My mom used to sew dolphin badges on all of my clothes, and I thought I was so cool.' Light bounces off his eyes as he laughs softly.

'Ahh, that's sweet. My parents used to buy me Happy Meals every time I was a bit down, and it just contributed to the problem.' Thinking about my parents sends a wave of pain through my stomach.

'Where are your parents now?'

For a second, I watch the condensation roll down the outside of my wineglass. 'They're in the Cotswolds still. I don't see that much of them anymore.'

'Oh.' He looks like he wants to ask why, but he doesn't. I like that he seems to be able to sense these things, but I find myself wanting to offer him an explanation.

'We had a bit of a disagreement a few months before Kev died. It was silly really, I'd overheard them saying they didn't think he took life seriously enough and I blew my top. We'd all been really close before that. For almost ten years Kev and I had gone and had Sunday lunch at my mum and dad's house and it felt like a huge betrayal to hear them say those things. After he'd gone, I couldn't really bring myself to forgive them and I couldn't live in that village anymore. I couldn't be around the people who went from knowing us as a couple to giving me pitiful glances when I saw them in the offy.'

'The offy?'

'Off-licence, or liquor store.' I put on my best American accent for 'liquor store' to lift the mood, and it comes out pretty good. 'Anyway, I had to get away so I moved to London. There was a small part of me that did it for Kev too – he loved to be spontaneous and a part of me wanted to keep that little spark of him going. It was a bit of a two fingered salute to my parents too at the time I suppose.' Ethan furrows his brow sympathetically.

'They adored Kev,' I explain. 'He was the son they'd never had, the person who'd brightened up their miserable daughter's life. He'd help my dad with DIY and my mum with the gardening. He'd make them laugh and call them nicknames that nobody else would get away with. That's why I was so hurt when I heard them talking so negatively about him. It was such a stab in the back. I realise now that they didn't mean it, they'd had a few glasses of wine and were having a bit of a bitch because we lived differently to them. It's taken me a while to see that and at the time, I just wanted to keep my memories of Kev pure.' I take a sip of my wine, and it hurts to swallow it.

Ethan stares down at his hands which rest upon the table. 'I totally get it, you know I do. Do you think maybe you've been a little hard on them?'

His words send heat through my body and I have to steady my voice before I speak. I know I'm only angry because he's right. 'If Kev hadn't died just a few weeks later, I probably would have listened to their explanations and forgiven them eventually. Maybe. But when he died, their careless words manifested in my mind and I couldn't bring myself to be around them. They were devastated by his death and filled with regret, of course they were. They even said they'd lost a son but I didn't want to hear about it. Your brain doesn't work properly when it's filled with grief, does it?'

'No,' he says softly. 'So haven't you seen them at all in eight years?'

141

I pause, trying to think of a way to word my answer that won't make me look like a total bitch.

'Not exactly.' He raises his eyebrow and I continue. 'Not face to face and not for a while but a few years ago I started sending Christmas cards and things. A year or so ago, I found a pair of my gran's old earrings and I texted my mum to say I'd send them over to her. Since then we've sent the odd text.'

'Don't you miss them?'

I don't need to think about it. 'Yes, of course I do. They tried so hard to be there for me after Kev died but I found it suffocating. It was so confusing after what they'd said, and too much in a short space of time. Out of anger, I told them I'd never forgive them and if they didn't stop trying to make amends, I'd disappear for good. So much time has passed that I don't see a way of changing things. The damage I've done is irreversible.'

'It may feel that way, but it's been eight years, and to them, they haven't just lost Kev. They've lost you too.'

His words hit me like a staple-gun to the chest, propelling painful tears up to my eyes.

'I know,' I say, my voice cracking. 'It's just been so long. I don't know what I'd say to them if I picked up the phone or turned up on the doorstep.'

He raises his eyebrow. 'As a parent, I wouldn't care. If it were Lexi who'd cut me out of her life and she turned up one day to apologise, I'd just be glad to have her back. I say if you want to patch things up, just explain how you felt.'

I blow my nose on my napkin. Not the most attractive manoeuvre, but fortunately for me, I'm not trying to be alluring. 'I'll maybe call them when I get back to the UK.'

'We have phones here too,' he says with a hopeful look.

'Don't push me,' I warn, jokingly.

'For me, family is the most important thing. Without them, I wouldn't have gotten through – even my dumbass brother was there for me,' he says fondly and laughs.

142

I don't even know myself why I had to get away. It was a feeling so strong, like a vice around my lungs squeezing me tighter after every encounter. I'm not sure there was a word for it but I knew it would only ease off if I left the village. It's so long ago now it's hard to remember. 'I don't know why, I just couldn't let anyone help me. Whenever anyone tried it was like the Thames Barrier came up and kept them out. I didn't want anyone in my life who wasn't Kev.'

'I needed help for Lexi more than anything. She was teething at the time, and I remember looking at her little pink face as she screamed and screamed and saying to her, "Your mother is dead, why are you screaming about nothing?" My mom overheard that particular breakdown, and she took over until I could think more clearly. My dad was great giving me a job, so I could be near her all the time. Giving up my career was a huge decision, overnight I'd lost my wife and my dream job.'

Life didn't feel fair after losing Kev. My universe was upended, and we didn't deserve it but taking a mother from a baby is something else. 'I don't know how people expect us to come back from tragedies like these,' I say.

He twists his mouth grimly. 'When Nicole died, the celebrant at her funeral said something that helped. She said grief is our unspent love.' He pauses and his eyes start to glisten. 'She said, when you lose someone you love, the love you feel for them has nowhere left to go, so it comes out in tears and emotion. The more you loved them, the more that comes out.'

'I hadn't thought of it like that.' Since my discarded tissues could have been packaged up and used to start an international wet wipe company large enough to rival Huggies, the evidence was there – I had a lot of unspent love for Kev. 'Does that mean I didn't show it enough when he was alive?'

'On the contrary, it had somewhere to go then, you gave it all to Kev.'

I dab my eyes with my napkin before my make-up is ruined.

'Going back to your question about how do we come back from losing someone we love? I don't think we do. But, in some ways, we get to have another chance at life. We can't replace those we've lost, but we can meet people who light up our lives in a different way.'

'One door closes …' I'm over-simplifying a broad range of emotions but it's true.

'Exactly. The courses of our lives may change, but we can still enjoy them. I get to see much more of Lexi now that I'm based in Provincetown and not Boston, and I get more of a balanced life. I meet great people, present company included …' He smiles warmly, and it's infectious enough to make me too, even if I know it was a playful dig at the comment I made to him when we met at the cocktail bar.

He's right. My career path has taken me in directions I'd never have dreamed of, and whilst being so career driven wasn't in my original plan, I'm good at what I do and I'm enjoying it. There's so much I have to live for and whilst my dream job is no way a replacement for Kev, it's not exactly a booby-prize either.

The sun has sunk below the horizon and the restaurant's fairy lights have come on, illuminating the decked patio area like enchanted hope.

'We should order some food,' I say, glancing at the menu, which seems dull in comparison to the views all around me.

'So, has there really been nobody else since Kev?' Ethan's question shocks me, and I put down the menu. I know we've been sharing, but my knee-jerk reaction to bristle kicks in, and I must get a grip of myself.

'Nope, nobody. No dates, no calls, no online flirting. Nothing.'

He raises both eyebrows before looking back at the menu. 'That's impressive.'

'It helps that all the men I work with are complete knobs.' I laugh. 'In all seriousness, I'm not out to impress anyone; I've just made a promise to myself which I'm sticking to.'

'Don't you ever wonder "what if"?'

'No.' Not until recently. 'What about you? Have you dated anyone?'

He shuffles in his seat uncomfortably, but if he doesn't like the question, he shouldn't have asked me.

'There have been a few dates. They were early on, and I just kept comparing the poor women to Nicole. They didn't stand a chance. Barney and Harry tried telling me to wait and heal, but off I went anyway. I think in some ways I was just trying to fill the hole that Nicole had left in mine and Lexi's lives, when in reality, we needed to let that wound heal first and then build on what Lexi and I had together as a duo. Now I feel like we're ready for someone to come along. I know Lexi would love it if I met someone.'

'But Harry and Barney said you're off limits.'

'Ahh, so you've talked about me?' He wiggles his eyebrows and smiles mischievously.

'Don't go getting all big-headed. It just came up.'

'It just came up, did it?' He's still grinning. I swing my napkin at him.

'Harry and Barney are a little protective of me and Lexi. They want to make sure I'm ready for a relationship and don't want me to jump into anything. They've seen the disasters of the past and want to make sure if and when something happens, it's right for us both.'

I smile at how sweet those two can be. 'I must admit, I thought they were trying to set you and me up at first. Everywhere they sent me I saw you.'

'No, they've been known to help singles out but they're not really the matchmaking type. They're actually quite reserved about things like that.'

'Oh.' Maybe I was stereotyping a little bit and I shouldn't have.

'They are good at sending business my way, though.'

'Hmm, so they were just using me to boost your profits?'

'Well, believe me, I did not thank them for sending me the uptight British lady with a chip on her shoulder.' His eyes dance playfully.

'Well, I didn't thank them for sending me to the arrogant bike guy who bit my head off.'

'I'm glad we've gotten to know one another now,' he says in a more serious tone, and any banter between us dissolves.

'I am too.'

The waiter comes over and hovers by our table for a few moments.

'Oh, we need to order.' I look at Ethan and pull a 'whoops' face.

'Actually, ma'am, the kitchen is closed now, but we can serve you another drink.'

'Oops.' I look at Ethan.

He shrugs. 'Pizza again?'

We leave the pretty restaurant (that I would like to return to one day) and grab a takeaway pizza.

'Where are going to eat this?' Ethan says. 'We could go to my place, but Lexi will be asleep, and my mom is there.'

'How about the beach?'

'Perfect.'

The lights from the restaurant we were at illuminate the sand just enough that we can see where we're going, and we find a spot near the shore to sit. The sand is cool and damp, and goose pimples pop on my arms.

'Here, take my sweater,' Ethan says, pulling a thin navy jumper from around his waist. I take it gratefully, and he hands me a slice of pizza. The moon is full and high above the dark water, casting its warm white glow across the calm waves.

'Well, you're a cheap date,' I say, nudging him playfully.

'I know, you got away lightly with the pizza. I was intent on the lobster back there.' He passes me one of the beers we bought.

I hold mine out towards him. 'Thank you again for helping to save my career last week. You really didn't owe me anything.'

He clinks his bottle against mine. 'I enjoyed it.'

I glance sideways at him, and he's looking at me intently.

'Me too.' Despite the jumper, a shiver runs up my spine, and I can't tear my eyes away. I know I need to. I know I should. But I can't.

He brushes the hair off my face and tucks it behind my ear, then he gently takes my hand, the one holding the pizza, and moves it away from my mouth. For what seems like an age, we sit like that, looking into one another's eyes, our faces partly lit by the moon, listening to the crash of the waves and inhaling the salty air. His hand is still clutching my pizza hand, and I want to joke about him trying to steal it, but something about this moment is so captivating that I don't want to spoil it. Instead, I swallow and realise my mouth is dry.

He leans in and I freeze. I know what's coming, and I want to bolt. But simultaneously I want to feel the lips of this beautiful man on mine, just for a moment. I brace for impact, but instead of our lips colliding, it's our foreheads. His is warm against mine. I can feel his breath on my face, slightly tinged with the smell of beer. He holds the side of my face, clasping mine to his, and I let my muscles relax. Then his nose presses against mine, nudging me into position so our mouths can meet. His hot, pillowy lips are on mine. I let it happen. When his start moving, I find mine are moving in sync. We're kissing and it feels amazing as my senses go into overdrive, his smell, his taste and his touch. It feels like it's supposed to. Nice. So nice I want to cry.

So much emotion wells up inside of me that if I don't get a grip soon, he'll feel the tremor in my lips or hear the hitching in my breath. It feels so right, so perfect, that if I were twenty-two again I would carry on for the rest of the night – or month, depending on my uni work requirements. But I'm not twenty-two. I'm scarily (just) old enough to be a twenty-two-year-old's mother, but that's by-the-by. Kissing Ethan is wrong on so many levels. I must make it stop.

Eventually, as his hand slides down my back, I pull away.

'Wow,' Ethan says.

Panic rises up inside me. 'This was a mistake. I'm sorry.' I get up and run across the sand to the road. The town is eerily quiet, and when I don't hear Ethan behind me, I relax. When I reach my hotel room I throw myself on the bed.

The pizza is still in my hand.

'What do you want?' I try to close the door but my mum puts her hand out to stop me.

'Sam, let us in,' she pleads.

I'd seen them at the funeral but I left before they could come over and speak to me. What the hell do they want anyway? To say 'I told you so'?

'Love, we know you're angry with us, but let us explain.'

I swing the door open and gesture for them to come in. They both hover for a moment, looking at each other, then my mum leads the way.

'So, I guess Kev crashing his bike proved your point nicely?' I fold my arms, unable to tell if I'm protecting myself from them or my own cutting words.

My mum's eyes are red and moist. 'Sam, we didn't mean any of those things we said. We loved Kev so much, you know we did. We were just exasperated with all the spur of the moment decisions and things. They were just words. Meaningless words.'

She looks me in the eye and I look away. These could be meaningless words too, or words born from guilt. Guilt of getting caught and guilt of Kev's death.

'Do you know what?' My voice trembles. 'Kev wasn't even bothered by what you'd said. He laughed and said you wouldn't have meant it seriously. He thought I was silly to keep cutting you off.'

I catch my mum smile. 'That was Kev.'

'Yeah,' I say bitterly. 'Too good for any of us.'

There's a moment of silent agreement from the three of us.

'Sam, we should come together,' my dad says. It hurts to look at them because deep down I love them and I know they're hurting but I can't forgive the things they said. Not now.

'What hurts the most, is that I know you loved Kev, I know you thought of him as a son and yet you still said those things.' I slump onto the sofa.

'We all say things we don't mean. I called your father a lazy lummox to my friend once but it doesn't mean I don't love him,' my mum pleads.

'Calling Dad lazy, isn't exactly the same as saying you hoped Kev and I would be divorced by now.'

'We didn't say that.'

'Semantics,' I bark.

'Let us help you come to terms with this,' my dad says.

'You could move in with us.' My mum puts her chubby hand on my shoulder, but I continue to stare at the same piece of peeling wallpaper that I've been looking at since she arrived. I'm empty. 'Look, love, I don't mean forever. Just let me and your dad look after you for a while, make you some proper meals, fend off the condolences for a bit, keep the well-meaning neighbours away.' She moves her hand down my arm and gives it a rub. It incenses me. I shuffle further up the sofa. Out of reach.

'You have to let us help you.' It's my dad's turn to speak. His tone is pleading.

If I have to listen to them any longer, I'm going to explode. As if a few home-cooked dinners are enough to fill the enormous hole Kev has left in my life. I can't stand their pity any longer. It's like my insides have been scooped out. All the warmth and love I ever had has gone. I'm a hollow shell, slowly filling with rage and hatred for everyone and everything that has the audacity to carry on living in a world where Kev does not.

'Are you kidding?' My mum and dad look taken aback, like they actually thought I was considering their offer.

'The two people who didn't think Kev was good enough for me want to help me get over his death?' I let out a small, dry laugh, 'You're always trying to control everything! Where Kev and

150

I went on holiday, what we spent our money on, and now my grief! Just leave me alone!'

'Come on, Jeanie, she's upset. Let her grieve.' My dad bows his head.

'We'll let you grieve,' my mum says. 'But we're here for you.' I chance a quick look at her red-rimmed eyes. Her mouth is drooping at the corners as though someone is yanking an invisible string that's been attached to them. My dad looks much the same. I go back to staring at the peeling wallpaper. From the corner of my eye, I see my dad take my mum's arm in his, linking her for support. My chest aches for them through the dullness I already feel, but I can't forgive them. They're alive; they have each other. I'm practically dead, and I have nobody. Nobody who understands this mess, at least.

***

A few days later, I open the curtains and the light almost blinds me. I shut them instantly, before opting for a compromise and leaving them slightly apart, allowing a thin ribbon of sunlight to stream in. I take a deep breath and walk to the doormat to scoop up the mail. When the doorbell rings I nearly jump out of my skin. I stay crouched by the mat, holding my breath. I see a shadow shuffle about outside through the frosted glass window, and they ring again. I daren't move. Eventually, I hear them walk down the path, and I exhale. That was close.

I scurry into the kitchen at the back of the house and sit at the table, fanning the mail out in front of me. Junk, junk, bills ... then something catches my eye. It's franked and looks official. I open it. It's about Kev's life insurance. They're paying me some money, and when I look at the sum, all kinds of thoughts fly through my head. It's enough to pay the house off with a bit extra, and for a split second, I feel a tiny bit relieved before I want to vomit with guilt. No amount of money can replace Kev.

151

I push myself away from the table. The air feels close and thick and I need to go outside.

I pull on my long coat, which doesn't match my joggers and sweater but I don't care. Grabbing my keys, I march outside and suck in a lungful of fresh air. It feels good. There are a few people walking down the road. Tourists, maybe? I ignore them and make my way towards the river.

'Sam?' I hear a woman's voice. I keep walking, but I can hear someone jogging to catch me up. I speed up.

'Sam?' She's getting nearer. 'Sam?' She pulls to a stop in front of me, and I have no choice but to grind to a halt. It's my mum's friend, Sue.

'Love, I wanted to offer my condolences. It's just awful what's happened, and if there's anything I can do …' She cocks her head to the side and creases her brow.

'Th-thank you, but there's nothing.' My dry lips crack as I force out the words. My voice sounds like someone else's; it's small and squeaky. I just wanted the words to come out and I used the front of my throat in haste. Now she's going to be all sympathetic and I can't stand it.

'Any time you fancy a brew or a chat, please, pop round. My kettle is always on, and I always have cake.' She presses her lips together, so the skin above and below squishes out.

Cake? Is she for real? Kev has been in the ground just a few weeks, and she thinks cake is going to cheer me up? My fingers ball up and I squeeze as hard as I can, pressing my nails into my palm. I manage to meet her eyes and nod before scurrying back towards my house. I walk as fast as I can, fixing my eyes on the path ahead, and don't stop until I'm putting my key in the front door.

Once I'm inside, I slam the door closed and slump against it. *I can't do this.* I can't be around these people who pity me. Most of them probably wish it was me who died and Kev who lived. He was the sociable one, the life and soul of the party, the one always up for a laugh. I was just the accessory always with him. I imagine life will get easier, someone else will die and the villagers will find someone new to pity, but I'll still be in this house, with the mirror in the hallway that's not quite central to the radiator cover because Kev had already knocked two holes in the wrong place and I said no to any more. We'd laughed about it and went for a curry. I stare up at it, as it taunts me with Kev's memory. Everything oozes with him, and whilst I love every inch of his soul left behind in this house, I can't deal with seeing it every day. Perhaps one day I'll come to look at it with nothing but fondness, but right now it just makes my angry wounds raw with sadness.

I need to get away. I could rent somewhere, just for a bit. I could get a temporary job for a few months. Somewhere busy where nobody knows me, or somewhere by the sea. It will be good for me.

***

The good thing about living in a quaint touristy village is that people always want to rent property. I listed the house with an online agency, and someone snapped up a six-month rental within days. So here I am, in London, south of the river, living in what barely qualifies as a flat. As I'm about to enter the converted townhouse it's in, my phone buzzes. I glance at the screen, which says 'Mum and Dad calling'. I hit decline and stuff the phone into the back pocket of my jeans before heading up to my new home. I feel guilty for not answering, but it's been weeks now and I still can't face talking to them. Plus, I don't have the energy to explain myself. I did send them a letter, so they know where I am and that I'm safe but I'm not ready for anything more.

I couldn't face a flat share, and I couldn't bear some of the less desirable areas, so I spent a lot more than planned on a lot less space than needed and ended up here. After a few weeks of applying for dead-end jobs, I decided it would be silly to ignore my field of marketing; it was never my job at a small marketing company that I needed to get away from. I love designing fliers and banners. Tomorrow I have a second interview for a marketing assistant post at an international company called Pink Apple Marketing.

CHAPTER 22

I didn't sleep at all last night. The rational and irrational parts of my brain argued without respite, and to be fair, they both presented excellent cases. The kiss with Ethan was amazing. It catapulted me back to my school days and fulfilled my teenage fantasies of snogging the fittest lad in the school, and all of the fluttery feelings I imagined would be par for the course were there. The attention scratched an itch that I thought I'd slapped calamine lotion on a long time ago, and I can't honestly say that's a bad thing. The moment could have swept me away in a new direction, and I wanted to let it. I really did. Ethan is gorgeous, honest, reliable, sweet and wholesome but he's also got this raw edge about him that gives me urges I haven't felt in years. If you could write down the perfect traits of a man, on little pieces of confetti and put them into a bag, shake them up and shout 'Hey presto', Ethan would emerge.

But – of course, there's a 'but' – what is the point in allowing myself to fall for someone? What is the point in having feelings for someone who isn't Kev and who I'll never see again once I go back to England? It's like swearing off meat and then enjoying a random burger ten years down the line. You might think you want it, it can do no harm, but you'd just feel disgusted with yourself afterwards.

This situation isn't good for Ethan either. If he's ready to start a relationship, it needs to be with someone more local to Provincetown than London. It needs to be with someone of a similar mindset. Having a fling with me would be awful for him.

And Lexi. I need to do us both a favour and be the logical person in this ... whatever *this* is.

'Wow' is Bridget's reaction when I fill her in after breakfast. 'I never thought I'd hear of the day when Sam Butterfield kissed a man.'

'I know,' I say solemnly. 'Two men, actually.'

She gasps.

'Don't get your knickers in a twist, the first was just a drunken mistake and doesn't count.'

'So, the kiss with Ethan counts?' Her tone is mischievous.

'Do you think it makes me a terrible person? It's like I'm destroying Kev's memory or something.'

'No, no, honey, not at all,' she soothes. 'You're a normal person continuing your life. It's what we all want you to do.'

'There's something I have to confess.' I pause as emotion bubbles up in the pit of my stomach.

'Go on.'

'I can't even remember Kevin's voice.' My own voice is a whisper as my chin trembles and a watery pain surges through the bridge of my nose and eyes. 'I don't remember how the love of my life sounded, and when I think about his face, all the images I see are from photographs, not real life.' I'm sobbing now, uncontrollably.

'Oh, honey, I wish I was there to wrap you up in a hug. Listen to me – you are not a bad person. This is just nature's way of letting you know that you should move on, that it's okay to live your life after losing someone.'

I sniff.

'You've dedicated eight years of celibacy to Kev's honour. Think about it, what would Kev say to that? Would he be pleased? Would he want you to do eight more years?'

I shake my head and realise she can't see me. 'No.' I sniff again. 'He'd call me a daft bint and tell me to be happy.'

Bridget laughs. 'There you go then.'

156

'I know, but my rationale is solid. Nobody can replace Kev, so I don't see the point in trying to. Remember when your favourite four-year-old gladiator sandals broke, and you bought six new pairs hoping to replace them? In the end, you threw them all in the bin in temper and ranted about the fact your feet would never be happy again.'

'Yes.' She sounds confused.

'Well, your feet equal my heart.'

There's a silent pause.

'But then I discovered espadrilles and my feet were happy again, just in a different style. Maybe your heart can be happy again on a different continent.' Her tone is musical, and I sense she's proud of that little retort. It makes me smile.

'Are you saying you don't want me to come back to England?'

'What? No. Shut up, it's your stupid analogy, and you know very well what I'm saying.'

'I know.'

'So, are you going to go and see this Ethan guy again?' she asks hopefully. 'He sounds much better than a pair of sandals.'

'No. He's in a similar place to me, and he has this sweet little girl. I don't want to complicate their lives. Maybe, just maybe, when I get home, I'll agree to go out with one of your third-floor-office guys.'

She squeals, and dolphins gather in the bay.

***

I spend the day by the pool and head to Harry and Barney's for seven. They've booked us in at the secret restaurant because, I tease, they are apparently more high-maintenance than Ethan, and pizza on the beach just doesn't cut the mustard.

'It sounds awfully romantic,' Barney says when I've told them the story of last night (minus the kiss).

157

I take a sip of my wine and look at the window, unable to make eye contact.

'There's more, isn't there?' Harry says, his voice thickened with interest.

I might as well tell them. At least it will make the other thing I have to tell them easier to bear. 'We kissed.'

Two gasps come almost too quickly.

'That's wonderful. Isn't it?' asks Barney.

I sigh. 'It was wonderful. It was perfect.'

'There's a "but" coming, I just know it.' Harry leans back in his chair in anticipation.

'There is a "but".' I tell them how I ran off and give them the shortened version of my rationale; London is a long way from Provincetown and I'm not looking for love.

They don't say anything, so I take it as my cue to drop my other bombshell. 'It's the reason I won't be coming back to Provincetown during the rest of my stay in the US.'

'Oh, Sam! Don't do this again. Just talk to Ethan and agree to be friends,' Barney pleads.

'I can't.' I shake my head. 'I've tried that, but every time I see him, we seem to get closer. Kissing was a step too far.'

Harry and Barney look down at the table but remain silent. I know they want the best for Ethan too.

'I'm going to miss you guys so much. You've made me feel so welcome here and saved me when I was ready to catch the first flight back to the UK and give up my career. I'll be back to see you guys, I will, but I need to put some distance between me and Ethan before things get out of control. The thing between Ethan and me isn't just attraction or lust. We've connected emotionally, and that's the dangerous part. We live on different continents – there is literally an ocean between us.'

'That's poetic,' Harry says.

'So poetic,' Barney agrees, eyes glistening.

'So, you understand.'

158

They nod. Barney blinks, allowing a tear to roll down his chubby cheek. I stand up and walk around the table to hug them both.

'You guys can come to Boston anytime and visit me.'

Harry looks at Barney and nods before looking back to me. 'We do love the city, and we don't go nearly enough. It will be good for us.'

'See.' I smile, reaching out and taking their hands.

'The idea of you and Ethan is just so fairy-tale,' Barney says, and I look down at the table.

'Maybe in another life.'

CHAPTER 23

Work is going really well. The team is busy sourcing locations and Patrick and I have been brainstorming slogans. It's been good to keep busy. When my brain idles, its default setting seems to be to fill the void with thoughts of Ethan.

'Play hard with an edge,' Patrick says, with a distinct lack of confidence.

'Hmm …' How do I say 'that's crap' politely? 'The whole 'work hard, play hard' thing has been done. What else have we got?'

He sits back in his leather office chair and puts both hands behind his head. 'Not much.'

I tap my fingers on the desk. 'It's like I'm having a mental block. I need to get my creative juices flowing a bit.'

'You're right. Let's head to the park, get some fresh air.'

'That's the best idea you've had all day.'

Ten minutes later, we're strolling through Boston Common. I'd managed to convince Patrick that ice creams were a good idea since the sun is out and it's a hot day.

'I've been trying my best to channel the brand but I don't know if we're overthinking the whole slogan thing. What about something simple like "kick back"?' I lick a dribble of ice cream off my cone.

'I like that, but it needs more – "kick back and relax"?'

'Not really in keeping with sporty footwear.'

'You have a point.'

'"Stride forward, kick back"?'

Patrick ponders this for a moment. 'I like where you're heading,

160

it suggests you can wear these shoes for being active and chilling out. What about "storm forward, kick back"?'

I nod. 'Storm forward … it packs more of a punch!'

'Did we just nail this thing to the ground?' Patrick asks.

I smile. 'We nailed it down.'

'A toast,' Patrick says, holding up his ice cream, 'to us!'

I knock my ice cream against his and with my other hand swipe the screen of my phone to turn the camera mode on. 'Hold on.' I snap a picture of our two ice creams together in the sunlight, celebrating our victory. 'We just worked together as a team.' I smile.

Later that night, I upload the picture onto the Pink Apple Instagram. The green grass behind the ice creams makes them pop and the sunlight striking them looks so arty that when I add a filter, it looks like the Instagram gods have taken it. 'Sod it,' I add it to my personal page too.

***

The following Monday I'm walking out of the office for the day when I spot Harry and Barney waiting outside. My heart leaps in shock.

'Surprise!' they chorus.

'Oh my god! I can't believe you came.' I clasp my hands to my mouth. After a busy week at work last week, a day at the Quincy Market, and Faneuil Hall and a sightseeing trip to Salem at the weekend, I'm ready for a drink with my pals.

'We told you we loved the city,' Harry says. 'Now, who's for a cocktail?'

We head to a bar at Long Wharf and manage to find an outside table amidst the bustle. It's in stark contrast to the relaxed feel of Provincetown, but I enjoy the vibrancy of this just as much.

'So how have you been?' Harry sips his drink. Because it's so busy, we decided to keep the drinks order simple: three beers.

'Good. Great. Work is great. I've managed to see new sights. It's great.'

Harry raises a suspicious eyebrow. 'You're saying "great" a lot.'

'I'm sorry, are my synonyms not up to scratch for you? I'll buy a thesaurus,' I say dryly and quickly regret my defensiveness. It's not their fault I miss Provincetown and feel crappy about it.

'Ooh, excuse me,' Harry says. 'It just seemed a little staged, is all. Are you sure you're okay?'

'Yes.' I let my shoulders slump. 'No.'

'Neither is Ethan, in case you're wondering,' Barney adds.

Oh? 'I wasn't.'

'We've never seen him so blue. We really think you should go see him. Just have a conversation.' As Barney speaks, Harry nods in agreement.

'There's nothing to talk about.'

'He misses you. I think you've ignited something in him that he didn't expect.' Harry's eyes are pleading.

'Well, why isn't he the one here telling me that?' I fold my arms and then realise they could take that the wrong way. The last thing I want is Ethan turning up. 'I mean, it seems like it's actually something *you* want and not him.'

Harry reaches across the table and takes my hand. 'Ethan knows why you're here and he respects that. It's why he didn't chase you down the beach, and it's why he's leaving you alone. He wouldn't want you to feel forced into seeing him. He'd want you to *want* to see him.'

I don't say anything. I feel like clinging to Kev's memory is taking more and more effort and that scares me.

'Sam, you and Ethan adore each other. We've seen it even if you're trying your best not to. We get it, relationships are scary things, especially when you've been hurt before. It took me a while to trust Harry,' Barney says softly.

'Oh?' After their romantic first-encounter story, I hadn't expected that.

'My ex of seven years ran off with his Pilates instructor – a woman too. Not only did I feel like a discarded piece of gum, chewed up and spat out on the street, I also felt like I was so repulsive, I'd put him off men for good.'

'It's true,' Harry says, 'Barney would pull away at every milestone. He didn't show up to the meal we had planned with friends to celebrate our six-month anniversary because he thought we'd be breaking up soon and he wanted to save face. When we got our first apartment together in New York he showed up on moving-in day with just an overnight bag with one outfit change in because he was sure I'd kick him out soon after. It took a lot of work.'

'It's not the same thing.'

'The circumstances are different, but the fear of commitment is the same,' Harry says.

'It's not so much the fear of commitment,' I choke. 'It's the fear of forgetting about Kev and not respecting his memory.'

'There's room in your heart for Kev and Ethan,' Barney says.

Tension rises in my chest and I shake my head. Whenever I try to explain it, it doesn't come out right and people don't get it. 'No, no there's isn't.'

Both Harry and Barney stare at me before Barney speaks. 'It just seems like such a waste to have you two to find a spark but fizzle out before you've even had a chance to throw on a little propane.'

'It isn't just Kev, I'm from a different *country*. You're saying I shouldn't be afraid to get hurt but anything between us is destined to end. We both get hurt in that version of the story so what good is a *fizzle*?' I bang down my beer with a little too much force and a little bit sloshes over the top.

'People make these things work,' Barney says.

'I'm not *people*. I'm odd and damaged and I'm not available for … for … relationships.' I sweep my hand to the left, accidentally sending Barney's beer crashing to the floor. My initial reaction is to apologise profusely and help him clean up the spillage, but instead, I stand up and shove my bag on my shoulder. The air is so thick it's choking me.

'Do you know what? I kissed my boss too, perhaps he's the one I should be fizzling with – at least that way, I wouldn't have two bored, meddlesome guys driving me insane.' Even as I say the words, I hate myself for them and know they aren't true, but I can't help myself.

Hurt is etched on both their faces and I feel a sharp stab of guilt. I can't deal with this. My heart starts to race. I hitch my bag higher. I like Harry and Barney so much that I don't want to say goodbye to them either. Leaving them and Ethan will almost be like mourning for Kev all over again. Instead of losing one person, I'll have lost three. It's better if they hate me.

'I'm not here for much longer. I think the best thing all round is for us to say our goodbyes before things get messier.'

Harry looks mortified. Barney looks like a puppy that's been stuck in an animal shelter for far too long.

'I'm sorry. I just can't take this. I can't take any of it. I have to go.'

With that, I leave, walking briskly without so much as a backwards glance until I reach the relative sanctuary of my apartment. As usual, I head straight for my room, walking past the men, who are sitting in the lounge watching whatever sport of the day it is they're watching. As usual, they ignore me.

I throw myself down face-first onto the bed and try to calm my breathing. Just two more weeks to go and I can put all of this behind me.

CHAPTER 24

'Great news.' Patrick looks like the Cheshire Cat when I enter the office the next day.

'Oh?' I ask, not really in the mood for his attempt at suspense.

'I've just been speaking to the rep from Rocks, and the guys want us to use Provincetown as the location. We presented several great spots – Hamilton Beach, York Beach, Plymouth – but they loved the vibe that came through from the Provincetown footage.' He is so enthusiastic, and I don't really know why. Wherever he and the film crew go is not really that interesting to me, and the last thing I want to do is think about that place.

'That's great.'

'I know, isn't it?' he says. The smile isn't going anywhere and it's starting to unnerve me.

'Yeah.' To my shame, a little bit of sarcasm laces the word.

'So, I hope you don't have plans this evening, because you'll need to go pack a week's worth of clothes.'

What the actual fuck?

Perhaps I've misunderstood. 'Sorry, what?'

'Well, you're coming of course. Don't look so surprised. You're the brains behind this campaign. Rocks want everything the same in the videos, apart from you and the dodgy phone footage obviously.' He laughs like I'm supposed to find it funny that they clearly wouldn't want the old bird in the video. I suppose if I wasn't about to throw up, I might have laughed along. 'I know you love the place and knew you'd be thrilled to be heading back there on expenses.' He winks. 'It would be great if you could get in touch with all the rental places for the car and bikes and stuff. I think we'll have four different models …'

His words are drowned out by the pulsating heartbeat that's pounding in my ears. If I tell him I can't go, I might as well ask for my P45. My UK boss will hate me for pissing off the US team, and Patrick will make my life miserable – if he doesn't send me straight back to the UK via cargo ship or whatever means available. I'd be throwing everything away by not overcoming this one last hurdle. Surely, I can bite the bullet and power through my last two weeks here?

'Oh, and one last thing.'

'Hm?' My attention is back on Patrick.

'You might want to sit down for this one.'

Now he wants me to sit. I've already been knocked sideways. I do it anyway because if that was only the *amuse-bouche* course of the bad news, this is going to be terrible.

'The feedback for your work has been so positive. You weren't afraid to go with your gut—' he punches the air '—even when everyone else in the room wouldn't listen.' Well, I'm glad he sees that now. 'You are exactly the sort of person we want on this team.'

I see where this is going. He wants me to join Tony, Dave, Carl and Steve and be a regular on this little jaunt. Well, thanks but no thanks, buddy. I'm going back to my simple life in my UK office, reunited with Coco in my little flat in a country where chocolate tastes good again.

Back. I'm going back.

'Which is why I want to offer you a permanent position here in Boston. It's based solely on your merits as a top marketer, not your sake drinking skills.' He smiles sheepishly. 'We can sponsor your visa, and the salary will be a big improvement. We have a great health insurance package that includes dental, and we'll put you in accommodation for six months until you're up on your feet. What do you say?'

166

Oh my god. Oh my god. Up until recently, this would have been my dream come true. I'm a career girl – I have few ties, and being a success is all that drives me. Not to mention sticking it to the men who initially thought I was useless. But I can't say yes. I can't live here with Ethan being so close. Barney and Harry must absolutely hate me now and … no. Just no.

'You take your time. No rush. I'm heading out of the office for the rest of the day to prepare, but we'll meet at the ferry port tomorrow morning. I'll email the details.' He doesn't wait for a reply; I gather he's too excited about the trip. Once he's gone, I sit there dumbfounded.

Why is it that when you want something bad enough and work hard enough for it, it doesn't come until the worst possible time?

CHAPTER 25

The weak morning sun casts a warm glow across the bay. Seagulls caw overhead, and the breeze is cool enough to warrant a hoodie and a fleeting bout of nostalgia for the UK. When I spot Patrick walking towards me, my stomach sinks. We're really doing this.

'Good morning,' he says, more chipper than usual. I can't even bring myself to reply. Instead, I pull the zip of my hoodie right up and shove my hands in the pockets. 'Did you manage to call all the rental places to arrange the stuff we need?'

I nod. 'Yes, it's all sorted.' By some miracle, Ethan didn't answer the telephone. I'd worked myself up all afternoon, forging an explanation for my behaviour the last time I saw him. I even came up with a convincing argument as to why he should let my company rent from him, just in case he was so mad at me he said no. Car rental in Provincetown is strangely limited. Thankfully, it was his brother, Zac, who I caught at the bike rental place, so I spoke to him about the kayak and cars too. He sounded pleased to hear from me, so I guessed Ethan hadn't been telling him how I bolted after we kissed.

'I'm going to sit inside and make a few calls while we're still near the mainland. An idle mind is work for the devil,' Patrick says as we board the ferry.

'An idle mind is the devil's workshop,' I mutter but he doesn't hear me.

It's even cooler at sea, so I put my lightweight quilted jacket from back home on over my hoodie and sit on the outside deck. If I followed Patrick, there would be a point at which we'd have

168

to make small talk, and he may even ask about my decision on the job front. I don't want to have to turn it down until nearer the end of my stay if I can help it. Doing so now may make him resentful of me, and I don't need that when he's technically the only person on this trip who doesn't hate me.

The hotel Patrick booked for us is more upmarket than the one I spent my weekends at, and it's at the other end of town. In a way, the change helps me to distance myself from the connection I had with the place. I just need to get the rentals out of the way, and then I'm pretty sure I can focus on my job.

I'm sitting on a deckchair by the small, freeform pool when Patrick comes out. 'I've just had a call from the film crew and they're about fifteen minutes away. We're hoping to get down to the beach and start shooting the kayak scenes within the hour, so I thought you could go on ahead to liaise with the rental guy and find a spot away from the sunbathers.'

Of course, it's a perfectly reasonable request from Patrick's point of view, but the thought of heading over there gives me a five-kilogram weight in the pit of my stomach.

'Okay.' I just have to be grown up about it. I'm only here for a week.

'Great. I'll catch you later.'

***

I go to my room and freshen up. Now the sun is higher in the sky the temperature has risen, so I put on some comfy grey jersey-style shorts and a white sleeveless T-shirt and tie my hair in a high ponytail to keep it out of the way. My skin glows with the colour I've picked up so I don't bother with make-up. When I can procrastinate no more, I make my way over to the kayak rental place. When I get there, I'm relieved to see it's Zac who is sitting in a deckchair outside.

'Hey, Sam.' He rises to his feet and smiles when he sees me.

'Hi, Zac.' I smile back, mostly with relief at not having to see Ethan.

'I've polished up a few of these for you because I didn't know what colour you guys wanted, so just take your pick. The film crew have basically paid for a full day's rental for all the kayaks, so I'm closed to the public today.'

'That's great,' I say, scanning the beach for the best spot. 'I think I'll take a couple over there.' The beach is pretty quiet, and the sunbathers are concentrated nearer the road, which makes sense because dragging your stuff across the beach is no easy task. I pick up the handles on two kayaks and start to pull them.

Zac reaches out for one of the handles. 'Here, let me.'

'It's okay,' I protest.

He holds his hands up in the air. 'Sorry, force of habit, what with Cindy being pregnant. I'll leave you to it. I'll be in the cabin if you want anything.'

I force a smile, glad to be left alone.

A little while later, as I sit looking out across the water waiting for Patrick, Zac jogs across the sand towards me.

'I thought you might want a snack,' he says, holding out a Tupperware tub of chopped strawberries.

'Thank you,' I say, taking one. I expect Zac to leave, but he sits down in the sand beside me.

'Cindy is obsessed with healthy eating at the moment. She said we need to form good habits for the sake of our child.' He pulls a Hershey bar from his back pocket. 'So I eat the fruit and stuff, but sometimes I waver. Want a piece?'

I laugh and shake my head.

'Ethan told me what happened between you guys.'

My body tenses, but Zac raises his hand, so I stay silent.

'He knows you haven't healed. He's been there, so he gets it. He's going to lay low while you're here. I just thought you should know that he isn't avoiding you or anything.'

My chest swells with something. I was genuinely relieved to

see Zac this morning, but ever since I sat down, I've tried to ignore the niggling feeling of disappointment at the fact I won't be seeing Ethan. For some reason, I feel done out of talking to him. The thing is, whilst my head knows that keeping my distance is the sensible thing to do, my heart misses his company, my eyes miss his face, and my body misses the feeling of his touch. They put up a rather compelling argument when they gang up on me.

'That's really considerate of him,' I say eventually.

'He's a nice guy. Hopefully, one day, he'll meet someone who is right for him. He deserves to be happy.'

I nod along and glance around. Patrick and the film crew are trudging through the sand towards us. 'Looks like it's time to start filming.'

'I'll make myself scarce.' Zac rises to his feet and I follow suit. 'I'll catch up with you later.'

'Sam!' Patrick greets me with an exuberance that is probably for the benefit of the film crew, who are a compilation of the fashion-afflicted and the severely miserable. Without acknowledging me, they begin to unpack their equipment and set up.

'So, are they all briefed on what they're doing?' I say quietly to Patrick.

'Yes. The models are too. They'll be here in just a minute.'

It isn't long before the filming is underway. People are milling, buzzing, ordering, shouting and drinking coffee from eco-friendly reusable travel cups. Patrick and I watch the footage through a monitor under a sun canopy, and it looks great. The edgy angles give the film a contemporary look, and the sixteen-year-old non-binary model just oozes 'cool', wearing those pink-and-black graffiti Rocks like a star. It's great. It's going to look perfect.

'That's a wrap,' the producer calls, resulting in some clapping and back-slapping. 'Bright and early tomorrow, okay, team?'

As the film crew make their way back to their van, Patrick announces he's turning in for the night. We finalise some plans for tomorrow, and I stay to watch the sunset for a little while, to

171

wind down after the excitement of the day. When my arms start to get goose pimples, I decide it's time to get moving and I head to walk across the sand in the eerie-blue twilight. As I round the corner, I bang into something solid.

'Ethan?' The sight of him causes my lungs to clutch my breath.

'Sam, I thought you'd be finished. I was just stopping by to do some paperwork.' His features slacken with shock or something else. I fight an urge to reach out to him.

'We're all done here. I just needed to take a minute to relax. It's been one hectic day.' I swipe my brow for effect.

He nods. 'Okay, I'll see you around.'

'Yeah,' I reply, but he's already unlocking the door to the cabin. I think about calling after him to thank him for being so understanding, and to tell him how great Zac has been, but he seems off. I suppose I can't expect to hurt his feelings and have nothing change between us. Instead, I go back to my hotel and get into bed. We have a 5.30 a.m. start, so an early night is in order. I close my eyes and try to clear my head of the buzz of the day. Removing each thought one by one, until all that's left is the image of Ethan's magnetic blue eyes.

CHAPTER 26

The alarm goes off after what feels like just minutes of sleep. My forehead is filled with tension, and there's a heaviness behind my eyes. It's far too early.

After splashing cold water on my face and brushing my teeth, I feel human enough to go down for breakfast. Patrick is helping himself to waffles when I get there.

'Ooh, those look good,' I say, filling my cup with coffee that looks strong enough to beat Jean-Claude Van Damme in an arm-wrestling contest.

'Fuel for the day.' He pats his stomach. 'We want to try and wrap up the bike scenes today if we can.'

'I guess I'll be needing a few of these waffles too then?' Like I need an excuse.

I take my waffles and coffee outside to sit on the terrace overlooking the pool, partly because it's nice out here, and partly because it's too early to try and make small talk with Patrick. Whilst I'm glad to be a valued part of the team now, I can't chat about baseball or whatever else the male team members discuss in the bars after work. A bird lands on the table next to me and starts pecking at a discarded muffin case. An opportunist. Perhaps it's in our nature to take the unexpected things handed to us in life. Maybe that's why it's bothering me to know that Ethan is around and I'm not going to see him. He's the unexpected muffin of the trip, a sweet treat that wasn't meant for me but one I could enjoy whilst I'm here all the same. I suppose any ordinary person in my shoes, without the baggage that I have, would just go for it without a second thought.

173

The bird flies away, leaving behind a now shredded paper case with crumbs strewn everywhere.

And that metaphor is exactly why I won't be tempted.

Patrick pops his head around the door. 'Need to leave in five.'

'No problem,' I say, draining the last of my coffee. The distraction is most welcome.

***

'Morning, Sam.' Zac's smile is a welcome relief. I know he's already told me that Ethan is giving me a wide berth, but I couldn't help but wonder if he'd be there anyway. I suppose seeing Ethan unexpectedly is what I've come to expect. My insides feel heavy.

'Morning, Zac.' I greet him with a hug, which I realise too late might be a little over-familiar for someone I hardly know. Is there such thing as familiarity by proxy? 'We're heading to the cycle paths to film, and I've no idea how these guys are going to transport all of their equipment. I don't think we've properly thought this through.'

'No problem. We have some cargo trailers that attach to the bikes. I can fix you up with a couple of those.'

'Perfect.'

Zac goes off to arrange trailers. The models, film crew and Patrick are all outside choosing bikes and giving it far too much thought, with the exception of Patrick, who already has a black one. I want to shout to the new, moody-looking model that the pink one *definitely* brings out her cheekbones, but there's a chance she'll think I'm being serious. I should be out there doing the same, but the peacefulness of the shop is too alluring. I wander along the compact aisles, absentmindedly looking at the bike accessories until I'm back at the till. A photo above the door to the back office stops me dead. It's Zac, Ethan and their father on a boat, hugging. They're the picture of happiness. In the photo, Ethan's hair is short and tidy, Zac isn't quite the man-mountain

174

he is now, and their father has fewer creases on his face, but each one of them is beaming with joy. Their happiness is so real it practically leaps out from the picture. It must have been before …

'Are you ready?' Patrick shouts from the doorway.

'Coming.'

When I step outside, they're all ready and waiting to go. 'Here's our number,' Zac says, handing me a business card. 'I'm not expecting to be too busy today, so call if you need anything. Otherwise, I'll see you later. But there's no rush to be back for five – if I'm gone just leave everything outside. It'll be safe.'

'Okay, thanks.' I smile and take the card. 'See you later.'

'Nice guy,' Patrick says when we're on our way. Once we hit the trail, the sound of the surf and the cool morning breeze makes conversation impossible, and it isn't long before my mind refocuses on that picture in the office. Something is bugging me about it. It could be because I understand Ethan's pain and why he never smiles like that now, but I think it's something else. It's the family thing. A sharp pain penetrates my chest, and before I can stop it, an image of my own parents pops into my head. Both cuddly, with slightly ruddy cheeks and wayward hair, always dressed in bargain something-or-others that they've got from the central aisle in Aldi or ordered from the back of a Sunday magazine. Always holding hands. Always smiling. The memory is filled with warmth. I haven't thought about my parents fondly for a long time and the happy memory sends a stab of guilt through my stomach. If losing Kev and learning about Nicole has taught me anything, it's that our loved ones can be gone in a flash. Ethan was right, it's time to make amends.

As if on cue, my foot slips off the pedal and smacks me in the shin. 'Jeezus!' I yell.

'You okay?' one of the film crew asks. There's no obvious concern in his tone.

'Yeah,' I say, forcing a smile through the smarting pain.

I deserved it. My parents used to smile all the time. People always described them as 'jolly'. I can't imagine what my leaving did to them. I'm a horrible, horrible person. All they've ever wanted was the best for me. Sometimes they were just too much. I was a grown adult and they still couldn't let me make my own decisions. Perhaps I did overreact to the whole Kev thing but I was so angry at the time because I felt betrayed. They'd welcomed him into their lives then said all those things behind his back.

'We'll set up here,' Patrick says. He's picked a great spot. It's a part of the trail where you can see the sea and grassy sand dunes. The camera crew start to unload the equipment, and the make-up artist starts daubing translucent powder on the two models' faces to get rid of the shine. I sit on a grassy dune, knowing that my presence for the next few hours will be largely unnecessary.

After a few hours of retakes of different angles, poses and positions, I offer to cycle back into town to pick up some bottled water. As I cycle to the little shop, I can't help thinking about my parents and what I've done to them and, on a whim, pick up a postcard. When I've dumped the bottles of water in my bike basket, I sit on the wall of the church and take out a pen.

Dear Mum and Dad,

I stare at the words. They look so unfamiliar, so odd. I haven't said the words 'Mum and Dad' in eight years, choosing to just write 'Sam' at the bottom of any Christmas or birthday cards and I certainly haven't sent any postcards. I tear the card in half and dump it in a nearby bin before heading back to the shoot.

CHAPTER 27

'So, have you had a chance to consider my offer?' Patrick's question comes as soon as I hand him his bottle of water, and it throws me. My head has been filled with Ethan and, strangely, my parents.

'Patrick, I'm so sorry. There's a lot to consider, and with the trip and everything, I've not had the chance to fully weigh it up. It's a great offer, it really is …'

'Look.' He pats me firmly on the back. 'Take your time. It's a big decision.'

'Thanks.'

I sit back down and still not tired of the excitement of being on a film set, take in the scene. I don't know how the models and actors do it. The same movements over and over again, with chants of 'Let's try that again' and minor tweaks every five minutes. I must admit, being here, in this life that's so far removed from the life I'd planned, is exhilarating. When Kev and I were together, designing fliers for local businesses was what I loved – it paid the bills, didn't stress me out, and I was happy; my ambition extended only to having a family and juggling everything that would bring. It wasn't until I got the job at Pink Apple that I saw how far I could take myself in marketing. Once again, I felt fulfilled, bar the niggling ambition to make the US team. I should be proud of myself; I am proud, and if I'm honest with myself, I would love to live over here. What's not to love? The scenery, the fact they have proper seasons, being so close to the beaches. What am I really leaving behind in London? My pokey flat? Of course, there are my friends, the number of whom I could count on one hand even if I lost two of my fingers in a terrible accident, but they would only be a Skype chat away. Besides, now Bridget is married, the likelihood is I won't see as much of her.

When I simmer it all down to the really sticky residue of truth, it's Ethan. I know how crazy it sounds – it's the complete opposite of why most women wouldn't want to move away. Most women would hate to leave behind a man they liked. The truth is, he's in my head, filling up all the free space that work doesn't occupy. I see his face, I replay his conversations over and over, and I can still feel the heat of his lips on mine. The space he takes up in my head is growing too, forcing his way into all the little cavities, firing up neurons I didn't know existed. I'm worried that soon there will be no room for any other thoughts.

Anyway, the conclusion is the same: I can't let a man get in the way of a once-in-a-lifetime opportunity, because, well, nobody should ever do that, so I at least need to give the move some serious thought.

Once we're all packed up and ready to go, we set off on our bikes. It's almost dusk; we finished just before we lost the natural light. We're all weary, grimy and thick with the heat of the day. I can't wait to have a cool shower and an early night. The film crew go on ahead, and Patrick and I set off after them. Cycling in the open air sure beats the stuffy tube as a way to commute. There's something so free about it. It's a similar feeling to the one I get on the top deck of the ferry when the wind blows my hair.

All of a sudden, there's a mighty bang and my bike stops dead, propelling me off the seat and over the handlebars. Everything happens in slow motion. I'm aware I'm flying. I'm aware I'm going to crash into the trailer of the suddenly, inexplicably stationary bike in front at any second, and I'm aware it's going to hurt.

'Ouch.' There it is. The edge of the metal rim cracks both of my shins, and my chin hits the back seat of the bike, knocking my head backwards. My neck bends unnaturally, sending a sharp pain down my back. It takes me a second to realise what's going on. My hands are clutching the sides of the trailer, and my knees are inside, on top of a metal equipment case, whilst my bike lies in a heap on the floor.

'Are you okay?' one of the female crew members says. I look up at her and realise she's not talking to me, but rather the woman on the bike, whose abrupt braking caused me to crash into her, and whose trailer I'm now in.

'Sam, are you okay?' Patrick is already by my side, helping me up.

'I don't know what happened. She just stopped.' My voice is shaky.

'Here, sit down.' He eases me onto the grass by the side of the path. 'Where does it hurt?'

'Everywhere.' I'm aware that I sound a bit whiny, but it does. 'I'll be okay. You go on ahead. I'll just sit for a minute.'

'Okay, we have somewhere to be,' the unsympathetic film crew lady says. I give a wave accompanied by a sharp, sarcastic smile. I was talking to Patrick anyway.

'I'm not leaving you. Your chin looks like it's going to bruise, and your legs are a mess.'

'I'll be okay.' They're a bit battered and bloody, but I don't think anything is broken.

'You can't ride your bike back.' We both look at the crumpled heap of metal. The front wheel is so badly buckled that I realise Patrick is right. 'I'm calling Zac.'

'No, there's no need. I can push it back; it's not that far.'

'It's far enough.' He's already dialling, and I feel like an idiot.

'The shop will be closed now,' I say, remembering Zac's instructions to just leave the bikes outside if he's shut up for the day.

'I have his cell phone number.' He turns away and paces as he waits for someone to answer. 'Hey, Zac ...' He steps just out of earshot, and I can only hope that he's not telling Zac some mistruth about how I can't ride a bike.

'He's going to bring a pick-up,' Patrick says, sitting down beside me.

Great! A full-scale rescue.

'I never did apologise for kissing you that night at the Japanese place.' Patrick's gaze is fixed on the grassy dunes ahead.

I feel my cheeks flush. 'It's water under the bridge.'

He sucks the air through his teeth. 'I know. I just really respect you and I want you to consider the job offer without thinking that I only offered it to you because I like you. I respect your work above all.'

Patrick *likes* me? 'Thank you. It's nice to hear that you respect my work. Especially after our rocky start.'

He flashes me a smile. 'I mean it. I'm a complete professional and kissing you was wrong. I got carried away in the moment and the drink.'

'It's fine. Let's forget about it.'

He rubs his hand down the side of his face. 'I just hope this means you can consider the job offer without wondering about any ulterior motive. There isn't one, I promise.'

It takes a lot to admit you made a mistake and I think I'm developing a deeper level of respect for Patrick. He's actually a really nice guy and I think we could work well together if I was planning to stay.

'I'll consider it on a professional level.'

We fall into silence and it seems like we're sat for ages in an awkward bubble by the time we hear someone approaching.

My chest clenches when I see him. 'Ethan?' He's dressed in a black vest and grey sweat shorts.

'Hi, Sam.' There's a long pause. As we stare at each other, my stomach does unusual things and I hate it. 'Cindy isn't well. I told Zac to go home.' His tone is flat.

'As you can see, there was an accident.' Patrick steps between us. 'Pink Apple will pay for the damage to the bike.' I grit my teeth. We shouldn't be paying for the damage; the stupid film company should.

'It's fine. Let's just makes sure Sam is okay.' His voice is deep and thick but his tone is short and he looks coldly at Patrick. It reminds me of the way he looked at me back in Boston. Oh god, I bet Barney has told him Patrick and I kissed.

Ethan slides his bag off his shoulder and crouches in front of me. 'Let's just take a look at the damage to your legs.'

He lifts my left leg and examines it. 'You're going to have a nasty bruise there. Let me clean these cuts up.' He rummages in his bag and starts unpacking antiseptic wipes and all kinds of other things.

'Patrick, you don't need to wait for me. It's been a long day.' He's hovering around like a spare part, and him being here serves no purpose.

He rubs his face. 'I should see you get back to the hotel alright.'

'I'll be fine.'

Patrick glances warily at Ethan and back to me. 'Only if you're sure.'

'It's okay, I know Ethan. We're friends.' My eyes lock on Ethan's as I say it, and they seem heavy under his furrowed brow.

'I could do with calling the office, and I have some things to go over from today …'

'Then go, honestly. Once Ethan's cleaned me up I'll be fine to walk back.'

'I'll sort the bicycle out,' Ethan says. Hearing his voice reminds me that his hand is still on my leg, and now that I've thought about it, it's all I can think about – my skin beneath his warm touch.

'Okay, don't let her lug that thing back.' I open my mouth to protest Patrick's instruction, but he continues talking. 'She'll insist, but don't let her.'

'I know she can be a little stubborn,' Ethan says.

'Excuse me! I'm right here.' They both look at me as though they'd forgotten.

'Okay, I'm going.' Patrick picks up his bike and waves before climbing on and cycling back towards the town.

'I'm going to dress these cuts, and then do you think you'll be able to walk to my pick-up at the end of the path?'

'Yes, of course. It's just cuts and bruises.'

Ethan cleans me up. It stings like hell, despite the obvious care he's taking not to hurt me – even though he's obviously upset with me. He dabs the cuts gently until the sandy grains that have embedded themselves in my shins have gone.

'Some of the cuts are pretty deep,' he says, unwrapping a bandage.

'The edge of the metal trailer I bashed into was quite sharp.'

He places a pad over the cuts and starts to wrap my left shin up tightly. I watch the movement of his bronzed, firm shoulders as he works.

'Next,' he says, placing my left leg down and picking up my right.

I let the silence go on as he tackles the next lot of cuts. There's so much I want to say to him, but so much I shouldn't. I appreciate that he's keeping things strictly first aid.

Ouch. I wince as he catches a sensitive spot.

'Sorry, almost done.'

'It's okay. Crashing the bike wasn't the first time I banged that shin today, so it's particularly sore. I think me and bikes are a bad match.'

He doesn't acknowledge me.

When he's finished bandaging my right leg, he stands up and holds out a hand. 'All done.'

I take his hand and he yanks me up. Once my full weight is on my legs, sharp pains shoot up my shins and I double over.

'Here, let me help you.' He tucks his strong, firm arm under my own to support me.

I force a laugh. 'I didn't expect that to hurt quite so much.'

182

'You've probably bruised the bone. C'mon, let's get you back.'
He scoops up my bike with his other arm and hangs the frame
over his shoulder, and we start to shuffle along.

'So, you're back in town?' he says after a hundred metres or so.
Has he been wanting to see me as much as I've wanted to see him?

'Yep.' He already knows why I'm here, so there's no point explaining.

'It's good to see you.' The raw honesty in his tone makes my
stomach flip.

'You saw me yesterday.'

'You know what I mean.' He gives me a little nudge, which
makes me smile.

'It's good to see you too.'

We don't speak again until his blue pick-up truck is in sight.
He tosses the bike in the back and hoists me up into the passenger
seat.

'Can we talk?' he says once he's climbed in the driver's side.

My chest clenches. I'm not really sure what there is to say. We
both know where we stand. 'What do you want to talk about?'

'It feels like we have unfinished business.'

So much for respecting my choice. I remain silent.

'I've tried to respect you because I thought we had a connection that you couldn't deal with. I was okay with you wanting to
keep your distance.'

When he pauses, I don't reply.

'I even understood when you ran off, but then I see you on
Instagram looking cosy with that guy Patrick, who you apparently
kissed! How is that supposed to make me feel?'

'Are you going to start the engine?' I say impatiently. My head
has started to spin. I thought I had everything under control.

His hands curl around the steering wheel and his knuckles
turn white. 'Do you do this to everyone you ever meet or just
guys who like you?'

'I beg your pardon?'

'Push them away.'

183

'I'm not pushing you away. I just don't want to encourage you and end up hurting you.'

'Damn it.' He bangs the steering wheel, and I jump. His face fills with regret. 'Sorry, you're just driving me crazy.'

'The Patrick thing was nothing, just a drunken kiss that meant nothing and you know that social media isn't real. It was a few pictures to generate likes for the business. The kiss with you *did* mean something and that's what's so hard to deal with.' My heart aches and I don't really know what to say. I thought he understood. He'd told Zac as much anyway. 'I'm trying to be upfront with you, Ethan. Why are you wasting your time with me?'

He takes a deep breath. I stare straight through the windscreen, unable to look at him. 'Because I'm falling in love with you.'

I continue to look ahead, but his words send waves of emotion crashing through me. Not just because I feel it too and I hate this situation, but because I'm hurting him without even trying and it's the last thing I want to do. When I don't reply, he carries on. 'When you left me on the beach, I understood. I got it. I thought I was the first person you'd kissed since you lost your husband. It's hard for you. Well get this, you *are* the first person I've kissed since losing my wife, and it was hard for me too.'

That was like a punch in the stomach. He'd been on dates – I had no idea he'd not kissed anyone. 'Then why are we doing this?' I wave my hand between us with anger. 'If it's so hard.'

'Because it feels too right to ignore.'

My eyes start to feel hot and damp. I turn my head to the side window before he notices.

'Sam?' he says softly. He puts his hand just above my knee, but I still can't bring myself to look at him.

Eventually, he reaches for the side of my face, carefully avoiding my chin, and I let him gently turn it towards him so that our eyes meet. His deep blue eyes and full mouth are so compelling to look at that it's hard to remember why I don't want this. He moves in, slowly placing his warm lips on mine. My stomach stirs, and it feels so delicious I can't fight it. I pull him towards me, closer, firmer, until our mouths are moving in perfect rhythm. One kiss can't hurt, can it?

When we pull away, neither of us speaks, and this time I can't physically run away. Not that I want to.

'Don't tell me that didn't feel right.' The breathiness of his voice makes me want to grab him and pull him tighter in. I tug at the hem of my shorts instead.

'Ethan?'

'Don't say you disagree.'

I shake my head. 'I wasn't going to. But you do know that we can't ever be an *us*, don't you?'

He runs both hands through his mop of hair. 'I don't think I can keep away from you as long as you're here in Provincetown.'

Oh, bloody hell! Me neither. It seems so pointless trying to avoid him when all I want to do is be with him and one week here won't be the end of the world … will it? It does confirm my decision though. I have to go back to the UK. I have to know this isn't going to spiral into something too deep. 'We can see one another, but I'll be leaving soon and that will be it.'

'It's better than not seeing you at all.' He turns the key in the ignition, and the engine rumbles to life.

When we pull up outside my hotel, he surprises me by climbing out of the truck.

'I'm not going to let you struggle to get inside,' he says, obviously reading my expression.

I place my hand on his shoulder and heave myself out of the truck. 'I think I'll be okay.' He looks disappointed, and, shockingly, I feel the same, so I add, 'But some company wouldn't go amiss.'

As we enter the lift, I wonder what on earth I'm doing. It's like my brain has been hacked. Even when I'm turning the key to my room, a part of me is screaming to make Ethan go away. But that part of me is drowned out by the part that wants him to stay close by.

185

CHAPTER 28

Ethan returns from the ice machine and hands me a makeshift cold-pack of serviettes and ice. 'Your chin looks swollen. It seems like quite a crash you had.'

My chin has started to ache and pressing the ice on offers some relief. 'The woman just stopped in front of me; I've no idea why. Then she scowled at me like it was my fault.' I shake my head.

'Those showbiz types, hey?' He grins, and it sends warmth through my chest.

'Ouch, it hurts to smile,' I say. 'If you're going to hang around, we need some kind of pact to be miserable together.'

We both laugh a little then fall silent. I wonder if he's thinking the same as me – that being miserable together seems to be our thing. It's the thing that brought us a step closer to one another on the beach in the first place.

'How about a drink?' I say. 'Perhaps some alcohol will numb the pain.'

'I can take you to a doctor if you want?' His brow is a map of concern.

'Honestly, it's nothing. The bruised ego is probably the worst of it.'

We sit out on the balcony, and I get some beers and snacks from the minibar. 'They're on expenses,' I say as I dump them onto the balcony table. It's dark now. Although we can't see the ocean, the sound of it crashing against the shore creates a pleasant background noise.

'I heard about what happened in Boston, with Barney and

Harry,' Ethan says after opening a packet of peanuts. 'I didn't get the full story, but Harry said you'd fallen out, thrown a beer and stormed off saying you were never coming back to Provincetown again.'

I sink back in my chair; the guilty feeling starts to swirl around in my stomach. 'I didn't throw a beer; it was an accident … I did get upset. They were pressuring me about you, and I couldn't take it. Sometimes my emotions get the better of me. I overreacted, but it wasn't quite as bad as what they told you.'

'They'll get over it. They're very forgiving guys,' Ethan says, and I can't quite believe he's being so reasonable about it. I'm still disgusted at myself for the way I spoke to them. I can't handle pressure or the feeling of being pushed but I need to learn how to deal with my own feelings without lashing out at others.

'That doesn't really make me feel any better about how I behaved. I need to apologise and make it up to them. I'm hoping to call round tomorrow.'

'That's a good idea,' he says offering me some peanuts. For a moment, the only sound is the gentle tide lapping against the shore. 'Now then, should we talk about all the kissing? Since we're having uncomfortable conversations.' My eyes dart to meet his, which are dancing mischievously.

'*All* the kissing?' I look at him with bemusement.

'Okay, both of the kisses.'

I take a sip of my rum and Coke. 'What is there to say?'

'You're going to make this as difficult as possible, aren't you?'

I put my glass down and turn to face him before softening my tone. 'Not intentionally, but what is there to say, really?'

'Well, you could start by telling me what a great kisser I am.' He raises his eyebrows expectantly.

'I'd only say it if it were true.' I pause, and he feigns hurt, pressing his hand to his chest.

'Okay, brushing that aside, since you obviously have issues with compliments, what would you say to doing it again?'

I swallow a little too loudly. 'To kissing?'

'You obviously need a little more persuading.'

Cymbal-crashing monkeys run around in my head. He couldn't be further from the truth. 'Okay.' He leans in and cups my chin gently before placing his lips on mine, and somehow it feels familiar. Nice, yet so alarming. *What am I doing?*

He takes my hand, pulls me out of my chair and sits me on his lap. My soft bottom cushions me on his firm, sturdy legs, and he lifts my arms and wraps them around his neck. The feel of his huge body against mine is so reassuring, so desirable, that I know when it's time to get up, I won't want to. This is very dangerous territory for me.

He runs his finger down my arm, tracing the outline, before lifting his eyes to mine.

'You're beautiful, Sam.'

A tingle runs down my spine. It's been a long time since anyone has said that to me. Anyone sober, at least.

'You're not so bad yourself.' It's a massive understatement, but like he said, I'm not good with compliments.

'You're so easy to be around. After losing Nicole, I couldn't imagine feeling anything for another woman ever again. But with you, all the lines are blurred. The boundaries that I set myself are no longer there, if that makes sense.'

It makes perfect sense. It's exactly how I feel.

'No one would judge you for moving on. A lot of time has passed,' I say, slightly avoiding the topic.

'Nobody would judge you either.'

'I know.' I've known that for a long time. Nobody but myself at least.

He squeezes me tightly. 'It's cruel that we've had this realisation when you have to leave so soon.'

'At least you've taken the first step. I'm sure Barney and Harry have enough friends in their phonebooks to line you up a few potential dates if you're no longer "off limits".'

'I've taken the step with you for a reason. They're great and everything, but I'm not sure Harry or Barney could find me someone I click with in the same way.'

I don't reply to that. I doubt there is a queue of Ethans waiting for me in London either.

'Do you have to go back to England?' he says, stroking my arm.

I almost say no as an instinctive reaction. It's true, of course, I don't have to go back to England, but I can't tell him about Patrick's offer. Not now I've decided I can't take it, not now things are so complicated. Ethan won't understand me turning it down when he knows I'm so career driven and he'll think it's him when the problem is me. As much as he understands me, he won't understand why I have to go home. I don't even know if I understand anymore so the last thing I want is a discussion about it. It's a feeling rather than a thought which boils down to the fact, I just need my life to get back to normal.

'As much as I'd like to stay here forever, England is my home. I can't just emigrate at the drop of a hat. Besides, don't you need the blood of a fairy godmother, half a shooting star and the wispy hair of five baby pixies just to get a green card to live here in the States?'

He smirks. 'You've done your research.'

I get a pang of guilt about lying to him. I have the star, blood and hair combo in my back pocket. Patrick handed it to me on a plate but crossing this line with Ethan is proof that I can't live here. A fling for a few days is one thing, but I can't risk giving him my heart. Not when I already gave it to Kev. Not when I'd be risking having it broken again.

'We can enjoy the time we have left,' I say, surprising myself.

Ethan kisses the top of my head and pauses to smell my hair. That tingle runs down my spine again. 'I'll take it.'

CHAPTER 29

The next day, I meet Ethan at his car hire place early. I'm pleased to report nothing (that would need pre-watershed censoring) happened between the two of us last night. We talked, cuddled and listened to the sound of the sea until he left at around midnight.

Zac is staying at home with Cindy today as she's on bedrest, so even if yesterday hadn't happened, I'd still be facing Ethan today. I'm glad it's on these new terms we have. Our understanding has given me a sense of peace, which reminds me, I need to go and see Harry and Barney later.

'Hey, beautiful.' Ethan picks me up in his strong arms with ease and kisses me.

'Someone's chipper this morning.'

'What can I say? I had a great night with a great girl last night.' My stomach flips, and he puts me back on solid ground.

'Morning, guys.' Patrick appears, and I groan inwardly. I was hoping for a bit more time alone with Ethan before work kicked off. Patrick must have spotted me leaving early and thought I was keen to get cracking. 'The crew are on their way.'

'*Delightful*,' I whisper under my breath dryly.

'We meet again.' Ethan stretches out his hand, and Patrick shakes it with vigour.

'I'm surprised you guys are even renting to us again after yesterday,' Patrick jokes.

'Let's hope the film crew can drive better than they can ride,' I snipe, feeling the need to clarify, once again, that it wasn't my fault. Patrick gives me a glance but doesn't respond. I understand him wanting the week to run smoothly, it's my neck on the line too. If I upset the film crew by having a go, they might head off in a strop, which will delay the project and we're already behind schedule. For that reason, I'm prepared to let it go.

'Well, you'll do a lot more damage if you crash one of these.' Ethan pats the bonnet of my favourite red Jeep as the film crew's van pulls up.

The random bike-braker gets out of the van and rearranges her short, black, spiky hair. When she notices me, she narrows her eyes at my chin and then walks over to Patrick to present some paperwork.

'She seems nice,' Ethan whispers.

'Don't get me started.' I shake my head. 'Are you going to come out with us today?' I ask, realising how keen I am for him to say yes.

'Dunno.' He runs his hand through his mop of hair.

I laugh. 'Are you trying to play it cool?'

'A little. Let me lock up and I'm there.' He kisses my cheek and darts off, leaving a warm glow on the side of my face. Still smiling, I turn around and come face to face with crash-girl, who scowls. Obviously, happiness is not contagious.

'Let's go.' Patrick claps three times and everyone starts to move. 'We'll go over to the main street while it's still quiet, then over to the beach.'

Patrick jumps in the driver's seat of the Jeep. 'You getting in?'

'Yes, I need to get in the back. Ethan is coming too.'

'He is?' Patrick raises an eyebrow at me as I climb in. 'So, is he coming to make sure we don't smash up his car, or did you and Florence Nightingale hit it off last night?'

'It's not like that.'

He holds his hands up in surrender. 'Hey, it's none of my business. I just saw that his truck was outside the hotel for a while last night and wondered if that means you're now considering my offer more seriously.'

191

My mouth feels dry and it's a chore to speak. 'Patrick, look, about that—'

'All ready to go.' Ethan appears from nowhere and jumps into the Jeep.

'We'll talk about it later, Patrick,' I say.

Ethan directs us to the carpark near the ferry pier, and we pull in just as a huge flock of seagulls passes overhead, flying towards a fishing boat that's just come in.

'At least it's not too busy,' Patrick says, climbing out. The film crew are already unpacking, and the models are in the van having their make-up done. Ethan and I volunteer to go on a coffee run. The irony doesn't escape me when I think back to how incensed I was when I used to get sent on them.

'So, I'm guessing today will be a lot of hanging around,' Ethan says whilst we wait for ten completely different styles of artisan coffee. Seriously, what's wrong with a good old-fashioned latte?

'You don't need to hang around if you have better things to do.'

'Not really. Jimmy, our store assistant, will be at the car rental place soon, and my mom had Lexi overnight. They're baking today and if I go pick her up too early, I'll be in trouble. I just meant that we should get the chance to spend some time together.'

'Oh, yes, we—' Something, or rather someone, catches my eye, and I run outside.

'Barney?'

His eyes almost pop out of his head. 'Sam?'

For a moment, I just look at him. How can I explain my behaviour back in Boston? My forehead is so tense I struggle to relax the creases down the centre. 'I need to apologise to you and Harry.'

Barney's face is hard. 'You really upset Harry, you know.'

I put my hand on his arm and speak softly. 'I upset you too.'

His face is still stony, and I can hardly blame him. 'I thought we deserved more than a yelled goodbye-great-knowing-you.'

'You did. You deserved much more. I was hoping to stop by tonight if that's okay? It's a long story, but I'm here with work.' Ethan steps outside carrying a large box filled with takeaway coffee.

Barney raises his eyebrows. 'Work?'

'Yes. Can I call round later to explain?' I glance at Ethan. 'I'll explain everything.'

'Harry and I were going to go out to dinner when we've finished work.' He juts out his chin.

'I'll come over after.'

'No.' He waves his hand and exhales. 'Harry will want to see you. Come about six. We'll cook.'

'Only if you're sure?'

'I'm off to see the seafood guy so we'll have plenty in.'

'Thanks, Barney.' I stretch up on my tiptoes to kiss him on the cheek, and the corner of his mouth twitches into a smile.

'Bring wine,' he says pointedly, and I give a captain's salute in response.

'That wasn't too bad,' Ethan says once Barney is out of earshot.

'I just hate seeing him like that. I seem to have this knack for hurting the people closest to me.' Somehow, seeing Barney put on a brave face makes me feel ten times worse.

'They'll forgive you.'

'That doesn't really make me feel any better about my outburst. I mustn't forget that wine!'

When we arrive back at the carpark, the Jeep has been rigged up with a camera. Two young female models are pouting in the front seats. There's a cameraman in the back and one on the road.

'It looks like they're taking still shots with the fishing boats in the background. We've got time to enjoy our coffees,' I say, sitting down on the floor out of the way. Ethan goes to hand out the rest of the drinks before coming to sit beside me.

'Not one *thanks*.' He shakes his head.

'These guys are great compared to the guys back in Boston,' I joke. 'To be fair, Patrick, as it turns out, is alright, but still …'

'But still …' He smiles and sips his coffee. 'Barney and Harry really like you. I know they have a lot of friends, but they don't connect with everyone like they have with you and me.'

'They have been really good to me. I hate that I've hurt them.'

'We all make mistakes. They'll forgive you. And they'll miss you when you leave.'

'I'll miss them too. I have good friends in the UK, but not many.' I get a pang in my stomach for lying to Ethan about the job offer.

The film crew start moving the car and equipment over to the main street, where a few early risers have gathered to watch. Ethan helps move a strange-looking piece of equipment while Patrick and I check some of the footage on the monitor.

'So,' Patrick says. 'My offer?'

I almost feel at peace having made my decision. I don't have any friends in Boston and awkward conversations over after-work sushi with Patrick isn't really a replacement. I still have a great career in England and there will be scope for promotion one day, I'm sure. I'm better off back in London with Coco, Bridget, Viv and Sarah.

'I'd love to stay in Boston and have all this just a ferry-ride away. I really love the place.'

'But?'

'But I have too much baggage at the moment. Perhaps in the future, next year maybe? But not now. It's a bad time.' I look at him and can tell he's disappointed. 'I'm sorry. It's a fantastic offer. Perhaps one of the other guys will be more suitable.'

'I'm in no rush. Keep an open mind,' he says, before walking off towards to the relocated Jeep.

When he's gone, I slump against a lamppost. I feel hollow. Formally turning the job offer down feels rubbish and pointless now I've done it. It reinforces how happy I am here and how much I'll be giving up by going home. But I've run away before, to London, and all that did was put my feelings on hold. I've not moved on from Kev.

'I've not moved on from Kev,' I whisper. It's like I was put in a vacuum pack the day he died and I need to get out. I love Kev more than anything, but I also have to live.

What I need to do is tackle my issues head-on and that means going home, back to the Cotswolds. I need to go and see my parents.

CHAPTER 30

'Harry, Barney.' I glance up at them from the doorstep and, for a moment, I can't tell if they're going to let me in.

After too long a pause, Harry sighs, 'Come in. Go straight through to the kitchen.'

I walk slowly down the hallway and hover by the breakfast bar. 'For you,' I say, sliding a wine carrier containing six cold bottles of Chardonnay over the counter to Barney.

Harry stands by his side in an obvious show of solidarity and folds his arms.

'I'm sorry. The way I spoke to you in Boston was out of order. Totally unacceptable,' I say. 'The truth is, I'm confused. In London, I thought I had everything figured out. I was getting on with my life, working hard and I thought I was happy. Then I came here and started to … feel things. It confused me and I can't process it.' I'm struggling to articulate what is essentially a churning mass in my stomach. 'I do like Ethan and I know it's going to be hard to leave. Saying goodbye to you two is going to be hard enough, never mind him too and the more time I spend with you all, the harder it seemed to be getting. I was trying to protect my feelings. It was silly of me, and my outburst was uncalled for. I feel terrible about it.'

They glance at one another. 'That was quite a speech,' Harry says, but not in a sarcastic way. 'Must have taken some courage to admit you're wrong like that.'

Barney juts his chin out and nods. For a moment, we all freeze. Then, they come around my side of the table and give me a big hug.

'We missed you, Sam,' Barney says.

'I missed you too.' My eyes prickle with tears as I squeeze them both tightly.

When they pull away, Harry gets out some plates and puts a platter of seafood and a bowl of salad in front of us. Barney gets out the wine glasses and starts to pour. 'Now we've got the yucky business of apologising out of the way, I'd like to hear all about what's been going on with you and Ethan.'

I feel heat flush my cheeks despite knowing full well this question would crop up.

'We kissed, again.'

Shocked gasps ensue.

'What?' Harry says.

'But you said ...' Barney adds.

'I know what I said.' I fill them in on my injury and how Ethan came to my rescue and how he'd forced me to confront my feelings.

Barney places a theatrical hand on his heart. 'You two are just perfect together. I can't believe it's all going to come to an end.'

'I know,' Harry says. 'I sort of feel bad about Boston now. I feel like we've had a part in all of this star-crossed lovers business.'

'No, no, guys, you're missing the point. We *know* we have a short expiry date, and that's okay. If I knew this was going somewhere, I'd freak out again. This way it's a fling and when I go back to England I'll slip back into my normal life. Ethan is fine with it too.'

Barney lets out a groan. 'I hope you kids know what you're doing.'

'We just care about you both,' Harry says.

'We know.'

'In that case, why isn't Ethan here with you?'

'I wasn't sure how you were going to accept my apology, so I thought I should come alone.'

'You silly girl. If we cut ties with everyone who we had a little to-do with, we'd have nobody left, not even each other,' Barney says, whispering the last part. Harry is already dialling Ethan on his phone.

About half an hour later, Ethan arrives with Lexi, who squeals with delight when she sees Barney.

'Uncle Barney!' He picks her up and spins her around.

She screams again when she sees me. 'Sam!'

'Hello, Lexi.'

'Hello, Lexi,' she says, mimicking my accent.

'Not bad,' I say in my best attempt at an American accent.

'Lexi, that's not polite,' Ethan warns her.

She pulls a face. 'Uncle Harry, can I play with my cars and dolls on the deck?' Harry nods and goes over to unlock the patio doors.

'How did it go?' Ethan whispers when nobody is around.

'They were great.'

'I told you.' He smiles and wraps his arms around my waist. My chest swells and I realise it's the first time I've *felt* happiness in quite a while. 'And did you miss me?'

I roll my eyes. 'It's been about two hours.'

'Exactly.' He grins and pulls me towards him before planting a kiss on my nose.

'Shall we eat?' Barney asks, and the interruption reminds me that I'm getting swept away by Typhoon Ethan. I actually feel okay about that.

'Eurgh, these shrimps still have eyes,' Lexi says, holding one up by its tail.

'You just peel them, like this.' Ethan starts to remove the head from his own shrimp. 'Anyway, I thought you wanted to be a mermaid? Mermaids have to eat them like that. Not all mermaids have dinglehoppers, you know.'

'I need a knife. A dinglehopper is a *fork*, which Flounder believes is a comb. Utterly useless in this situation,' she replies matter-of-factly, and I stifle a giggle.

'We need to limit your TV time,' Ethan says, defeated.

CHAPTER 31

The rest of the week is spent getting some still shots of the models in their various gear and capturing some of the scenery. We re-shoot some of the footage of the main street and spend time watching what we've got. When I'm not working, I'm with Ethan. Sometimes that includes Lexi, Barney and Harry; sometimes it's just the two of us. Yesterday afternoon, Ethan and I went on a whale-watching tour. It was an impromptu trip. We'd been walking back from filming and Ethan spotted a sandwich board advertising the last sailing of the day. We had five minutes to run down the pier and buy a ticket and when we boarded, I was out of breath.

We weren't that far from the shore when a huge, dark tail hit the water no more than ten metres from the boat. I'd been in awe. We were stood by the rail in silence watching the dark shadows of a pod swimming beneath the surface when suddenly, a humpback whale breached. Its whole body left the water exposing its tummy. Almost as soon as it happened, it crashed back into the water like it was playing to its audience. It made me feel a little bit emotional and, without thinking, I'd wrapped my arms around Ethan's neck and kissed him. It was perfect.

When we wrap up for the day, Patrick tells me I can have tomorrow off as he thinks we have all the footage we need so we're just about done. It's only 3 p.m., and I know Ethan and Lexi are on the beach with Barney and Harry, so I head straight there to meet them.

'Let me take you out on a date tomorrow,' Ethan says as we sit on the beach watching Lexi build sandcastles.

My chest flutters. 'A date?'

'Yeah, I was thinking Martha's Vineyard.'

'Is that where *Jaws* was filmed?'

'Does it matter either way?'

I laugh. How odd is it that Eighties excitement took over when it was the word *date* that should have stood out. Why am I not more alarmed by this?

'No, it doesn't, I just loved the movie when I was a kid. I'd love to go on a date with you.'

'Sam, Sam. Look!' Lexi shouts. I heave myself up and go over to the sandcastle village she's built.

'That's fantastic, Lexi,' I say, stroking her silky hair.

'I'm going to miss you when you go back to England.' She continues to build as she speaks. 'It's nice having another girl around.'

My chest pangs. That's the nicest thing anyone has ever said to me. I'm going to miss Lexi so much. 'Ahh, sweetie, you have your grandma.'

'I know.' She glances up at me. 'But she can't braid my hair as well as you can.'

'I'll come and visit you if I ever come back.'

'Will you visit my dad too?'

'Yes, I suppose I would.' My eyes catch Ethan's and I get a zap like I'm a fly hitting one of those blue lights in a café.

Her face breaks into a huge smile. 'Good. He likes you.'

I swallow hard. Explaining our situation to a six-and-three-quarter-year-old is not within my remit of expertise. 'I like your dad too. And Harry and Barney and, of course, you.'

She regards me for a moment, as though trying to organise her thoughts. 'He's happier when you're around.'

It's hard to know what to say to that. I believe her. I'm sure if Bridget were here, she'd say I was happier with Ethan around too, but it doesn't change anything. 'I'm sure it's you that makes him happy.' I kiss her on the head. 'Now then, how about some ice cream?'

200

Later, Harry and Barney join us, and whilst they build a sand palace, Ethan and I head to the shoreline. I slip off my sandals so I can walk in the shallow surf. 'Being in the sea makes me strangely uncomfortable.' The panic I felt when I fell out of the kayak comes back to me.

'I'm not sure being in an inch of water counts as "being in the sea".' He kicks his foot at a wave, purposely splashing my legs.

'Hey!' I scream, kicking water back at him a little too hard. It drenches his T-shirt and shorts.

'Oops,' I say, stifling my laughter.

'That's it!' He puts his hands together and stoops down, scooping up a huge amount of water. I try to run, but it's hard because I'm calf-deep. Icy water pounds against my back. Even my hair is drenched.

'Oh, you've done it now,' I say. He turns to run, but he's having similar trouble to me as he's even deeper. By the time I reach him, the freezing water is above my knees, but I manage to pounce on his back. My intention was to try and topple him, but now I'm hanging from his huge, solid body, I don't think I have a hope in hell.

'Well, that was a silly move,' he says, walking deeper into the ocean.

'No, please, no,' I beg. If I jump down, I'll have to swim. 'I don't have any spare clothes. Harry, Barney!' I scream.

'Sorry, we can't hear you,' Barney yells back. We've moved quite a way down the beach and they're just dots.

Ethan leans backwards slightly, purposely dunking the hem of my dress in the water.

'There's nobody to save you,' Ethan whispers devilishly.

'You're wetting yourself too,' I say.

'You're right.' He takes both my wrists in his big hand and uses the other to pull me around to his front. I scream as the swift action takes me by surprise. 'Sorry, I can just dunk you better from here.'

'You wouldn't,' I say, although I'm worried that he maybe would.

He leans forward, and I clutch his waist with my legs as tightly as possible. My lower abdomen stirs as the top of his shorts rubs against my thighs. 'I remember how you don't like being manhandled, so I should just let go, right?'

I plead with puppy eyes.

Just as the tip of my ponytail touches the water, he hoists me back up and plants his warm lips on mine, sending a wave of heat through me.

When he pulls away, he kisses me on my nose. 'Let's get out. A man could freeze in here.' He carries me back to the sand and places me down on my feet. Despite the heat of the sun, the damp parts of my dress and skin feel freezing, and I get goose pimples as I fasten my sandals.

'I don't know about you, but I wish we had brought towels and a change of clothes,' I say, rubbing my arms.

Ethan puts his arm around me and rubs too as we walk along the sand. When we arrive back to the others to looks of bemusement, I'm almost dry. I'm sure it's from my body heat rather than that of the sun.

***

My phone shrills at seven the next morning. It's Ethan letting me know he's outside. I grab my beach bag and chuck in some sun cream, a towel, my purse and sunglasses before heading downstairs.

When I'm close enough, he takes both of my hands and pulls me in for a kiss, he smells all citrusy and delicious. 'Good morning.'

'Good morning,' I say. He kisses me again, causing a swarm of butterflies to take flight in my stomach.

'Hop in, we have quite a drive to Falmouth.' He holds the passenger door of my favourite red Jeep open, and I climb in.

Remembering my bird's nest locks after my last trip out in this car, I scoop my hair into a topknot so I don't have to worry about it until later.

'Let's get some music on.' He puts a CD in the player.

'How retro.' I laugh. 'Wait a minute, is this Justin Timberlake?'

'The one and only.' He takes his eyes off the road momentarily to flash me a smile that turns my insides to liquid. I'll never get tired of seeing those white teeth against his honey tan.

As we drive, Ethan sings along to Justin, and I'm slightly impressed that he can hold a tune.

'You're a dark horse.' I have to shout because the speed we're travelling at makes the wind impossible to talk over. The less appealing side of travelling in a topless soft top.

'I've been known to do a bit of karaoke in the local bars in my time.'

'Well, that I have to see.' I get a pain in my chest when it hits me that I'll be back in England in a week, and I probably won't ever get to see Ethan do karaoke, or anything else for that matter.

'We're here.'

Falmouth, it transpires, is as quaint and pretty as its Cornish namesake, and as we drive past all the shops and cafés, I'm tempted to suggest ditching Martha's Vineyard in favour of strolling the high street here. That is until we drive down towards the harbour and spot the 'Island Queen' Ferry. 'Ooh, that looks like fun,' I say as Ethan pulls into the carpark.

Ethan buys the tickets, and then we wait in the busy holding area to embark. Ethan stands behind me and wraps his arms around me before kissing my neck. My body is in defiance of my head, because every part of me from the neck down wants him.

'You smell nice,' he says, kissing my neck again. The people around us are probably thinking we're a couple in love. If that were the truth, I'd have bolted the second I caught wind of it, but it isn't. We're just enjoying one another's company because we clicked. Soon, we'll go back to our ordinary lives. It's the only reason I'm allowing myself to do this, and there's no more than cuddles and a few kisses going on. It's harmless.

People start to shuffle forwards and board the boat. We manage to get a seat at the front, so we have great views of the harbour as we sail out. Martha's Vineyard is only thirty-five minutes away, and we can see it ahead.

'So, this is the second boat trip in two days. Still no seasickness?'

I roll my eyes. 'Can we forget about that now?'

'You're the only person I've ever known to get sick in a kayak. I don't think I'll ever forget.'

'I think I have a problem with small vessels, that's all.'

'Alleged manhandling aside, you hated me that day.' I can't see his eyes because he's wearing sunglasses, but I know they will be twinkling with amusement.

'I did. You weren't a very nice person,' I say, pointedly.

'Wait, I get that I was a little grumpy at first, but you did stand me up the week before.'

'I did n—' I stop talking when I see the corner of his mouth twitch with amusement.

***

We disembark at a place called Oak Bluffs, which is a town on Martha's Vineyard with another eye-pleasing array of colourful clapboard buildings. We browse the shops along Circuit Avenue, where I pick up a couple of souvenir tea towels and a fridge magnet.

As we head back down towards the water, Ethan slips his hand into mine. The feel of his skin on mine sends fizzes of warmth through my whole body. I allow myself to wonder how I'd feel if we were in London and our *thing* didn't have an expiry date. It's hard to imagine hating this but it's different here. I know going back is the right thing to do. There is too much left unre-

204

solved at home. I'm ready to face up to things I haven't been able to before. I'm ready to see my parents.

After a while, Ethan grinds to a halt.

'What's going on?' I ask, desperate to go and see the beach.

'This is The Flying Horses carousel.' He's already pulling me inside the old wooden building. 'It's supposedly the oldest carousel in America. We have to ride it.'

Oh no, no, no. We'll look like fools. 'Perhaps if Lexi was with us, but two grown adults can't ride this.'

'Of course, we can. It's iconic.' He pulls me inside towards the ticket counter, where we join a small queue of families.

'I can't believe you're making me do this,' I whisper as he buys our tickets.

'Stop worrying about what other people think.'

We stand by the gate waiting for the carousel to come to a stop. It's not even a very big carousel, and the horses don't move up and down like modern ones. It's definitely meant for kids.

I choose a light brown horse on the outside, and Ethan goes behind me. 'You need to try and catch the brass ring,' he says as the ride begins to turn.

'What brass ring?' I ask, before noticing the boy in front grabbing at an arm sticking out of the wall. On our next rotation, I'm poised and ready, and when we come up to the arm, I reach out, grabbing the ring.

'Yes!' I shout.

To my surprise, I enjoy riding around on the wooden horse. Those few moments of the breeze blowing my hair give me a chance to be alone with my thoughts. Well, as alone as I can be with Ethan filling my head.

'Admit it, you loved every minute of that,' Ethan teases as we climb off.

I smile. 'I suppose I enjoyed it more than expected, and I won this,' I say, waving the brass ring in front of him.

'You're quite competitive really, aren't you?'

I pull a smug expression. 'Only when I'm winning.'

I give the ring to the child who was sitting in front of me and tried to catch it.

'You just gave away your free turn!' Ethan says.

'What can I say, I'm competitive *and* generous.'

The bright sunlight stabs my eyes when we step outside, so I scramble around in my bag for my sunglasses whilst Ethan pops to a nearby ice cream parlour to get us each a chocolate ice cream in a waffle cone. We walk towards the beach to eat them.

'There are better beaches than this, you know,' Ethan says as we arrive at the skinny strip of sand packed with tourists. Half a bench becomes free when a woman and a child stand up, so I dive on it, scooching up so that Ethan can squash onto the end. It's hard to eat my ice cream whilst being pressed up against him, but his skin prickles mine with warmth and the awkward eating is a small compromise.

'I'm sure there are but this one was close by.'

'A low-maintenance date. I like it.' He nudges into me playfully.

A date? I'm on a date, I remember. I say the words in my head and they flow with surprising ease. A comfortable silence ensues whilst we sit, looking at the boats, birds and people.

'This is perfect.' I lick a dribble of ice cream off the side of the cone and catch Ethan watching me. 'Well, I'm not going to waste good ice cream.'

He laughs.

'Are you looking forward to getting back to London?' His tone is casual, but I sense a pensiveness.

I nod as I swallow a chunk of cone. 'I suppose so. It's a completely different kind of place. It's so bright and colourful here, and London is so dull and grey, but there's always something to see or do. It's my home and I've always been happy there.'

'It's your home,' he echoes and squeezes my knee. I can't help but think about Patrick's offer and I get a pang of guilt. 'C'mon, I have an idea.'

He pulls me back towards the shops and we stop at a car rental agency. Funnily enough, there are a few Jeeps outside; that car should be the symbol of Cape Cod.

'We might as well see the island,' he says as he comes out swinging the keys.

I jump in the passenger seat and open the illustrated map. 'We have to see the beach *Jaws* was filmed on. Oh, and the bridge,' I say excitedly, and Ethan laughs.

We drive past Ocean Park, which, if you excuse the brightly painted wooden houses around it, looks very English. 'This reminds me so much of being a kid,' I say. For a moment, I feel a little nostalgic when I think of going to the seaside with my mum and dad when I was little. 'My parents used to take me to the seaside in the summer.'

'Great memories hey?'

I nod but Ethan's focus is on the road ahead.

'Are you going to go see your parents when you get back to England?'

The question is like a blow to the abdomen. Obviously, I'd been considering it, but Ethan doesn't know that, and nobody else knows anything about my parents, so it makes me uncomfortable to be quizzed about them.

'You can talk to me, you know,' he prompts, but it's not permission to talk that I need, it's some sort of instruction book – *Reconciliation for Dummies*.

I look out across the water stretching as far as the eye can see. 'I've been thinking about it.'

'That's good.' He glances at me before looking back to the road ahead. 'I think if you don't, a day will come when it's too late. You can't turn back time, but you can work with what you have right now. I don't know them, but I'm sure they'll just be relieved to have you back in their lives.'

His words bounce around my ears and mix with the reverberation of the wind before I let them sink in. I know he's right about going to see them, but, after all this time, I'm not sure he's right about the reception I'll get.

'Did you not feel like pushing everyone away after losing Nicole?'

He slips his hand from the gearstick and entwines his fingers with mine. 'All the time. The difference was that I had a baby to think about. I needed to take all of that help people were offering.'

'I'm a horrible person, aren't I?' I've reflected enough to know that I am. Just spending time with Lexi yesterday was enough to show me how heartbreaking it would be for Ethan if she grew up and disappeared one day without so much as a goodbye.

'Don't say that. We all respond to grief differently, and our priorities don't often sit within the "be a good person" category when we're hurt. We lash out at those closest to us. Maybe it's our natural instinct to protect them from our pain or something. I don't know. You acted out of grief, but you have a chance to put it right.'

'Over eight years later? I'm not sure they'll listen.'

'It's better than not at all.' He squeezes my hand, and I know he's right. 'C'mon, I have an idea.'

We continue down Seaview Avenue, which lives up to its name. The thin strip of road is surrounded by water on either side, and a gorgeous golden sandy beach runs down the length of the left.

'We're here,' Ethan says as he pulls the car over at the side of the road.

'Where?'

'That's Joseph Sylvia State Beach.'

'The *Jaws* beach?'

He shakes his head 'Yes the *Jaws* beach ... and I thought you were a *Jaws* fan?'

'I am,' I protest. 'It looked further away on the map and, in my defence, it may have been the Eighties when I last saw the film.'

'Well, you're on the tour now, ma'am.' He jumps out and I follow.

'I can't believe I'm actually here,' I say. 'And it is a gorgeous beach.'

'Let's take a walk then. Unless you fancy a swim?'

'I might dip my toe in, I don't think my new tea towel is up to drying two grown-ups.'

After a paddle, we stroll the surprisingly quiet and unspoilt coastline as I'm hit with a bit more of that Eighties nostalgia mixed with some stomach-stirring memories of being in the sea with Ethan yesterday.

'There's nobody around.' He pulls me into him. 'Which means I can do this.' He presses his mouth to mine and runs his hands down my back. Cupping my bottom, he lifts me up as the rhythm of our lips picks up pace. I want to wrap my legs tighter around him but I'm scared of cutting off his circulation.

We drive a little further down the road, taking in the stunning views of the beach, which still runs alongside us. Then I notice the bridge.

'I do recognise that,' I say. A handful of people have gathered by the rail and are peering over the edge. 'You don't think there's something in the water, do you?'

'What, like Jaws?' he jibes as he pulls the car over.

'Funny,' I say dryly. 'What are they doing then?'

'They're jumping in. It's a thing.' As if on cue, a young woman climbs over the wooden fence and plunges into the water below as the others cheer. 'Want a turn?'

'Ha, no thanks.'

'That no towel thing is really holding us back today,' he says.

I watch another person plunge in to the sound of squeals and it reminds me of how routine my life has become. Kev had been the Yin to my Yang in that respect. I've always played things safe unless he encouraged me to do something daring. Perhaps it's

209

time I did something brave for myself. I know I've spent three months in another country, but I'm still doing the same work for the same company. It wasn't really very daring. This looks fun and I should start having more of it.

'Actually, I think I will jump in.' I smirk.

'You're kidding, right?'

'Nope.' I open the car door. 'Are you coming?'

He follows me as I walk past the 'No Jumping' sign onto the wooden walkway of the bridge. It isn't a high bridge by any means, but the thought of jumping off it is still a little daunting. But after all my big talk, there's no way I can back out now. I take off my sandals and place them near the edge. As Ethan crouches down to take his trainers off, I watch a few more jumpers. It's unnerving that most of them scream as they're doing it. I climb onto the wooden rail and stand up straight. It seems even higher now.

'Three.' I glance at Ethan, who wears an expression of bemusement crossed with something that looks a little bit like fear. 'Two, one!' I grab my nose and plunge into the freezing water before I have a chance to chicken out. When I come up, there's a second splash, and Ethan surfaces next to me with a 'Whoo!'

'That was fantastic,' I say, almost trembling with adrenaline, and perhaps borderline hypothermia. I can't believe I just did that. My heart is racing.

'You don't think there are sharks in here do, you? Maybe we should get out of the water just in case.' A sudden tension forms in my chest.

'We do get them.' He starts to look from left to right, nervously. 'In fact … Chief?' he yells. 'Chief Brody?' he yells again and people are starting to look.

Chief Brody as in the main character in *Jaws*. Very funny!

'Shhh, you absolute knob!' I splash him and he bursts out laughing. 'Now I'm getting out just so nobody thinks I know you.'

We swim over to the side and climb over some rocks to a

sandy beach. It's even colder once we leave the water, and my saturated dress clings to me.

Ethan shakes his head to dry off, like a wet dog. 'You surprised me back there.'

'I may never get the chance to do that again,' I say, with a sad realisation. 'I thought I should live for the now and at least I have a cool story to tell.'

He takes both of my hands and kisses me. His lips taste salty. 'This is living for the now.'

I close my eyes and lift my face to the sun, enjoying the fullness in my chest for a moment. I need to spend more time 'living for the now'.

As we head back towards the car, I pick up my bag, which I'd dumped near the 'No Jumping' sign. 'I think we need evidence of this moment.' I take out my phone and hand it to Ethan, expecting him to take a picture of me, but instead, he pulls me into him and takes a selfie of us both.

By the time we get back to the car, I'm shivering uncontrollably.

'Take my T-shirt, you look freezing.' Ethan hands me the T-shirt. His body is almost dry, bar a few glistening droplets.

I put it on and slide the spaghetti straps of my dress off before pulling it down and wriggling out of it. When I climb into the Jeep, I tie it around the roll bar. Ethan looks at me and raises an eyebrow.

I shrug. 'It will dry off.'

'I know that. It's the half-naked girl in my car I'm having trouble with.' He flashes a mischievous grin.

'Well, don't go getting any ideas, Mr!'

We carry on towards Edgartown where we park up. I put my still-damp dress back on, and we take a walk up to the lighthouse and sit on its concrete base.

'I can't believe I'm going to lose you in a few days,' Ethan says, putting his arm around my back and squeezing me tight to him.

It's come too soon. My heart aches for a few more weeks. 'We knew it would happen. You said—'

'I know what I said. It doesn't make it any easier. I just wish you could stay a little longer so we can figure out what's going on between us.'

I swallow the word 'nothing'. It seems too harsh, but it also doesn't feel as right as it should. That word could have tripped off my tongue a few weeks ago but now, the deceit of it chokes me.

'Is there no way you could extend your stay, for just a few weeks? Could you talk to Patrick?'

My stomach rolls. 'I really wish I could. My visa is up. Immigration will be banging on my door come next Sunday.'

He traces my arm with his finger until he lands on the heart of my charm bracelet. 'It feels wrong to let you walk away.'

I raise my eyebrow.

'Not "let you". You know what I mean.'

Of course I knew what he meant. I needed to stall because walking away does feel wrong but I can't admit that to Ethan. Nor can I tell him I had the option to stay – it will only hurt him, knowing I'm turning my back on him. 'Leaving you is going to be one of the hardest things I've ever done, but we knew what we were getting into.'

He squeezes me in his arms again as we look across the sand, to the blue water of the Nantucket Sound beyond.

The drive back to Oak Bluffs is quiet. As are the ferry ride to Falmouth and the long drive back to the tip of Cape Cod. I sense that Ethan is angry that I've not tried harder to stay for a while, but he shouldn't have asked me to. It isn't fair – I've only just come to terms with our arrangement, and now he wants to dial up the intensity and move the goalposts. I try and block the whole thing out as we make our way back to Provincetown, but the problem is, the feelings Ethan's having are echoed inside of me. Spending time with him hasn't felt like I've been cheating

212

on Kev like I thought it would, it hasn't felt wrong, yet I know I have to go back to England. Being with Ethan this week has felt safe because I haven't had any false expectations. What if there was no end date and I expected him to be around forever? What if I expected him to be around forever and then one day he was gone? I can't go through that again.

A ball of emotion flares up in my throat and as I choke it back, tears prick my eyes. I turn my head to the side so Ethan doesn't notice.

'Goodnight, Sam.' He leans across the armrest to kiss me on the cheek. A huge part of me wants to ask him in, but it's late, and it would send out the wrong message.

'Goodnight, Ethan.' I climb out of the truck, and before I close the door, I pop my head back in. 'Patrick and I are going to view the stills in the morning, but I'm free in the afternoon. It would be great to see you, Lexi, Barney and Harry one last time before I go.'

'I wouldn't miss it,' he says with a sad smile.

'See you, and thanks for today. I loved every minute.'

It will stay in my memories forever.

CHAPTER 32

After a few hours of work at the hotel, I check my phone. There's a message from Ethan asking me to meet him, Barney and Harry at a beach bar near the harbour.

'Since it's our last day and we've got a lot to celebrate, I thought we should go for a drink,' Patrick says before I can make my excuses to leave.

'Oh.' He picks up on my tone and his expression falters and I feel bad blowing him off, especially after we've worked together so well this week. 'I was just about to head out to meet some friends, but you should come along with us,' I say, trying to mask my disappointment.

As Patrick and I walk to the bar, he talks animatedly about the project, and how thrilled Karma and Peace will be with our final campaign. I can't help but brim a little with pride. I have my rung on the ladder and it's much further up than I could have anticipated. It won't be long before Rocks trainers will be seen everywhere, and I'll always know that I played a part in that.

The closer we get to the bar the more apprehensive I feel. This is the last time I'm going to see Ethan. Butterflies tied up with little knots fill my stomach.

'Hi, everyone.' I feign a cheery tone as we find the others at a table near the water's edge. I do all the introductions, then Patrick heads to the bar.

'Sam!' Barney says. 'I can't believe you're leaving us tomorrow.'

'Me neither, but it had to come to an end. I'm just glad I met you guys.' I reach across the table and grab their hands. 'All of you.' I look meaningfully at Ethan.

'Barney and I have talked, and we're going to try and visit London in the winter, so you'll have to show us all the sights,' Harry says.

'And of course, we'll be stalking you on social media,' Barney adds.

'Of course, and likewise.' I laugh at the honesty we share.

Patrick returns with some interesting pink cocktails with sparklers in. 'The barman said if I was at this table, I had to get these.' He shrugs, placing the tray down.

'Glad he was listening,' Barney mumbles.

'They're special cocktails. We're calling them The Sam,' Harry says.

'The Sam?' I say, picking one up and taking a sip. 'Oooh, sweet.'

'Yes, sweet like you, but there's a hint of chilli in there because we think you've got a kick to you.' Barney gives Patrick a pointed look which, fortunately, he doesn't seem to pick up on.

I take another sip. 'Mmm, I taste it now. I like it. Thank you, guys. I've never had my own cocktail before.'

Everyone takes a cocktail from the tray and Barney raises his glass. 'To Sam.'

'To Sam,' the rest chorus.

'I can't believe we're losing our star employee,' Patrick says, taking another sip of his drink. My stomach starts to tighten. Oh god, this conversation is heading towards dangerous territory.

'I know.' Ethan wraps his big hand around mine. 'We don't want to lose her either. It's a shame you can't keep her on.' He laughs. It was a flippant remark, but Patrick's face is one of confusion.

'Haha, well he can't,' I blurt, hoping Patrick takes the hint but it doesn't come out in the light-hearted way I intended it to.

'I tried my best to keep her but she's a tough nut to crack. I even offered her dental.' Patrick takes a sip of his cocktail. It's like slow-motion as I watch Ethan's expression change from one of jollity to one of confusion. My throat feels thick and I can't swallow. As I glance around the table, I notice Barney and Harry's faces have taken a similar turn. My chest clenches and I don't quite know what to do or say.

'Guys, I …' When I speak, Ethan looks at me with deep hurt in his eyes. I can't bear it.

'I'm sorry, I have to go pick up Lexi. She's expecting a picnic on the beach,' Ethan says, standing up. A shard of glass pierces my chest. *He'd planned that for me.* As he walks off, I freeze before running after him.

'Ethan, wait!'

He turns to look at me, his eyes watery and full of sorrow. 'Why did you lie to me?'

'I didn't, not really, not in the bigger picture. I told you I wasn't looking for a relationship. I told you that this … thing between us was just temporary. The way I chose to live my life eight years ago hasn't altered.'

'You told me there was no way you could stay for a little while longer. You lied to me.'

I bite down on my lip. His face is twisted with anguish. I hate seeing him hurt like this. It hurts me and I'd do anything to take his pain away, but I know what I'm going to say next might as well be a twist of the knife.

'Ethan, we can't *be* anything. I like you, and I don't doubt that I could fall for you, but it isn't what I want, not really. My heart belongs to someone else. At some point down the line, I'd realise that and end up hurting you more.'

He looks like he's about to protest but exhales instead. Then he gives a small nod of his head. 'Whatever. Look, I don't expect you to leave your life in London for me. I'm not mad at you for turning down the job, because that's your decision. I just wish you'd been upfront about it in the first place. Instead, you gave me some kind of hope that maybe there was something between us, but you knew all along there was nothing.'

'Ethan.' I sound pathetic.

216

'Those two guys in there are going to feel the same. They showed you so much kindness, and you weren't honest with them either.' His mouth is set in a hard line. 'You pretend you've got this tough shell, that you're preserving the memory of Kevin and you're all noble and shit, but you know what, you're just scared. You're scared of letting anyone in. You're fooling yourself like you've fooled yourself for the past eight years and now you're running away from me like you ran away from your parents because you can't face anything head-on.'

He might as well have stabbed me in the chest – it would have been less painful.

'I'm so sorry.' My voice is a pathetic whisper.

'I wish you'd never set foot on that ferry from Boston.' With that, he turns and storms off. There's a sharp pain in my chest as a wave of emotion hits me. Tears fill my eyes and I start to sob uncontrollably. I want to run after him, but what's the point? He hates me and the bottom line is that I'm leaving. This is too confusing. I need to go home where everything makes sense.

CHAPTER 33

I slump against the wall. I don't know how long I've been out here, and I don't want to go back inside the bar to face Barney and Harry, but I haven't really got a choice.

'Arrgh!' I yell.

'You alright, honey?' a man in higher heels than I could ever wear asks as he walks past. I nod and force a smile, so he continues on his way.

Wiping my eyes, I head back into the bar. I'm met with two frowning faces and a look of utter confusion from Patrick, who looks at me and then back to them before standing up.

'Look, I'm sorry I misread that situation. I hadn't expected … well, you know.' He pats me on the back. 'I'm going to go pack. I'll see you later.'

Barney and Harry look like the air has been squeezed out of them, they can barely even bring themselves to look at me. I sit down opposite them. 'Guys?'

They both stare at their almost empty cocktail glasses.

'It doesn't matter that I turned down the job. I was always going home and nothing serious was ever going to happen with Ethan. You know that.'

They both shuffle uncomfortably. 'We know,' Harry says eventually.

'So why are you so upset?'

'Because you didn't tell us about the offer, and because you hurt Ethan.' Barney fiddles with the base of his glass.

'But why would I tell you if I wasn't even considering it?'

Silence.

'And the reason I didn't tell Ethan was because I didn't want to hurt him. I didn't think he'd find out about the job offer and I wanted to keep things casual and uncomplicated.' I look between each of them for a response but neither one replies. 'You know what? I need to pack too.' I stand up. It's not the way I wanted to leave things, but what choice do I have?

'Sam, wait,' Harry calls. When I turn to look at him, he casts Barney a nervous glance.

'We don't want you to leave on bad terms.' He holds his arms out, and I step forward so he can wrap me in a hug. I squeeze him tightly.

'I'm sorry,' I whisper.

'We'll miss you so much.'

'I'll miss you too.'

'And me.' Barney stands and wraps both Harry and me in his arms, and for a moment, we stand there, embracing.

'Ethan will get over it. He just really likes you, and you make such a sweet couple,' Harry says when Barney frees us from his grip.

We did. The thought is tinged with so much sadness. 'I'd have loved to say goodbye to Lexi, but I can't go and see her now.'

Barney rubs my arm and purses his lips. 'I'm sorry, honey.'

'It isn't your fault. You're right, I should have been upfront. I see that now.'

'Ethan will calm down. Write to him and Lexi when you're back home, once he's had a chance to cool off.'

I nod; that's a good idea. 'Yes. I'll do that.'

Since the picnic has been cancelled and there's little more to say to Barney and Harry, I decide to go back to the hotel. 'I'm going to go and pack too. But I'll miss you guys so much. Definitely come and see me in London.'

Barney's eyes glisten. 'We will. I'm going to miss you too.'

Harry leans forward and kisses me on my cheek. 'Me too. Look after yourself, Sam.'

'You too. Look after each other, and Ethan.' They nod, and I kiss them both before saying a final goodbye.

When I leave the bar, I feel hollow.

Back at the hotel, I glance at my clothes strewn over the little chair in the corner, the towel in a crumpled heap on the bathroom floor, and my beauty items scattered around. The thought of having to pack it all away daunts me. So instead, I take a small bottle of rum and a can of Coke out of the minibar and sit out on the balcony. There are some paddleboarders out, and a few swimmers, and some small boats bob around nearer to the horizon. The sun has started to head towards the west, and it casts its golden glow across the water. It's not just wonderful people I'll be leaving behind. It's this too. I sip my drink. It's strong. I wish I'd gone to get some ice.

There's a knock at the door, and my heart leaps. *Could it be?* I jump up, straightening my clothes and hair as I dash to the door. I take a deep breath before I open it.

'Patrick?' My heart sinks.

'Sorry to disturb you. I was just booking a table for dinner and wondered if you'd like to join me at around seven? We can wrap up this week in style and it can be my way of apologising for causing a problem earlier.'

'I'm sorry, Patrick, I'm tired and you don't need to apologise. It's my fault.'

'No worries.' He gives me a knowing look. 'Are you okay?'

I nod, then close the door and slump against it.

CHAPTER 34

The following morning, I wake up feeling a little more hopeful. I had an early night; thankfully, I managed to drift off. I think I was so drained after everything that happened, my body needed to reboot. As a result, I'm feeling better, brighter. There's a small ember of hope that Ethan will come to say goodbye today. Leaving on good terms is all I can really hope for.

I have breakfast, if a tiny nibble of a pancake constitutes breakfast, then finish my packing and find myself waiting in the lobby for Patrick with ten minutes to spare, so I chance a look at my phone.

Nothing.

There's still time.

'Morning, Sam. All set?'

Patrick settles the bill with the company credit card, and then we head to the pier in silence for the ferry ride back to Boston. As we walk down the wooden boards of the Macmillan Pier, I can't focus on looking straight ahead. My eyes dart about, searching for Ethan amongst the crowds. I know I've hurt him, but surely he wouldn't let me go back to England without a proper goodbye.

People are already boarding the ferry, and Patrick joins the line and my heartrate picks up. I can't go yet. It's too soon. There's a man walking down the pier. I squint, he's a big build, athletic with brown messy hair. My heart skips. As I watch him hopefully, willing him to get nearer so I can see properly. He joins a woman at the end of the queue and my insides turn to a solid, heavy rock. It isn't him.

221

'You're miles away,' Patrick calls, his voice further away than it should be. I turn around to see the queue has moved on. The man behind me clears his throat impatiently, so I walk on, still scanning the crowds for Ethan. There's still time. We're walking down the ramp to the jetty now. Still no sign. The queue moves quicker, and I'm swept along, but if I just caught a glimpse of Ethan, I'd go against the tide, I'd catch a different ferry. I walk up the gangway. In a few more steps I'll be on the boat; if he's coming, he's almost too late. A crewmember greets me onboard as I take another step.

It's too late.

I sit outside, where I can still see the pier. The last few passengers board, and the crewmembers remove the gangway. A horn sounds, and we're off.

And just like that, it's all over.

CHAPTER 35

When I was a child, I used to wonder if the world was black and white in the 'olden days', because that's how old movies were. When I emerge from the Underground, it's like I'm in one of those movies. Everything is monochrome. The Thames is a murky brown-grey. The sky is a pale white-grey, and the damp, soggy buildings are just grey. The kaleidoscope of colour I'd become accustomed to in the States has gone, and I can't help but wonder whether stepping back into my past was so necessary.

When I get into the lobby of the office building I work at, the theme continues: grey suits and shift dresses, black suits and shift dresses. I'm thankful for the sight of our quirky receptionist, who almost always dresses like a rainbow.

I check my emails. Hundreds. There's one from Patrick saying that he hopes I got home safely. He'd tried to convince me to stay once more. Once we got back to Boston, I had one more day in the office before I flew home, and he spent most of it trying to convince me to take the job. He thought I'd made some good friends there and was a much happier person than the one who arrived. But what did he know? I told him I was happy to be going home and that I was miserable when I'd first arrived because I was homesick. It couldn't have been further from the truth.

Tony perches on the edge of my desk. 'I can't believe you came back here.'

I roll my eyes.

'You're single, you live alone, you have no ties and you had the chance to move to Boston and you turned it down.'

Word travels fast. 'You heard then?'

'Yes, Patrick let slip that he'd offered you the job the day before we were due to fly back. The rest of us were on eggshells for that last afternoon, wondering who else he'd offer the job to instead.'

I shuffle in my seat. Any one of those blokes would have sold a kidney to take that job, but I know he didn't offer it to anyone else. He'd already told me that he'd created the role for me and they didn't really need anyone else. He'd called it a shift in resources. In the end, he asked if I'd be happy to give input on US campaigns remotely, and I agreed.

'I was just lucky Rocks liked my ideas.' I wave my hand dismissively.

'You made yourself heard, and I think Patrick liked that too.'

'Maybe not at first, though.' I wink.

He shakes his head. 'I still can't believe you didn't take the job.'

I just shrug. There's no way I'm getting into it with Tony.

At lunchtime, I go downstairs to meet Bridget.

'Finally, you can take that cat back!' She greets me with two air-kisses.

'That cat you've had in every Instagram picture you've posted over the past three months?' I say dryly.

'I suppose she's cute!'

'How's the world of accounting?' I ask.

'Never mind that, how was the rest of your trip? I want to know everything, apart from all the work stuff.' She lifts her over-sized mug and sips her cappuccino.

'Cape Cod is beautiful. It's got that lazy, beachy American feel to it, like the movies always portray – clapboard housing, unspoilt, rugged shorelines, a nice breez—'

'Enough about clapboards and breezes. I want to know about the men.' She snuggles back into her seat, ready for a long and juicy story.

I knew this was coming and in all fairness to Bridget, she's even waited long enough that I've had time to take a bite of my sandwich. Marriage must have calmed her down. 'There were men there, lots of men in fact. There's a large gay community in Provincetown.'

'Funny.' She bangs her cup down. 'Tell me about Ethan.'

Kind, sexy, toned ... perfect. 'What is there to say? He's gorgeous, we had a bit of a holiday snog, and now I'm back.' As I sip my coffee, one of the other guys, Dave, from the Boston trip walks past.

'Hi, Sam. Can't believe you're back here. Who turns down a chance like that?' He shakes his head with disbelief and walks off.

'What was that about?' Bridget asks.

'Oh, nothing.'

'It's not nothing. Why wouldn't a colleague expect you back? What was the chance you turned down?' She rests her elbow on the table and props her head up in her hand. If I don't tell her, she won't drop it.

'Okay,' I sigh. 'I was offered a permanent position in Boston.'

'What?' Her eyes practically jump out of their sockets.

'The team over there liked my work, and Patrick, my US boss, asked if I'd consider joining them, but obviously, I said no.'

'Obviously.' Her tone is laced with sarcasm.

'I can't just leave the UK. This is where I live.' I laugh nervously.

'You live by yourself. You can do that anywhere in the world.'

I try to appeal to her sentimental side. 'I'd miss you.'

'And?'

I forgot she doesn't have a sentimental side.

'And, I'd miss you. Isn't that enough?'

'Nonsense.' She waves her hand dismissively. 'You didn't even call when you were there. There's more to this than you're letting on, and I know it's to do with that guy.'

I can't bear to hear her call him 'that guy'. 'Ethan?'

'That's the one.'

'It's not as simple as that. He's part of the reason. Things were

225

getting complicated between us, and I did call you, by the way.'

'Things were getting good!' Bridget says sharply. 'And you hardly ever called me.'

I inhale noisily through my nose in the hope she gets the hint to drop the conversation.

'You can't do this forever, you know.'

'Do what?'

She leans forward and looks me directly in the eye. 'This silly self-preservation act, where you push people away.'

Her words remind me of the last thing Ethan said to me and I'm suddenly not hungry. I look at my watch animatedly. 'Oh dear, my lunch break is over. I'll catch you another time.' I lean over and kiss her on the cheek as she scowls at me.

'I'm not finished with you,' she says.

'Bye.' I wave as I walk away.

CHAPTER 36

It's been a week and a half since I arrived back in London, and life has almost fallen back into place. I haven't heard anything from Ethan, but I have had a few text conversations with Barney and Harry.

They haven't mentioned Ethan, and I haven't asked. It's better this way. I was going to take on board their advice and write to him, but somehow I haven't found the courage. Today though, that changes. I hate to think of hurting him, and I need to tell him how sorry I am. I've bought a little card from an independent card shop near my flat. It's plain, thick cream card and has a blue sequined dolphin on the front, which I hope will soften him a little. I take my favourite gel pen out of my desk drawer and start writing.

Dear Ethan,

I pause, tapping my pen on the desk whilst I think of what to write, but it's no good. It's like when I tried to write to my parents back in Provincetown. I'm just useless with words. I stuff the card and pen in my bag and get on with my work.

***

The following Saturday, Bridget invited me over for dinner with her and her husband. When the time comes around, it surprises me that I find myself hoping she'll cancel. Bridget is my best friend, but since I got back things have been different. Obviously, she's spent the last three months with her new husband, and I've not been around. I'm not blaming her for the fact she no longer wants to go for drinks after work five days of the week or shopping on a Saturday, but I suppose I feel a little ... cut out. It's nobody's fault, and I know I'm being childish, but I thought I'd come back to England and slot right into my old life. Viv and Sarah are preoccupied with their partners too. I suppose I'll just have to get used to these differences.

'Come in.' She kisses me on the cheek as I step inside her flat.

'I brought you this, in the hope you'll go easy on me.' I thrust a bottle of vintage red her way, and she gives a double eyebrow raise to show she's impressed.

'Hi, Sam.' Bridget's husband, Alex, appears, wrapping his arms around Bridget and kissing her affectionately on the neck. It makes me feel squeamish. Bridget must sense that and wriggles free.

'Can you open this so it has a chance to breathe?' she asks, thrusting the bottle of wine at him. We walk through to the kitchen-dining area and take a seat at the breakfast bar where she has put out bread and olives. 'Sorry about that.'

'You're *newishlyweds*, it'll wear off.' I wink to show I'm teasing, and she narrows her eyes at me playfully.

'You'd know all about new relationships.' She shrugs and pops an olive into her mouth.

'Touché,' I say, spearing an olive of my own with a cocktail stick.

'Have you heard from him?' she asks with fake nonchalance.

I pick up a piece of bread. 'No.'

'Are you going to get in touch with him?'

I tear off a chunk. 'No.'

'Why not?'

I shove the bread in my mouth and point to my lips and shrug.

Alex comes in, offering me a little respite. 'Sorry, couldn't find the corkscrew.'

'Sod the wine. Let's have margaritas,' Bridget says. 'We can't wait for that to breathe; this girl needs a drink.' Alex starts getting

228

bottles out of the cupboard and a blender from under the counter.

'At least you've finally let someone in,' she says, placing her hand over mine.

'Eh?' Alex says.

Bridget rolls her eyes. 'I'm talking to Sam. You let every bugger in,' she says to Alex before looking back at me. 'I came back from work the other day and he had two Jehovah's Witnesses sat on the sofa. Anyway. You!'

'I did a little bit. But it reassured me that my decision to stay single was the right one.'

She eyes me suspiciously. 'I almost believe you, but I'm going to need an explanation.'

The sound of the blender cuts in as I try to organise my thoughts.

'Alex!' Bridget shouts over the noise.

'Sorry. I can't make frozen margaritas without blending the ice.'

I use the interruption as a chance to change the subject. 'Would you like to see some pictures from the trip?'

'Of course,' Bridget says. I take out my phone and open the camera roll, scrolling back to the start of the trip. She skips through them rapidly. 'Looks beautiful.'

She stops scrolling. 'Is this him?' She turns the phone around and there we are. It's the selfie Ethan took of us in Martha's Vineyard, wet through, in front of the 'No jumping' sign. Ethan's gloriously tanned, naked torso is on display, but that's not what's causing my chest to tighten. It's the carefree happiness in his eyes. It's not something I saw that much of, but when I did, his whole face lit up and it lifted me. To think I could be the reason for that look to be locked away again is too much to bear.

Bridget notices me staring at the picture. 'Why did getting close to Ethan make you realise being single was what you wanted?'

I swallow. 'Because it scared me.'

'Oh, honey.' She wraps her arms around me just as Alex places two margaritas down on the counter. She shoos him away and he disappears. 'Obviously, I never met Kev, but he doesn't sound like the sort of bloke who'd want you to stop living your life. I think he would have wanted you to meet someone who makes you happy. It's okay to let someone love you again.' Her words remind me of what Harry told me about Barney and how he was scared to commit after being hurt. Maybe I could try it again.

'I do feel like I'm the only person keeping Kev's memory alive, and it scares me that my memories seem to fade each day, and I'm worried that if I fall in love again, they'll fade altogether. But … I'm not just scared of forgetting about Kev, I'm scared of falling in love with Ethan and then losing him.' My voice is small and fragile. I've never confessed this to anyone before.

She squeezes me tighter. 'Oh honey, loving someone doesn't always end in tragedy and heartbreak.'

Maybe losing people has been my biggest fear all along.

CHAPTER 37

I stand outside the stone cottage I grew up in. Bridget was right. It is okay for someone to love me, so I thought it was a good idea to start with the only two people in the world who already do. A light is on in the lounge, even though it's morning. It always was a dark room. A shadow moves past the window. Could it be one of them? The longer I stand here, the harder it's becoming to force myself to walk down the short path and knock on their front door. I should just go. Too much time has passed and coming here was a bad idea.

'Samantha, is that you?' I turn my head to see an old lady I don't recognise straight away.

I narrow my eyes. 'Mrs Hanson?' I say to my old neighbour. She smiles kindly.

'Look at you. I'm glad to see you looking well.' She reaches out and squeezes my hand before walking down her own path. 'Nice to see you back.'

Before I have a chance to bolt back to London, the front door to my mum and dad's house opens, and my mum looks at me with pursed lips and a furrowed brow. For a few seconds we freeze, until her expression melts away. 'Sam?'

'Mum?' My voice wobbles. The sight of her is a number-twelve bowling ball heading for a strike and I'm the centre pin.

'Oh god, Sam.' She clasps her hands to her face and bursts into tears. Her shoulders bob and shudder. Then my dad appears by her side.

'What's up, love?' he says, putting his arm around her. She's still looking at my damp, tear-stained face.

He follows her line of sight. 'Sam?'

I twist my mouth in an attempt to smile but the muscles don't want to work.

My father dashes towards me and wraps me tightly in his arms. The smell of his familiar musky aftershave makes me feel like a little girl again in the safety of his arms. Emotion that's been welling up for the past eight and a half years is suddenly free. Sadness, guilt, absence. It's all there, soaking my dad's T-shirt as my body heaves it out.

My mum pulls me away from my dad. She wipes her face on her sleeve before cupping mine in her hands. 'We've been worried sick. Eight years of not knowing how you are or where you've been living and having to rely on a Christmas card to know you've not dropped off the face of the earth.' Her voice is laced with an understandable tremor of anger, and her eyes search mine for an answer I don't have.

'I'm sorry,' I sob. 'I just couldn't stand being here, reminded of Kev every single day.'

'We don't need to talk about this now. We're just glad to have you back,' my dad says. 'Come inside. I'll put the kettle on.'

My mum sits on the sofa, and I sit in the armchair by the window. 'I like your wallpaper,' I say. They've updated the brown and cream they used to have and gone for a modern grey and silver theme.

'Your dad did it. Needed to keep busy, you know.' She wrings her hands and glances around the room, unable to look me in the eyes.

'I know what I did to you and Dad was unforgivable. I wasn't thinking clearly.'

'You could have come to visit us. We were grieving for Kev too, you know, and then *you* left, it was like we'd lost you both.'

'I know,' I whisper. 'I was wrong, but I was upset about Kev. I wasn't thinking clearly and I was upset at you for what you'd said about him. I couldn't let it go.'

232

'We told you it was just meaningless chatter after a glass of wine. We loved Kev.'

'I know. I'm not upset about that anymore, I'm ashamed of how I reacted and I shouldn't have said those things.' I look down at the thick, grey carpet. A wide strip of which is worn down between the door and my dad's favourite armchair and I get a pang of sadness as I imagine him shuffling between there and the kitchen for fresh cups of tea. 'Once I got to London, I was determined to get through things by myself. I felt like you'd betrayed Kev and I didn't want your help coming to terms with his death. I shouldn't have called you controlling, you were just looking out for us and I've felt guilty about it ever since. Then, so much time passed, it got harder and harder to come and see you. I thought … I thought by then, you were probably better off without me.'

She furrows her brow and the corners of her mouth pull down. 'Don't ever say that.' She walks over to the armchair and perches on the arm. 'We were worried about you.'

She lifts her arm, and for a moment I think she's going to hug me, but then she puts it back by her side. *Too soon?*

My dad comes in carrying a tray of cups and a teapot. 'Tea is ready.'

'Thanks, Dad,' I say as he pours some out and hands me a cup.

It tastes just like it always used to. I haven't drunk tea since I left because the taste held too many memories, and now it's like I'm drinking them all up and it's a little hard to bear. 'I'm so sorry,' I croak, then start to sob again.

'You're here now,' my dad soothes.

'So, how have you been?' I look up at my mum, who is jutting out her chin. She's looking at my dad, and when I glance at him, he gives his head the tiniest of shakes at her. 'I know I've put you both through a lot of pain. I just … I meant otherwise.'

'We've been plodding along,' my dad says.

233

My mum looks at him, her face reddening. 'We had plans, as a family. We expected that, after a while, you'd come back for Sunday lunches with us. We thought there would be holidays, trips out and Christmases together. Eight years ago, you left us and took all of that away.'

'Jeanie,' my dad says in a soothing yet firm manner. I stand up. 'I shouldn't have come. I've made things worse. I'm so sorry.'

'You sit back down,' my mother says, and I do it instinctively, and for a second, I'm nine years old again. 'Now I may be angry and upset, but that doesn't mean I want you to disappear for another god knows how many years. We need to talk about it. Starting with where you've been and how you're doing. I know nothing about you anymore. You don't write much in those cards and texts you send. Are you remarried?' I shake my head. 'Kids?' She clutches the front of her sweater with anguish, and I'm glad I can truthfully answer no. If I'd robbed her of watching her grandkids grow up, I doubt she'd ever forgive me.

I tell them everything. How I'd felt angry with them for what they'd said and suffocated by the rest of the village, how I'd lost the only man I ever loved and how nobody else would compare. How I needed to be a tiny pin in a haystack in London, rather than a flashing beacon of sorrow in this village.

'It sounds like you've done well career-wise.' My mum is able to force a tight a smile.

'Yes, we're proud of you, love,' my dad adds.

'You know we never meant those things you heard us say,' my mum says again. Obviously the guilt has consumed her.

'I know, Mum. I was angry and upset and I think I turned part of my grief into anger.' I smile. 'I know Kev could be a bit of a bugger.'

Mum lets out a soft laugh. 'He was a good man.'

Dad and I nod, then there's a silence whilst we all sip our tea.

'So, are you with anybody?' my mum asks.

I shake my head. 'No, but that doesn't bother me. I've not

really been looking, either. I'm a widow, so I'm not technically alone – I have the wonderful memories of Kev to keep me going.'

My parents glance at one another, and as my words rattle around in my head, I realise how they must sound to Mum and Dad, two people who also knew Kev and haven't listened to me being stubborn about it for eight years. They sound, well, a bit crazy.

'Sweetheart, you have to move on,' my mum says, touching my shoulder.

'She's right, love. It's not healthy to think that way. Kev worshipped the ground you walked on. He'd hate to think you were doing this for him,' my dad adds.

'Kev only ever wanted you to be happy, he loved you so much, Sam. He'd be turning in his grave if he knew this. You're a beautiful woman in your prime, I can't imagine you've been short of offers.' My mum's eyes are full of concern, she must think I'm trying to punish myself or something. Suddenly, she lets out a small laugh. 'Remember that time he said if Ryan Gosling wanted to kiss you, he wouldn't stand in your way because "he couldn't compete with that" – he was joking, but later he told me he really wouldn't stop you because seeing your face filled with joy would be worth it.'

I think of Ethan, and my stomach twists.

I stand up. 'Mum, Dad. There's something I've got to do.'

My mum looks ashen.

'I'm going to come back soon, I promise. Let's go out for tea, my treat,' I say, dashing to the door. I glance back at them and bite my bottom lip. 'I love you both. See you in a couple of hours.'

'If I died, would you meet someone else?' I'm snuggled up in bed with Kev. There's frost on the outside of the window and the central heating is broken, so I know leaving the cosy duvet isn't going to happen anytime soon.

'That's a bit morbid for a Sunday morning,' he says, squeezing his warm body up against mine.

'But would you?'

'I don't know. Why would you even ask that?' Kev rubs my leg with his warm feet.

'Plenty of people talk about this stuff. I don't know, say I was run over by a bus tomorrow, would you *eventually* meet someone else?'

'I don't know.' He kisses me on my head and I snuggle up to him. The little spoon to his bigger one.

'Well, we're only young, so I suppose you would.'

'I'd rather not think about it.'

'What about if you were hit by a bus?'

'Why does it always have to be a bus?'

'I don't know, it's just an example of a random accident.'

'Then I could only hope and pray it was a Matchbox bus and not a big double-decker.'

I elbow him. 'Be serious.'

'I'd want you to be happy. I'd hate for you to be alone and sad. Obviously, not straight away or anything, but if you found someone who treated you right and made you happy, I wouldn't want you to push them away.' He squeezes me tightly.

'Me too.' When he puts it like that, I'd hate for him to be sad and miserable.

'Now can we talk about something else, like who's going to pop to the café for some bacon sarnies?'

CHAPTER 38

The iron gate creaks as I open it, like it could do with a good oiling. I follow the narrow lane round the bend and take the second footpath off it, which leads down the row of headstones where Kev's is. When I reach the vicinity, I have to squint to read four of the headstones to find his; each one is thick with green moss. I use my bare hand to wipe the one I think is Kevin's. It is.

I wipe a tear from my face as I take in the familiar headstone. White and crisp with a simple inscription:

KEVIN BUTTERFIELD
A light in the darkness.
Loved by many.
1980–2010

I wipe the rest of it and sit on the firm earth before it. There are a few dead flowers in a vase in front. The teddy bear his parents left after the funeral is long gone. They live in Spain and flew in for the funeral. I doubt they've visited his grave much but I imagine my mum pops over now and then and tidies things up.

'Eight years,' I whisper, sitting on the damp grass. The moisture soaks through the seat of my jeans. I only ever came here once, about a week after the funeral. I sat here for hours on the spongy earth that hadn't had a chance to compact. The brown, water-logged bear was surrounded by dying bundles of flowers, each with a generic message of condolence written in ink that heavy rain had caused to run. That's how long it's been since I was last here, preferring to remember Kev alive rather than as a piece of marble. 'Sorry I haven't been coming. I think about you every day though.'

The tired appearance of the stone reminds me of how much time has passed since Kev died. Ethan, Bridget and my parents are right. It is time to move on. I can't do anything, though, until this headstone is cleaned.

There's a Tesco Metro on the high street, so I head there and grab some essentials – cloths, a bleach spray, a bottle of water and some fresh flowers – and head back to Kev's grave. I spray the whole thing, wait a few minutes, wet my cloth and wipe. I repeat the actions several times until the stone is gleaming white again, then I replace the remains of the fragile, skeletal flowers with the fresh ones. It's like new now.

'To be honest, I was scared to come back here, Kev.' I stare at his name on the stone. 'I thought my memories would suffer if I kept reminding myself you were dead. When I was in London, it was just like I was working away. On a bad day, I could even imagine you at our house, waiting for me to come home.'

A couple walk past so I shut up, but I don't doubt for a second that they noticed me talking to myself.

'But all that time spent pretending you were here, in our old house, wasn't going to bring you back. It was just holding me in limbo.' Another couple walk by. 'I know you'd just want me to be happy,' I say quietly when they're out of earshot. 'You wouldn't want me to forget you, but you'd want me to move on. I know that.' I pause to rearrange the flowers. 'On some level, I've always known that. I just wasn't ready.'

I glance upwards searching for a sign but there's nothing but cloud above.

'I met someone, in Boston. It wasn't Ryan Gosling.' I let out a small, humourless laugh. 'It's over now but leaving him behind reminded me how happy love can make you, and I suppose it's opened me up to the idea that maybe I could love again.'

I look at Kev's grave, shining. One day that will be me. Do I really want to live my life alone only to become nothing more than a gravestone myself one day? Or do I want to take a risk and love someone again? Because falling in love is special and to deny myself that for fear of losing someone again is a ridiculous argument.

'I can love again. I should love again.' I stand up and pack everything away in my carrier bag before leaning over Kev's grave and kissing the cold stone. 'I'll never forget you though. My first love, you'll always be in my heart.'

***

I go and take a seat in the Teacup Café, which was a butcher's shop last time I was here. I'm pleased to see it's quiet, and an unfamiliar lady is serving behind the counter. I order a coffee and add a Florentine to the order as an afterthought.

I sit down and take the dolphin card out of my bag.

Dear Ethan,

There's so much I want to say, but I can't seem to get the words to assemble in my head. In the end, I decide to just write whatever comes first.

I should never have lied to you. The last thing I wanted to do was hurt you. I just knew that I couldn't take that job, so it seemed pointless discussing it. I didn't want to get your hopes up and it seemed best to bury the idea. The truth is, coming home has helped me re-evaluate a few things. I've come to realise that I can move on from Kev, and it's you who helped me to see that.

239

I'm running out of space, despite my squashed-up writing, so I have to go over onto the left-hand page. I draw a little arrow to show how the letter carries on.

> *You are a beautiful man, and leaving you was one of the hardest things I've ever had to do. Perhaps I should have taken the job and given us a try, but I still would have been in Boston, and I don't think it could have worked. Not whilst I still had issues to deal with.*
>
> *I just wanted to apologise. What I did cost me a proper goodbye with you and Lexi, and that's hurt me every day since I left Provincetown. I've written my address on the back of this card, but I'll understand if you don't reply.*
>
> *Live happy.*
>
> *Always.*
>
> *Sam xxx*

I read it through, but the words don't seem to convey the emotion that I want them to. I could throw the card away and buy a new one tomorrow, but there's no saying that I'll have better words then either, and I'll only keep putting it off. I just need to post this card and have done with it.

CHAPTER 39

I hadn't realised how lonely London could be. I'd always loved being part of the city set, walking purposefully at ten miles per hour and jumping on the tube with a flat white in hand. But just because there are people everywhere doesn't mean you connect with them. In fact, it seems that the more people there are around, the more people go out of their way to *not* connect. In the village, for instance, someone would spot a stranger from twenty metres and say hello and ask where they're from, just like they would in Provincetown. That small connection helps you to feel something for others, and that chips away at loneliness. It drove me away once, but now I see it as something wonderful.

I guess I'm feeling it more now because Bridget has got into a new routine and I don't have anyone to have fun with. The job in Boston seems so appealing, but had I taken it, I'd just be transferring my problems to another city.

My parents have invited me round for Sunday lunch. I agreed almost instinctively, but when I turn up, I'm nervous. My mum greets me kindly with a hug, and my dad looks up from his paper when I walk into the lounge and says, 'Hi, love.' It's almost as though nothing has changed in eight years. My mum refuses my offer of help, shooing me out of the kitchen to go and relax, because, 'There won't be much time for that in London.' I don't protest and tell her we have TVs and sofas there too. Instead, I sit uncomfortably in the lounge with my dad. Sky Sports is on. I want to change the channel, but I remember how he'd say 'Oi, I was watching that,' when I was a kid, despite being fully engrossed in the back pages of the paper. I pretend to be interested in whichever football teams are playing and try to ignore the noise of the crowd which is akin to tinnitus.

'Bill, can you set the table?' my mum calls.

'I'll do it,' I say, almost too quickly.

'Don't be silly, love, you're our guest,' my dad says, folding his paper up.

When he goes through the double doors into the dining room, I pick up the remote control and start to flick through the channels. The familiar smell of my mum's roast with all the trimmings fills my nostrils. A bouquet of nostalgia.

'Oi, I was watching that,' my dad calls, his back turned to the TV. I smile and put Sky Sports back on. Nothing has changed. I'm fifteen again.

'So, what are your plans, love?' my mum says once dinner has been served. She shovels a large piece of broccoli into her mouth.

'There's a teatime train I can catch from Oxford which will get me back to London at a reasonable hour,' I say, enjoying a bite of Yorkshire pudding soaked in gravy.

'I mean in life. Do you think you'll stay in London?'

'Perhaps. I'm not sure.' I hack at Mum's signature beef which she prides herself on cooking 'right the way through'. I never knew beef could be juicy and tender until I moved to London and discovered medium-rare.

'Are you happy there?'

She isn't prying, and I don't sense an ulterior motive in her tone, so I decide to be open. 'I have been, but since I got back from Boston, it doesn't feel the same.'

'Oh?'

'My friends have moved on a bit. It's nothing really. I think I just made some really good friends in Boston who I grew really close to and coming home made me realise how I don't really have the same thing here. Obviously, I miss the sun and beaches and stuff too.'

Concern is etched into the features of both my mum and dad.

242

'There's always room for you here, love,' my dad says, and my eyes prickle. I have to blink several times to keep the tears at bay. It's touching that he's said that, but I can't move back here. I'm glad to have a relationship with my parents again, but the thought of coming back to the village seems like a step backwards.

'Bill, it sounds like her heart isn't in the Cotswolds. It sounds like her heart is in Provincetown.' My mum gives me the smallest of smiles.

'I turned down a job there,' I blurt. Jeez, what's in these Yorkshires, truth serum?

'Why ever did you do that?' my mum asks. 'You've just said there's nothing for you in London anymore.'

'There was a guy. It's a bit complicated.'

My mum puts her hand on her heart and gasps. 'So you *have* moved on.'

'I don't think so. She's back here, isn't she?' my dad says.

'Rekindling my relationship with my parents, I think you'll find.'

'Hiding from reality more like,' my mum says. 'It sounds like you've made a huge sacrifice coming home just because your relationship got a bit "complicated", love.'

I open my mouth to protest, but for some reason, I can't seem to form a sentence that validates my actions. I'd never thought of my mum as insightful before. I don't think I ever listened to her.

'There's a chance the job would still be available, but I've only just found you guys again. I can't leave now. I have a lot of lost time to make up for.' I realise how much I mean those words.

'Honey, this time you'll keep in touch. This time we can visit you; you can visit us. This time we won't have lost you.' She reaches out and clenches my hand in hers.

My eyes sting again, and no amount of blinking can hold back the next torrent of prickly, salty tears. 'Thank you. I love you both,' I sob. 'I'm going to get in touch with Patrick and ask about the job.'

'Good for you, love,' my mum says.

'Why are you being so kind to me?' I can't help but ask. The last eight years must have been hell for them.

'You're our only child. We don't agree with what you did, but we understand. Sort of. We're not going to pretend that we weren't hurt by it though.' My mum shuffles slightly in her chair, and when she looks up at me next, her eyes are full of sorrow.

'I know. I'm so sorry for what I did.' The shame I feel is physically painful.

She shakes her head and waves her hand about in front of her face. 'You're here now. I just hope you've healed.'

I hadn't considered that. Am I healed? I got close to Ethan, so that must mean I'm heading in the right direction, and, recently, I've found myself thinking of Ethan even more than Kev. A wave of guilt hits me.

'Maybe,' I say. 'I went to Kev's grave last week. I've not been able to do that since the funeral.'

'So now maybe it's time to be happy again,' Mum says.

CHAPTER 40

It's been three days since I emailed Patrick, and a week and a half since I posted the letter to Ethan. Both should have been received by now, but neither have replied. It's put me on a floor of eggshells, smack-bang in the middle of limbo. The more thought I've given to moving, the more I believe it's the right thing to do.

'Sam, I've got a call for you,' our receptionist shouts across the open-plan office. For some reason, she'd rather yell than use the telephone system, and since I don't want to enter into a loud conversation about who it could be, I shout for her to put it through.

'Hello?' I say cautiously, hoping it isn't the CEO of that organic milkshake start-up chasing me for free logo designs again. I swear crowdfunding has a lot to answer for. Nobody wants to pay for anything anymore.

'Sam, hi, it's Patrick.'

'Oh, Patrick. Hello.' I sit up straighter in my chair.

'I got your email. Why didn't you just call?'

'I wasn't sure if the offer still stood and I didn't want to put you on the spot.'

'Don't be silly. We *want* you here. I thought I'd made that pretty clear. When do you want to start? I assume you have a lot to sort out.'

I think about it. My lease is just rolling monthly now. I have to sort things out with work, and the project I'm working on will take another month to see through. Then it will be close to Christmas, which isn't a great time to uproot. I should probably stay until after then, for my parents' sake.

'How about January? New year, new start,' I say, although I can't help but get a niggling feeling that Ethan will slip further away the longer I put off the move.

'January works for me. I'll make the necessary arrangements at my end, and HR will be in touch to sort out all the details. We'll also sort your accommodation, insurance and contracts.'

'Excellent.' Oh my god, I'm really doing this.

'We're excited to have you. I'm glad you changed your mind.'

246

CHAPTER 41

The streets are cold and still. Lined with cars parked bumper-to-bumper, which are unlikely to be driven until tomorrow. Almost every house is sporting a wreath, and twinkly Christmas tree lights are visible through most of the front windows. I dumped my easyCar about five minutes away, where I managed to squeeze the thankfully compact Fiat 500 into a tiny spot.

Struggling with my giant gift bag, I ring the doorbell and stand there patiently, as the aroma of cooked turkey somehow spills out.

'Hello, love,' my mum says, pulling me into a hug. 'Merry Christmas.'

'Merry Christmas, Mum.'

'Ho, ho, ho.' My dad appears wearing a fuzzy-felt Santa hat.

'Merry Christmas, Dad,' I say, kissing him on the cheek.

'Dinner is almost ready,' my mum says. 'Shall we eat first and do presents after?'

I'm shepherded to the table as 'Last Christmas' belts out from my dad's CD player. Three prawn cocktails, complete with Thousand Island Dressing, sit waiting on the same gold charger-plates I remember my mum buying from Wilko sometime in the early noughties.

'Let's eat.' My mum comes in from the kitchen with a bottle of prosecco and three champagne flutes. My dad sits down and holds out his cracker for me to pull.

'When is it you fly to Boston, love?' he asks, replacing his Santa hat with the purple paper one that has just fallen out of his cracker.

247

'The sixth of January,' I say. 'This prawn cocktail is good.'

'Thanks, darling.' My mum holds out her own cracker, and I pull the end weakly, ensuring that she wins. 'Come on, pull yours too.'

I oblige, even putting on my orange paper hat. 'Ooh, some golf tees,' I say sarcastically.

'I'll have them,' my dad pipes up.

'What do you call a line of men waiting for a haircut?' my mum says. It takes me a minute to realise she's reading the joke from her Christmas cracker.

'Oh, erm, I don't know.'

'A Barber-queue.' She chuckles whilst Dad and I groan.

'So, has it just been you and Dad for Christmas these past few years?'

'Yes. Pretty much,' she says.

'We went to the pub one year, but it was so overpriced we decided we weren't doing that again. Eighty-five quid a head, plus drinks.' My dad shakes his head so hard the underneath of his chin wobbles.

'What have you usually done for Christmas?'

'I didn't celebrate it for the first couple of years. I couldn't face it. Then, my friend Bridget forced me round to her house once she found out I spent Christmas alone and I've gone there ever since.'

'That was nice of your friend to make sure you weren't alone.' She smiles and stands up. 'I'll clear these plates and get the turkey out.'

'Have you got much to sort out for the big move?' my dad asks as he tops up my glass.

'My flat here is furnished and so is the one in Boston, so I don't need to worry about shipping sofas and things. I just have to pack up the rest of my stuff. Most of it I'm going to send over to Boston. The rest I can donate to charity.'

My mum starts bringing through steaming hot dishes of

248

sprouts, carrots, roast potatoes, stuffing and turkey, whilst my dad unscrews the lid on the cranberry sauce. It all smells delicious.

'What about your house here?' my mum asks, catching the tail end of the conversation.

I wring my hands under the table. 'Actually, I think it's time I sold it. I can't see myself ever moving back there, and I could do with the money to help get me set up in the States.'

Mum nods, but an air of sadness surrounds her.

'It just wasn't meant to be,' I add. 'Me in that house, building a family.'

'You still have time to build a family, love. You're not that old.'

'I know, and plenty of people do. I just don't feel like I could do the whole baby thing now. And let's not forget, I'd need a partner first.' My mum looks crestfallen but being an only child of parents desperate for grandchildren is a lot of pressure. Perhaps they should have given me a brother or sister and increased their odds a little. Of course, I don't actually say any of that.

Once we've eaten our Christmas pudding with brandy butter, we collapse in three stuffed heaps in the lounge, just in time for the Queen's speech. Which we listen to, in a fashion, as my mum makes her commentary about what the Queen *really* means by her comments on community and coming together.

'Shall we do presents?' I say ten minutes later.

'Good idea.' My mum gets up and walks over to the tree, where she picks up one of the gift bags.

'We had no idea what you were into, so I've put gift receipts in.'

'I'm sure I'll love whatever is in here.' I smile, taking out the first item, which is wrapped in red tissue paper. 'Slippers! I love them, thank you.'

'Let's have a look,' my dad says.

I laugh. 'You mean you didn't choose them?'

'I was at work earning the money to bloody pay for them,' he says.

'Fair point.'

'Open the next one.' My mum is on the edge of her seat, leaning forward in my direction.

I tear open the next package. 'Pyjamas! These look so comfortable. Thank you.'

'I just bought things you could easily take to Boston,' Mum says.

'I appreciate it. Thank you.' I hug her, and then my dad.

'Now, I've got you guys some presents too.' I start unloading my bag. 'I figured I missed eight Christmases, so I've bought you a present for each year I was gone.' Pangs of guilt bolt through me. I don't know if I'll ever stop feeling those. 'Plus one for this year. I know it doesn't make up for what I did, but I'm hoping it shows you how sorry I am.' I take the first two gifts, labelled '2010', and hand them out.

'I was feeling pretty low on the Christmas of 2010, so I figured I'd have bought you something sentimental. Open them.'

My mum tears hers open. It's a photo frame with a picture of me and Kev in. It had been taken by my mum during a meal about six months before Kev's accident. Mum had asked for a copy to put in a frame at the time, but I'd forgotten all about it. On the back, I've written a message, thanking her and my dad for trying to offer their support after I lost Kev.

My mum regards me with watery eyes. 'Thanks, love.'

My dad is inspecting his gift curiously.

'It's a spirit level. It was Kev's. I know he used to love helping you with DIY, and he'd have wanted you to have this. He'd have found it funny in his own dry way since he's now a spirit and all.' I shrug.

He gives a small, sad laugh, that comes out like a puff of air. 'He was far from level.'

'Okay.' I clap my hands together. 'Next.'

250

I pass out the envelope marked '2011'. 'This is the first year I was earning decent money, so I figured I'd have wanted to treat you both this year.'

'It's a minibreak to the Lake District, Bill.' Mum hands Dad the envelope. 'Thanks, love. I'll look forward to that.'

'2012 was a busy year for me, so I'd have probably grabbed something that looked nice on the shelves at Selfridges but required very little thought.' It's a Jaeger wallet for my dad and a purse of the same brand for my mum.

'These are lovely, Sam,' my mum says. 'But you shouldn't have spent all this on us. It's too much.'

I cock my head to the side and give her a meaningful look. One that says it's the least I could do. The side of her mouth curls into a tiny smile.

'In 2013, I had a thing for microbreweries.' I hand them some artisan beers, packaged in a neat little recycled box.

'In 2014, I did an Italian cookery course and spent three months eating own-cooked meals, made from organic ingredients from the best wholefood shop in London.' I hand them the heavy, wrapped cookery book. 'It's called *The Essentials of Italian Cooking*,' I blurt, as my dad turns it over in his hands. 'I had to find one that was already out in 2014 but I don't think cooking has changed much since then.'

'2015 was the year I tried to go plastic-free,' I say, handing them two identically shaped cylinders wrapped in gold paper.

'A water bottle!' My mum smiles. 'This will come in handy. Thanks, love.'

'And 2016 was the year I'd started hot yoga.' My dad's face goes from content to deeply concerned in record time. 'Don't worry, I didn't buy you a course of Bikram yoga. I made you a relaxation package.'

My dad opens the box, which has some bath salts, candles and a CD of relaxation music inside. He places a relieved hand on his chest. 'That's lovely that. Thanks, love.'

'Last year, 2017, I did my Christmas shopping in Edinburgh with a few friends, so I figured I'd have picked you up something like this,' I say, tossing them each a soft parcel.

'Tartan scarves. Fabulous,' my mum says.

I put my hand on my chest. 'That brings me to this year. This year, I spent a while in Boston and Cape Cod, and the place stole my heart. So, this Christmas, I wanted to get you something that would reflect that.'

'It's not a wrapped up cod, is it, love?' my dad says, shuffling nervously.

I hand them another envelope. 'No, but, in hindsight, that might have been a bit cheaper.'

'You open this one, Bill,' my mum says with a slight tremor in her tone.

Tentatively, my dad tears his thumbnail along the crease. 'Oh, my goodness,' he gasps.

'What is it, love?' My mum is already out of her seat.

'Return flights to Boston.' There's a tense pause as they absorb what the gift is. 'We will come and visit you, but we can't accept these, it's too much.'

'Well, I hope you do accept them, because they're non-refundable,' I say.

'Oh, love, thank you. Thank you for doing all of this. You didn't have to,' my mum says jumping up to give me a hug. 'I do feel like we know you a little better now though.'

'I know, I can't believe *you* did a cookery course.' My dad chuckles. 'Your mother only used to do a Sunday lunch because she was convinced it was the only proper meal you ate all week.'

'Hey!' I laugh. 'I was pretty good, I'll have you know. So, you'll come to Boston?'

They look at each other and smile. 'Of course we will.'

CHAPTER 42

The arrivals hall at Boston Logan International is swarming with people. It seems quite formidable second time around. Partly because I have so much more stuff, and partly because this time it's not just a three-month work jolly. When I've collected Coco, I heave my trolley to the pick-up area of the arrivals lounge, where a driver is waiting to take me to my apartment. It seems surreal. As we make our way through the rush-hour traffic, snow starts to fall. A yellow school bus pulls up beside me, pinching me into consciousness as I watch the red-faced children bounce energetically in their seats. *I'm really here.*

We pull up outside the apartment, the same one I stayed in when I was here last, only this time I'll have it all to myself. That is, until I'm on my feet, then I'll need to find a place of my own. The driver helps me up the steps with all my luggage. When I close the door, everything seems still until the noise from the city seeps in. I start to hang my clothes in the wardrobe and put up a few photo frames. There's not that much to unpack until the rest of my stuff arrives so I make a cup of tea. I'm desperate to see Ethan. I don't know what kind of response I'll get since so much time has passed, and he never replied to my letter. His silence speaks volumes, and part of me thinks I should respect that he's probably moved on, but I have to know. I can't head to Provincetown just yet because of work. The best I can do right now is settle in and focus on work. Coco wraps herself around my leg.

'You're not at all fazed by the move, are you?' I scratch her just under her chin, and she purrs with delight. I'm glad to have her with me. Home doesn't feel quite so far away.

I sit on the thick window ledge and glance out at the city. The months that have passed since I was last here have seen a wintery turn. Gone is the sunshine, glistening across the city. Instead, everything is white. The air is a frozen chill, though people are still wandering around, burrowed in their thick winter coats.

My phone buzzes.

Hope you've landed safely. Mum & Dad xx

I smile and tap out a quick reply, before I put my phone away and begin to unpack. I have the next day free to settle in before I officially start work, so there's a little bit of time to make the place a bit more homely and enjoy the city.

The next day, I have a bit of cabin fever so decide to take a walk. The snow has melted but the cold still takes my breath away when I step outside. It's what I need to wake up. I find myself ambling down to the harbour. The water is the colour of stone and the bustling crowds of summer are long gone. It's strangely peaceful and it gives me chance to reminisce about summer a little. I can picture the queue for the ferry and climbing onboard carrying excitement and anticipation in my stomach. It makes me think of Harry and Barney. I can't wait to see them, I've missed them so much. They never came over in winter as they ended up doing make-up at a theatre in Boston for a few months. We've sent emails and Skyped a few times, but they never mentioned Ethan and nor did I. I can't be sure if he'll give me the time of day when I do see him but I have to see him, I have to explain I was wrong and tell him that I love him. I shouldn't have needed to go back to England to realise that, but I did and I'm sorry and now I just need to tell him the truth. I run my hand through some water droplets, which have gathered on a railing. Maybe I could squeeze in a trip to Provincetown at the weekend.

CHAPTER 43

The bus takes an age to arrive in Provincetown, but when I'm finally here, I'm staggered by how different the place is. The buzz I'd become addicted to is now damp and calm; the bright rainbow of colour is now covered with a blanket of snow. I stomp through the cold, white crunchy stuff to the start of the Macmillan Pier. The beach to the left is covered with patches of white snow, and the water beyond a steely grey. A brave dog walker pulls his or her furry hood tight around their face to shield them from the elements. It's a little hard to believe that just a few months ago I was relaxing in a bikini at this very spot.

I'm desperate to surprise Harry and Barney. When they emailed to say they couldn't come to London, I was a little disappointed. I figured if they didn't come then, they'd probably never make it over and that would be that. As I head towards their house, my stomach starts to feel all twisty. They've been as friendly as ever in their emails, so I don't know why I can't shake this feeling of unease. Perhaps if I'd have just told them I was coming rather than making it a surprise I'd feel better. My mind keeps wandering back to Ethan, with it being winter and all, I don't even know where to find him. I never went to his house, and it's not like there will be much call for kayaking at the moment so I have to see Harry and Barney first.

The door to Harry and Barney's is framed by fluffy snow. There are a number of footprints up the steps and across the deck. I hope they don't have company. Tentatively, I knock on the door. I can hear voices coming from inside, laughter and music. Then the door swings open.

255

Harry's eyes goggle, and for a few seconds, he seems unable to speak. 'Sam?'

'Ta-dah!' I cast my arms in the air pathetically.

'What on earth are you doing here?' He steps outside and pulls the door to behind himself.

'It's a longish story and I'm freezing. Can I come in?' I try to peer behind him, through the crack in the door, but he blocks my view.

'Sam, it's great to see you, it really is and I'm so excited to catch up. It's just not really a good time right now.' He visibly winces as he speaks.

'Oh, of course. Sorry, I'm here unannounced. I just wanted to surprise you and couldn't wait to see you guys.'

'I'm so pleased you're here. Can we meet up tomorrow?' he says. 'It's just ... we have company, but it's not really an "invite everyone" type of thing.'

I look down at my frozen, snow-covered boots to mask the disappointment I know I'm wearing.

'Sorry, that didn't come out right. It's just—'

Suddenly, the door swings open. 'Honey, it's freezing! What are—'

Barney clasps his hands to his face. 'Sam? What are you doing here?'

'I just called to say hi, but I know you're busy. I'm going to catch up with you tomorrow.'

'Well, at least give me a hug,' he says, stepping into the snow with only socks for protection. 'It's so good to see you,' he whispers, and I fold into his familiar, cuddly warmth.

'You too. I'll see you tomorrow,' I say, turning to leave. As I do, I happen to glance through the lounge window. Not on purpose, and not because I want to be nosy – it's more of an instinctive reaction, involuntary even. *Ethan*. The quick glimpse I catch is enough to explain Harry and Barney's caginess. Ethan is with that dark-haired woman, Kimberley or something. She has her hand resting on his chest, and his arm is draped around her waist. There's a thud inside me as everything sinks. What did I expect?

I pull my coat tighter and carry on walking. I can feel my cheeks prickle with the heat of embarrassment despite the freezing temperature. Harry shouts that he'll text me about tomorrow. As they shuffle back inside, I hear Barney say, 'Poor thing. She looked like she'd seen a ghost.'

I feel like there's a kettlebell in my stomach as I trudge through the silent snow towards the hotel.

A few moments later, there's an energy behind me; slouchy footsteps and panting. Someone is jogging towards me.

'Sam?'

My heart stops. I recognise that voice.

I turn around to see Ethan standing there.

'Your nose is red,' he says. Of all the imaginary greetings I'd conjured up in my head for the first time we saw one another, that wasn't one of them.

'So is yours,' I reply, trying to be funny, but instead of laughing, his eyes search mine.

'What are you doing here, Sam?'

'Work.'

He nods. 'Another three months?'

'Actually, it's a bit more permanent than that.'

He lifts his brow. 'What?'

'I took that job Patrick offered me,' I say, kicking at the snow.

'Wow, congratulations.' He does that thing where he runs both hands through his hair, and it sends tingles through my stomach.

'Thanks. I just came to surprise Harry and Barney, but I didn't know they had guests. I never imagined it would be snowing in Cape Cod.' I chuckle nervously, and Ethan takes my hand. All the things I wanted to say to him dart around my brain but I'm too late.

'I'm sorry I never replied to your letter. I kept it though.'

'Of course you did. It had a dolphin on.' I wink, and he smiles.

'Exactly. Listen, I didn't reply because the only things I wanted to say I'd already said.'

'I know. I just had to apologise for lying. I hated thinking that I'd hurt you.'

He shrugs. 'I had a bruised ego for a few weeks, but in hindsight, you didn't owe me anything.'

'So, are you with someone now?' I force cheer into my tone.

He nods. 'Kinda. It's nothing serious. You were right about Harry and Barney and their never-ending list of friends. I had to reign them in once I told them I wanted to try dating again.' He laughs. The pain in my chest is unbearable and it takes every fibre of my being to hold back the tears which are about to surge from my eyes.

'I told you. I bet they had no trouble finding you a date.' I force a smile. Ethan has every right to be with someone. I had my chance and blew it. All I can do is pretend to be happy for him. 'Maybe they'll find me one now I'm in the state permanently.'

He pulls down the corners of his mouth and purses his lips. 'So, you're ready?'

'I did a lot of thinking back in England. I faced things head-on, got a bit of closure and stuff.' I notice Ethan is shaking beneath his thin wool jumper. The urge to take him in my arms and warm him up consumes me.

'Good.' He lets go of my hand and I let it fall to my side.

'You're freezing. Go back inside and enjoy your evening.' I put my hand on his upper arm and rub his bicep. *Damn*, I'd forgotten how thick they were.

'Look after yourself, Sam.'

He turns and heads back to Harry and Barney's, leaving me standing alone in the silent blizzard.

CHAPTER 44

Bang. Bang. Bang.

'I'm coming,' I yell as I towel-dry my hair.

Through the peephole I can see Barney chewing the corner of his nail. I open the hotel room door. 'Come in.'

'Sam, I need to talk to you about last night,' he says, plonking himself down on the bed.

'What about last night?'

'Harry and I loved you turning up out of the blue. We're both thrilled to have you back, and the surprise was perfect.'

'I know there's a but,' I say, folding my arms impatiently.

Barney exhales like he's forcibly evicting all the oxygen particles in his lungs at once. 'The thing is …'

'What is the thing?' Whilst I know this is going to be Ethan-related, I'm not sure exactly what I did or said to Ethan to cause Barney's grave expression. Evidently, it was something quite terrible.

'The thing is … Ethan …'

I want to shake Barney.

'He's been so happy these past few months—'

Ahh. 'And you don't want me coming along and spoiling everything?'

He ponders this. 'No, honey, no. That's not what I was trying to say. I just mean that seeing you may have stirred up some old feelings that he spent weeks trying to bury.'

'Dress it up however you like, Barney, but the sentiment is, you think I'm going to ruin whatever it is he has with Kimberley.'

Barney opens his mouth to speak, and I hold up my hand to

259

shush him. 'Save it. That's what you mean. But listen, Barney, I didn't come back over here for Ethan. I came out here because I loved my job here and the life I'd started to build. I loved spending time with you and Harry, the place is beautiful, and yes, I enjoyed my friendship with Ethan, but that is just a small part of it.'

'So you're not upset about him and Kimberley?'

I feel like a harpooned orca. 'I was a little surprised, but then that woman flirted with him at every opportunity. I'm more surprised it's taken so long, actually.'

'Ethan never noticed the flirting.' Barney laughs. 'It took me and Harry a whole evening to convince him that she liked him.'

'He wasn't really looking though.'

'No,' Barney replies quietly.

'How long have they been together?' I ask as naturally as I can.

Barney sucks the air in through his teeth. 'About six weeks. It's nothing serious.'

'That's what Ethan said. Maybe it will be, one day,' I say.

'It's certainly heading that way.' Barney looks up sharply, to gauge my reaction no doubt. 'I mean, well, you know – they get along. Kimberley is super-keen.'

Who can blame her? 'Barney, it's fine. I'm happy for them.'

'You are?'

What else can I be?

'Yes. Ethan deserves happiness more than anyone I know.'

'As much as you do.' He looks at me pointedly.

'My time will come.'

'What made you change your mind? About coming here, and relationships and stuff?'

I slump down on the bed beside him. 'I faced some of the issues I was trying to bury. I went back home, visited Kev's grave, made amends with my parents and put my old house on the market. When I was in London, I realised how little it actually offered me. What used to feel like a big plaster—' Barney furrows his brow '—Band-Aid,' I explain, 'felt like a downward spiral of hopelessness and loneliness when I went back there. Friends had moved on, and I felt so alone. I'd been so happy here, it's so full of colour and life, that it took the trip home to highlight how dull and meaningless my life actually was.'

'Well, when you put it like that …' Barney forces out a small laugh, like a puff of air.

'Sad, isn't it?'

'Listen. It can take people a lifetime to figure out what makes them happy. At least you've figured it out while your jowls are tight and you don't have cataracts.' He catches my puzzled expression. 'I just mean you're young enough to enjoy your life change.'

'You could have just said that. Now I'm worrying about jowls and cataracts.'

'Forget about that. Anyway, new topic, Harry and I are meeting Ethan and Lexi later to build a snowman. Would you like to come?'

'Will I be at risk of ruining Ethan's happiness if I do?'

'There's no need for sarcasm, missy.'

'Sorry, I couldn't help that one. I really don't think he'd want me to be there. Anyway, the answer is no. I'm happy to let Ethan get on with his life with Kimberley, and I'm heading back to Boston anyway.' That's a lie, because my bus is booked for tomorrow, but I plan to sit tight in my hotel room until then.

'That's a shame. There's a little girl who I just know would love to see you.'

My chest pangs. 'I miss her so much.'

'At least you're not on the other side of the Atlantic Ocean now. You'll see her soon enough.'

'I suppose. Anyway, enough of all of that. Tell me about you and Harry. What have you been up to these past few months?'

Barney and I chat for a good hour. He tells me all about their huge Halloween party and how he's lost ten pounds by following the juice cleanse.

'Oh, dear lord, is that the time?' he says suddenly.

'You'd better go. Snow-folk don't build themselves.'

He clasps his hands together. 'Are you sure you can't come?'

'Sorry, not this time. Maybe you and Harry could come to Boston to visit soon? I know it's a bit difficult now the ferry has stopped running for winter.'

'We can look at flights.'

'Super,' I say.

After Barney leaves, I flop on the bed. I don't feel like I expected to feel. I'm not sure if it's the change in weather, the fact I've been away for so long, or the fact that Ethan has moved on before we even managed to start anything. Really, it was silly to come back to Provincetown expecting everything to be the same. I expected to be, dare I say it, *embraced* a bit more. Now I feel a little bit ridiculous. Why would they? Anyway, I'm here to focus on my career and that's a huge, positive step for me. Things are exciting enough.

By mid-afternoon, I'm going stir-crazy. The last thing I want to do is go outside and risk bumping into anyone so I pace the room. When that gets dull, I go out on the balcony and then when that isn't enough, I wander downstairs to the reception. The place is deserted. Even the receptionist has gone off somewhere and it's a little unsettling to be so alone in a hotel. Horror story plot lines start to manifest in my mind as I glance around in search of life. I start off imagining that someone is watching me and within minutes, it progresses into full-on *Shining*-infused terror. That's it. I have to get outside.

I take the lift up to my room, grab my coat and decide to brave a little walk to blow the cobwebs away. Stepping outside is like being slapped in the face with an ice lolly, but I brace myself, put my head down and march on anyway. The sun is out and the sky is a cloudless blue, which was quite deceptive through the glass of the hotel room. Everywhere is dead. Commercial Street is closed, and there are just a few people sitting in the only open bar I've seen. I turn towards the pier and carry on walking.

'Sam!' a small voice screeches. And where I'd expect my stomach to twist, the feeling is more akin to being speared. I turn around to see Lexi running towards me before she collides into me. 'Sam, you're back.' She squeezes me so tightly tears press my eyes. I wasn't sure she'd remember me actually; we only met a few times, and she's so young.

'Lexi, it's great to see you,' I say. Realising that six-year-old children usually come with a parent, I scan the street behind her as my heart rate starts to pick up. 'Lexi, is your daddy here?'

'No, it's—'

'Lexi! There you are.'

Lexi freezes as a woman comes running over. 'Oops,' she whispers.

As the woman nears, I recognise Kimberley's dark hair. My heart sinks. 'You had me worried, young lady.' She takes Lexi by the hand.

'I just wanted to see Sam,' Lexi whines.

Kimberley looks at me and furrows her brow. 'Have we met?'

'I think we did briefly, back in summer,' I say.

'Oh, you're the English lady. I thought I recognised you.' She smiles but there is no real warmth behind it.

The English lady? 'That's me.'

'Well, it's lovely to meet you properly. Barney and Harry have mentioned you a few times.'

I smile tightly and indulge her as she holds out her hand to shake.

'Well, little miss, if we're going to finish our snowman before dark, we'd better hurry.' Kimberley readies herself to leave.

'But wait! Sam could come help us,' Lexi says. Kimberley flashes me a look that might as well have said 'Not even if my life depended on it'.

'Thank you, Lexi, but I can't today.'

'Why not?' She looks up at me, and I'm not sure whether she means to or not, but she looks so cute it's hard to maintain my resolve.

'I have to go back to Boston.'

Her face falls.

'Lexi, we need to go,' Kimberley insists.

'Will I see you again?' Lexi asks, ignoring Kimberley.

I crouch down so I can look her in the eye and take both of her hands in mine. Kimberley clears her throat loudly, but I ignore it. 'Of course you will. When I went back to England, I missed you so much. This is just a quick visit but I'm going to be living in Boston now, so it will be much easier to come and visit. Especially in the summer.'

'Good. I really like you, Sam,' she says. Her matter-of-fact tone doesn't fail to surprise me.

'And I really like you too.'

'Lexi.' Kimberley speaks abruptly and I raise my eyebrows with surprise. She must have noticed because she softens her tone. 'We need to finish before it gets dark. We can always just use the carrots I brought along for the nose, then we wouldn't have to go home.'

'Kim, our noses are made from the same stuff as the rest of our face, so why would a *snow*man have a carrot nose?'

'Okay, then we'll walk all the way home for a popsicle,' Kimberley says unable to keep her impatience at bay. 'But you do realise that none of the popsicles we have are the same colour as snow, so the nose will still be different to the face.'

'Your nose is red, but your face isn't. I'll use a red one,' Lexi states. At this point, I'm trying my best to stifle a grin.

Kim sighs. 'Fine, but there's no su … Do you know what? Let's just go get the popsicle and get back to your dad and the others.' She takes Lexi's hand. 'Bye, Sam.'

'Nice to properly meet you,' I say without conviction.

Running into Lexi feels like I've been whacked in the abdomen

264

with a bag of spuds. I was just coming to terms with Ethan's relationship and how happy he is, but the vibes I got from Kimberley weren't great. I'm sure she was just tired and cold. She's probably very nice.

I head back to the hotel and soak in the bath until the water no longer feels warm. As I'm wrapping myself in my towelling dressing gown, there's a knock at the door. My heart thumps in my chest. It's probably Barney coming to catch me out, but at least I have a good explanation.

I swing the door open and freeze on the spot.

'Sam.'

I swallow hard.

'Ethan. What are you doing here?'

CHAPTER 45

My hands tremble at the shock of seeing him.

'Lexi told me she bumped into you.'

'Did she tell you I was leaving?'

'Yup. So did Barney. Only there are no buses running today. You know these things when you rent out cars for a living.' He takes in my dressing gown and wet hair. 'Can I come in?'

I stand aside to let him pass. When I turn around, I find him looking at me.

His head is tilted to the side and the look in his eyes is so intense, it envelops me.

'Sam, seeing you last night threw me.' He rubs his hands over his face.

'I'm sorry. I didn't think my coming here would be a big deal.'

'It isn't.' He shakes his head. 'Wait, no, it is. It's great to see you.'

What is he saying? 'Why has everyone gone completely weird all of a sudden? Is it the snow?'

'It's you.' He takes a step closer, the way he looks at me sends a shiver down my spine.

'I'm sorry,' I say again. 'I'm leaving for Boston tomorrow, and we don't need to cross paths again.'

He takes my hands and wraps them in his. 'I don't want you to leave again.'

His words shimmy across my skin leaving goose pimples in their wake. I think I know what he's saying but I have to be sure. He's with someone else after all.

'But, Barney said ... Ethan, what's going on?'

'Forget what Barney said. When you left, I tried to move on, and for the past few weeks I've been happy. I thought my life was going in the right direction … but seeing you last night blindsided me.'

'Ethan, I didn't know. In England, all I could think about was you.' The words sound foreign on my lips. It's been over eighteen years since I said anything like that to anyone new.

He intertwines our fingers, and I relish the warm tingly feeling as he presses his forehead to mine. 'You should have put *that* in your letter.'

'When Kev died, people used to say to me "it will get easier" and I'd "move on". But the truth is, I didn't notice things get easier. To cope with the grief, I'd resigned myself to staying true to our marriage vows, it helped me get through the initial pain but then I became so absorbed in it, I shut people out and didn't allow myself to move on. I didn't notice things had gotten easier. When I went home, I visited his grave and it gave me closure. The timing was bad but what the heck.' I smile unconvincingly.

I have to stop this, only this time I'm not the reason why. He's with someone else. 'It just wasn't not meant to be,' I say.

Instead of backing away, Ethan puts his hand on my cheek and leans forward and presses his lips against mine. The rush I get is addictive, impossible to tear myself away from. Soon, our mouths find their rhythm, and the familiar comfort that comes with it.

Then Ethan pulls away and his big zaffre-blue eyes meet mine. 'Why now? Why didn't you come back sooner?'

'I had to sort things out. Otherwise I could never have moved on, not properly.'

He places his hand under my chin and strokes my cheek with his thumb. 'Did you come back for me?'

'No!'

Not that I'm going to admit now.

Instead of the relief I expect to see on his face, he rubs the back of his neck with his hand, and I see something more akin to disappointment.

'Ethan, look, I really like you, and perhaps I did come here hoping we could pick up where we left off. But I also came back for the job, and the place, and to see Harry and Barney. Don't think that my being here has to make things awkward between us. I know that I messed up and you're with Kimberley now, I don't want to jeopardise that. Apart from the kissing, just now.' I glance up at him shyly.

'The kissing was good.' He flashes a wicked grin that tingles through my chest.

'But wrong,' I say, glaring at him.

'Kimberley and I are not that serious,' he says.

'It doesn't matter. I don't want to ruin what could be there. You should give your relationship a chance. She seems nice.' Impatient, but nice.

'But—' His phone starts to ring. 'It's Kim. Listen, do not leave town. I've got to go, but we're not done talking.'

They're close enough that he calls her 'Kim', close enough that he can't ignore her call and close enough he leaves her alone with Lexi.

'Goodbye, Ethan.'

268

CHAPTER 46

The next day I drag my bags through what's left of the snow to the Chamber of Commerce, where my bus will come in. Hopefully. Ethan never came back last night. I imagine that once he saw Kimberley, he fell back into routine and felt guilty about our kiss. He'll have been trying hard to push me out of his mind no doubt. I'll be glad to get back to Boston and put this whole sorry trip behind me.

I can see the coach coming. A few more people with wheelie suitcases form a line behind me. When the doors of the bus open, I'm first to climb into its warmth. I get comfortable in my seat and take out a true crime book, which is probably what caused my irrational fear and, in turn, all the trouble yesterday. I wouldn't have felt the need to leave the hotel if I'd been reading a good old Sophie Kinsella book. The driver closes the doors and then the engine rumbles to life. I feel relieved to be leaving.

All of a sudden, the coach stops, and the doors open again.

'Can't people just be on time?' I hear a lady near the back grumble. I can't say I disagree, but I'm happy enough reading my book. It's a long trip and a few moments delay is hardly going to matter.

'Is this seat taken?'

Of all the empty seats on the bus. I snatch my bag off the spare seat with irritation but then the voice registers. 'Ethan?'

He slides into the seat next to me. 'Hi.'

'What are you doing here?'

'I have to be in Boston tomorrow to catch a bus,' he says casually. 'Thought we could ride together.'

'O-kay.' I draw out the word. 'How come you never mentioned this last night?'

'It's a last-minute thing.'

I eye him suspiciously but don't say anything.

He rummages in his rucksack. 'I've brought chips.'

The thought of a bag of chips doused in salt and vinegar rouses me, mmm. I'm slightly disappointed when he produces a sharing sized bag of crisps. Silly me.

'Anyway, four hours is a long time to be stuck on a bus,' he says.

It depends how the conversation goes. 'I know.'

'After I left you last night, I went to see Kimberley.'

'Oh?'

'She's a really wonderful person – kind, attentive, great with Lexi …'

I don't believe this. Is he really here to tell me how wonderful Kimberley is? Is he just trying to justify his choice? The thought is nauseating.

'That's great, Ethan. I'm pleased you've found one another but you don't have to explain.'

'Sam.' He leans forward, forcing me to look at him.

'What?'

'I'm trying to tell you something here.' He takes hold of my hand, and the familiar zings of electricity snap between us. My eyes meet his. 'She's great, and I felt really bad telling her that I had feelings for someone else.'

My hearts leaps. I almost ask who, but I'm not that stupid. Instead, I swallow my words.

'Sam, it took meeting you to make me want to have a woman in my life again. Kimberley told me that she'd wanted to date me for ages but I'd ignored her. It took you to change that. You made me want to be with someone again. Only *someone* isn't enough. I want *you*.'

Dancing butterflies multiply and fill my insides. 'What are you saying, Ethan?'

'I'm saying I want us to give things a go. I want to make us work.'

I'd not noticed how long his hair had got. It's wavy and flops down past his ears. It suits him. 'Ethan, I want it too.' Tears start to form as I smile. 'I want to take a risk with you.'

Ethan squeezes my leg and leans in to murmur, 'I'm here for you. Always.'

I kiss him on the lips. How did I get so lucky? Again. Ethan pulls me closer and kisses me harder, his hand sliding higher up my leg. My lower abdomen stirs with something unfamiliar and I start to feel very hot. Then the coach comes to an abrupt stop.

'Hyannis,' Ethan says. 'We have to change here for Boston.'

'Well.' The word comes out all breathy. 'The driver should have made a timely announcement.'

Once we've taken our belongings off the coach and we're waiting for the next one, I remember Ethan said he had to catch a bus tomorrow and can't help but feel a little deflated we can't spend more time together.

'What bus do you need to catch in Boston?'

'Oh.' He looks sheepishly at his feet. 'It's the mid-morning bus back to Provincetown. Can't miss that.'

For a moment I'm puzzled. 'What do you mean?'

'I booked this bus so I could have a chance to talk to you. If I'd have known how easy it would be to win you over, I could have just booked the bus to Hyannis.' Mischief plays on his mouth.

'If you're needing a place to stay in Boston, I suggest that you're nicer to me.'

***

It's late when we finally reach my apartment. We spent the whole coach journey talking, and nothing feels more right than taking him back to my apartment. I glance at his overnight bag. 'Where were you planning on staying?'

271

'I had no idea. But I couldn't let you walk away again.'

'Come here.' I pull him in to me and kiss him. As I run my hands down his defined, firm torso I find myself wanting more. Bravely, I slip my hands under his sweatshirt and help him wriggle out of it. Then I kiss his warm chest, breathing in the familiar citrusy scent of him through the fine sprinkling of hair as I do. The feeling of his hands running down my back and cupping my bottom is heavenly. He picks me up and I wrap my legs tightly around his waist.

'Go into the bedroom,' I whisper, pulling his earlobe gently with my teeth.

'Are you sure?'

'Yes, I'm ready.'

***

When the golden morning sun streams through my window the next day, I snuggle into Ethan.

'Morning,' he whispers into my hair.

'Morning,' I say back, stroking his chest. For a while, we both doze off again.

'Ethan?' I ask later.

'Mm?' he says sleepily, a sign of a good night, if you ask me.

'How will this work?'

He turns onto his side to face me. 'I know you need to be in Boston. We can work it out. We saw each other plenty through the summer. We can both travel back and forth. If we want it to work, then it will.'

'I want this to work,' I say, and I mean it.

I kiss his chest, and for the first time in a long time, I'm happy. I'm not scared of being with Ethan anymore. 'I know.'

He kisses my forehead, and I can't think of anywhere I'd rather be.

EPILOGUE

Summer

'Mum, Dad!' I scream as they emerge, bewildered, from the arrival's hall at Boston Logan.

'Hello, love,' my dad says, giving me a squeeze.

'Look at you, all tanned and beachy looking.' My mum gives me a kiss on the cheek. 'Who is this then?'

'I'm Ethan.' He holds out his hand to shake but my mum pulls him into a cuddle.

'Good grief, feel the muscles on this one, Bill. You could learn a thing or two.' She winks.

There's a cough. 'Ahem,' Lexi says patiently holding out her hand. My mum and dad turn to her and when she has their attention, she introduces herself.

'Oh, look how adorable she is, Bill,' my mum says.

'You're a little love alright, aren't you?' My dad smiles at her and shakes her hand.

'It's a pleasure to meet you,' Lexi says. I'm still in awe of her confidence.

'Shall we get to our house then?'

Ethan takes my parents' cases as we shuffle through the airport to where we've parked our car. We've rented a Suburban for the week while my parents are here and have both taken time off work to show them the sights.

'Please excuse the mess,' I say once we're on our way to our house in Quincy, which is on the outskirts of Boston. 'We've been working flat-out since we moved in and haven't unpacked yet.'

'That's fine, love. We'd have been happy in a hotel.'

'Nonsense,' Ethan says. 'You are family.'

I get a warm twinge inside at the word 'family'. It's taken me a long time to get one, but now I have it. Ethan, Lexi, my parents and not to mention Ethan's parents who've been great. When Ethan decided to go back into marine biology, it made sense for him to move to Boston and although it was quite soon, it made more sense to live together for childcare and financial reasons. Lexi loves our new home and settled in well at her new Elementary school. Ethan's mum comes and stays a few nights a week and we spend most weekends in Provincetown, which means Lexi gets to see her old friends too. Now it's warm again, Barney likes to gather people each weekend for a cookout and Ethan's mum cooks on a Sunday. Having my parents here completes the picture and the swelling in my chest feels like my broken pieces have been stuck back together.

'Here we are,' I say, as Ethan swings round onto the driveway.

'Wow,' my mum says, taking in the view of Boston Harbor from the front of our house.

'You should come up to the veranda,' I say, taking her by the hand and pulling her inside. We go upstairs to the first floor where the lounge and kitchen are and I pull back the folding doors to expose the large decked balcony.

'This is wonderful,' my dad says coming in behind us. The vast harbour is golden under the warm sun. We live on a narrow road and just across from the house is a stairway down into the water. When the tide is out, Lexi and I go and collect pebbles but right now, it's in and perfect for swimming.

'Take a seat and I'll make some drinks,'

As I place ice cubes in tumblers, Ethan snakes his arms around my waist and kisses my neck. 'Your parents seem very sweet.'

My chest pangs. 'They really are.' I spin round to face him. 'I have you to thank for having them back in my life, you know.'

He kisses me on the forehead. 'You reached out and admitted you were wrong. That's all you, baby.'

'Baby?' I smirk. 'That's a new one.'

'I'm just feeling the love today. What can I tell you? I'm happy!'

The doorbell rings. 'I'll get it!' Lexi screams.

'Hello, I'm Barney.' He makes a beeline for my mother. 'Now you, young lady, must be Sam's sister.' He kisses her hand and her cheeks redden as she smiles coyly. I shake my head and fill the tumblers with some fresh mango and orange juice that I blended earlier.

'Hey, honey.' Harry gives me an awkward kiss as I balance the tray of drinks in the kitchen. 'Look at him.' He points out of the window to Barney who is talking animatedly to my dad. 'He's in his element with new people. Before I go and say hi, do you need a hand?'

'I'm fine thanks, Harry, go and sit down.'

As Harry goes outside, I take a moment to watch them out of the window. Harry is already talking to my mum, Ethan and Lexi whilst Barney is still chatting away to my dad. Zac and Cindy arrive with their new baby, Lilly, and suddenly everyone is desperate for a cuddle, I smile as my mum gets in there first – like anyone else stood a chance. If Bridget could be here, I'd have all my loved ones together in one place. It's hard to describe how complete I feel. When I used to think about Kev, the happiest of memories were always tinged with gut-wrenching sadness, but now, I find myself thinking of him with pure fondness. It's weird how I thought my memories were enough to keep me happy. It's taken finding real happiness to see that. It's okay to love Ethan and still remember my love for Kev. I know that now. Ethan, Lexi and I marked the anniversary of Nicole's death a few months ago by sending a white rose out to sea and we're going to think of a way to mark the anniversary of Kev's death when it comes around next month.

The smell of the barbecue brings me round and I carry the tray of drinks outside.

'Here she is,' Barney says, standing up to give me a hug. I raise my eyebrows in confusion. 'I was just telling your dad all about the Ethan rollercoaster you went on last year.'

'Thanks,' I say dryly before giving my dad a sympathetic look.

'Anyway, I was also telling your dad that we could go whale-watching and maybe have brunch at our house and do some cycling and take a trip to Nantucket and—'

'Barney! Calm down,' says Harry. 'They're not here to see you, they've come to spend time with their daughter.'

'Uncle Barney, the tide is in. Will you take me swimming?' Lexi asks before he gets a chance to look downhearted.

As the two of them go off to swim, Harry goes to help Ethan with the barbecue and I finally get to sit down with my parents.

'You've got a lovely life here,' my dad says, patting my knee and I know it's his way of acknowledging that I can make good decisions for myself.

'I know. Things have finally turned around.'

'We're so glad to have you back in our lives,' my mum adds. 'I just wish it hadn't taken you so much time to discover happiness again.'

'I know, but if I'd have rushed it, I wouldn't have Ethan and Lexi.'

'That's true. Us parents just want to see their children happy.' I wonder if that's my mum's way of apologising for being too involved all those years ago. I give her a warm, meaningful smile.

'Right,' my dad says. 'I'm going for a dip too. Are you coming, Jeanie?'

I glance at my mum; there's no way she'll get in.

She glances out to where Barney and Lexi are splashing about with squeals of delight. 'Oh, go on then,' she says. I giggle as they both go off to change.

Harry and Ethan are stood drinking beer by the grill. The sun is lower now and deepening in colour. Swaths of yellow, orange and pink are cast across the bay. There isn't much swimming time left. I take a sip of my juice and enjoy the all-encompassing feeling of contentment. When I look down at the water, my dad jumps in with a splash and my mum is ankle deep, stood rigid on the step. I think she's about to change her mind when Barney takes her hand and yanks her in with a splash. She's laughing when she comes up for air. I smile. I have everything I need.

I have my second chance at happiness and I feel like the luckiest woman in the world.

Acknowledgements

As always, it takes many fabulous people to pull a book together and this one was no exception. Firstly, Cara Chimirri, thank you for your honest, constructive feedback, knowledge and incredibly helpful editorial notes. Secondly, Kia Thomas, thank you for your invaluable critique notes. Thirdly, thank you Dushi Horti for correcting all of my mistakes, typos and randomly strewn commas.

The book wouldn't exist at all if it wasn't for my publisher, HQDigital, so thank you for believing in me for a sixth time and for designing such a wonderful cover.

I'd also like to thank my army of supportive writer friends for their virtual hugs, humour and for always providing great procrastination fodder. Rachel Burton, Sarah Bennett, Maxine Morrey, Rachel Dove, Lucy Knott, Darcie Boleyn, Audrey Davis, Mary Baker and Rachael Stewart. There are so many more who know who they are. Finally, I want to give a huge shout out to the bloggers who have been so supportive in trying to help get my little books into the hands of readers. You rock!

**Turn the page for an extract from *It Started with a Note*
by Victoria Cooke …**

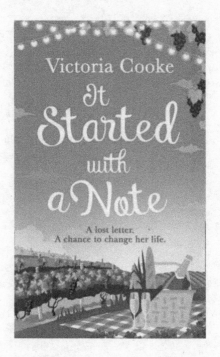

CHAPTER 1

I clutch the envelope tightly to my chest – so tightly, in fact, my nails tear into the crumpled paper, which has been softened by my sweaty palm and the relentless downpour. I release my grip slightly. It's too precious to damage, but I'm so scared of losing it. I feel like one of those mad scientists in a James Bond film who has developed a mini nuclear warhead and has to transport it somewhere with the utmost care to avoid detonating it at the wrong time. I'm not sure comparing myself to a villain is wholly accurate, though. Perhaps I should have laid it on a velvet pillow or something, like a prince carrying a glass slipper. Yes, that's better – a prince, not a villain. A princess? *I shouldn't be in charge of something like this.*

As I scurry down the high street, the eyes of passers-by rouse suspicion. *Do they know what I have? Are they after me?* I walk faster, heart pounding. It's difficult because my bloody shoes are killing me. Pleather. Man-made leather. Plastic-leather *pleather* sandals – a bargain at £12.99, but seriously, I've already spent double that on plasters for all the blisters they've given me.

The quicker I walk, the harder my bag-for-life bashes into my legs. Dented tins of peas, beans, stew and whatever else I'd salvaged from the 'whoops' shelf after work all unleash their fury on my shins. It isn't uncommon for certain staff members to accidentally-on-purpose cause a few *whoopsies* themselves. Not me, of course; it's a sackable offence and I can't risk losing my job since I'm the sole breadwinner in our house and my baby boy has just gone off to university so I need every penny.

Thirty-seven years old and I've already packed my Kieran off

283

to university while most of my friends are waving their kids off to high school. It makes me feel so *old*. When I looked that handsome six-foot-two beanpole in the eye and kissed him goodbye, I blubbed like a baby. He was still my little boy, even if I had to stand on my tiptoes to get close enough to grab his cheek. Of course, he'd just grunted and wiped the residue of tears, snot and my kisses off on his sleeve almost instantly. *Boys*. He's turning into his uncle Gary.

I'm still scurrying, every step causing me to wince in pain. Bag-for-life. *Bash*. Sandals. *Chafe*. And so continues the pattern as I dash through the town centre towards the bus station. Rain is forecast, thunderous downpours no less – an amber weather warning had been issued by that gorgeous weatherman, David Whatshisface, on the TV. He could make any weather seem bright and cheery. *I'd weather his storm.* I chuckle to myself, not even sure if that would even make sense to anyone other than me.

A deafening roar rips through the sky. *Uh-oh.* I try walking even quicker. *Bash, chafe, bash, chafe.* I don't have a brolly, though I know they're unwise in a thunderstorm anyway – David said so. I can see the bus station in the distance all lit up in the dusky evening like a heavenly portal to refuge. Just one busy road, several passers-by eyeing me (I'm still suspicious), and a plume of smoke from the smokers outside the pub to negotiate and I'll be home and dry, literally.

Just as I allow myself to dream of being home, the heavens open. Of course they do. They couldn't have waited just five more minutes – where would be the fun in that? The rain is so heavy it soaks through to my skin almost instantly. My denim jacket is leaden with liquid and the nylon of my uniform is soaked. I'm cold and sticky and my feet are squishing about in my sandals, squelching with every step. The envelope is getting quite soggy now so I stuff it into my handbag and tuck my bag tightly under my armpit for safety.

I slow my pace, unable to keep it up because my mascara and

foundation have run straight into my eyes, partially blinding me. I wipe them with the back of my hand and notice it's streaky black when I pull it away. *I must look a sight.* I've reached the road and the cars are coming thick and fast. Headlights, taillights, headlights, taillights. *Gap.* I make a dash for it, landing in a huge puddle by the kerb as I do. Brown water droplets dribble down my American Tan tights. *Why didn't I wear trousers?* David promised rain!

I make it across the road and begin negotiating the shrunken smoke plume, which is now concentrated to the little canopy above the door. My task is made all the more difficult by the next torrent of foundation and mascara liquid streaming down my face. The smoke makes me cough and splutter and I'm flapping my arms about as best I can with a one-ton carrier bag on my arm and a stiff denim jacket shrink-wrapping my body.

As I near the edge of the smoking circle, I bat the air one last time – one time too many for my so-called bag-for-life, which bursts open, spewing bargain tins aplenty all over the pavement. As I scan the devastation, I notice that the pesky little pokey thing you never quite know how to work has fallen off the corned beef tin. *Typical.*

I never swear.

Ever.

But if I did, Hells Angels would blush at the words I'd choose right now.

'Cath, you idiot!' I mumble instead.

A tatty-haired man bends down and starts to pick up the tins and I follow. Warmth in my chest grows from the seed of his kindness. He has a lit cigarette in his mouth and the smoke from it is so close and raw that it's burning my nostrils, but he's kind enough to help so I do my best to ignore it.

'Thanks, love,' I say, my voice thick with implied gratitude. He just nods and hands me four of the five tins he's picked up. I look at him, confused, as he stuffs the corned beef in his pocket and shrugs. The rain is beating down still, pummelling into my bag, and I'm shaking with the cold. Or shock. Before I can organise my thoughts and string together a sentence of scorn, he's stubbed out his cigarette and vanished back into the pub taking my tea with him. As my eyes sink to the ground, I spot the glinting little silver twisty thing off the corned beef tin, and it's mildly satisfying to know he'll never get to enjoy my tin of deliciously processed meat.

Striking corned beef hash off the menu tonight would be one more thing for Gary to moan about. Still, I have the envelope and no amount of whinging from my freeloading brother would change that. Hearing those words in my head makes me feel a little guilty. I'm supposed to be helping him, supporting him, but instead, I'm slowly losing my patience with him. I make it to the bus station and can see my bus has pulled in at stop number sixteen, which is right at the other end of the station, of course. I start running. I'm holding my shopping in two arms, cradling it like a precious baby so I don't lose any more tins. *Gary will have to have the stew.*

Just as I approach stop fifteen, there is a miracle. My bus is still in! *Thank God!* I slow to a walking pace, panting – the smoke, the bus fumes and the fact I haven't done any exercise since my last year eleven PE lesson all contributory factors.

Juggling my groceries, I stuff a hand into my bag, fumbling for my purse, which I locate quickly, and glance down at it to find some bus fare. The rumbling sound of the bus engine coming to life alerts me to the fact it's about to leave. I have no choice but to barge past the people queuing at stop fifteen and pop my head and arm outside; I wouldn't make stop sixteen. I'm waving frantically, balancing my precious tin baby in the other arm. 'Please stop.' The headlights get closer, but they're gaining speed. *Please stop.* 'Stop!' I yell.

He doesn't stop.

The next bus comes an hour later.

CHAPTER 2

When I finally arrive at the end of my road, I'm trembling, battered, and bruised, and all I've done is commute home from work.

The off-licence near the bus stop is open, and I have an idea to salvage the evening. My spirits are still high; I still have the envelope and I'm almost home. I plonk a bottle of cava on the counter and rummage in my purse for six pounds.

'Celebrating tonight?' Jim, the owner, asks.

'Ooh, yes I am.' I can't help but grin. 'But I can't tell you why – I don't want to jinx it.' I smile and give a little shrug.

'Well, whatever it is, you enjoy it, love.' Jim smiles back. 'How's that brother of yours doing?'

I want to offload and explain how exasperated I've become with him, how he never helps around the house and has yet to find a job, but I find myself unable to. I don't know if it's embarrassment or loyalty, or a complete unwillingness to bore the lovely Jim to death with my woes.

'He's good,' I say instead.

'Glad things are working out.' He smiles. 'I told him he could have a few shifts here to tide him over, but he said he thought things were looking up.'

Oh, did he now? 'Yes, apparently so,' I say.

Jim smiles again and hands me my penny change, which I pop into the charity box by the till.

When I finally make it through the front door, relief embraces me, tighter than my shrink-wrapped jacket. I'd make tea, then pull out the envelope and ask Gary if he'd help me celebrate, we'd have the bubbly and then I'd run a nice hot bath, putting that awful journey home behind me. Perhaps I'd book a meal for us at the weekend, at that new pub in town. I could even ask Kieran to come over and make it a real family affair. It would cheer Gary up and I'd quite enjoy the company and change of scenery. I smile dreamily as Gary approaches me.

'I'm goin' down the pub,' he mumbles, barging past me and causing a few tins from my precariously balanced bag-for-life to tumble to the floor.

My heart sinks. Gary always goes out for an evening drink, so it was silly to feel so deflated when tonight is no different. I should have expected it, and it wasn't like he knew I had exciting news to share with him. I contemplate asking him to stay in but as I turn around, the front door slams shut in my face.

At least I could have a bath and then make tea in my own time; that was something. My feet sting as soon as the bloodied blisters hit the hot soapy water, but the rest of my body needs a soak just to warm up because apparently it would have killed Gary to pop the heating on. The house is like an igloo and will take a good few hours to warm up. As much as I love him, I could batter him with a cut-price baguette at times.

After my bath, I heat up the tin of stew and butter some bread, which has started to go a little hard. It isn't mouldy thankfully, but bread never does seem to go mouldy anymore, which is a little odd come to think of it; I wonder what on earth goes into it nowadays. Still, this piece is okay – it just isn't deliciously fresh. I could have brought some deliciously fresh bread home if Gary had managed to send a simple text message to let me know we needed some. I shake my head as I take a bite.

I'd taken pity on him after our mum died. It had hit us both hard as we never knew our father and she'd been both mum and dad to us. I was so close to Mum and she was always there for me and Kieran – so much so that I'd never felt like a single parent. Gary was close to her too and after she died, he'd sunk into depression. He'd already lost his girlfriend, and a year or so after Mum died he lost his job too, but two years have passed since she died and I shouldn't need to be looking after him anymore. I'd let him move in about six months ago while he got himself back on his feet, but so far he's not displayed any signs of getting a job and moving out, and he only uses his feet to walk to the pub.

I place my bowl and bread on the kitchen table and remember the bottle of cava in the fridge. Celebrating alone seems a little sad but what choice do I have? A little glass wouldn't hurt, would it? One now, and perhaps Gary would have a glass with me when he got back from the pub, I reason. Maybe we could even have a chat about him moving out if he comes home in good spirits. The bottle is disappointingly warm despite having sat in the fridge for a good few hours. The blooming thing has two settings: frozen and lukewarm. I've asked Gary a million times to look at it for me or call someone out, but evidently, it's been too much trouble for him.

Remembering how fast corks can pop, I take a tea towel from the drawer to catch it in; I'd seen someone do that before at a party. Placing the towel over the cork, I begin to push at it with my thumb as hard as I can. It isn't budging so I place my hand over it, trying to ease it out, but the thing is stuck fast. I try my other hand: more wiggling, more pulling and even a twist here and there, but it is no good. I even hold the bottle with my thighs and try with both thumbs but it's useless and my hands are red and sore. Resigned to the fact I won't be having a glass of bubbly, I dump the bottle on the side and put the kettle on instead before sinking into the kitchen chair, where I cry.

I hate myself for it because I try so hard to be upbeat and positive, no matter how hard things get, but sometimes things pile up and the weight becomes too heavy to bear. It's not just the fact I've had an awful journey home or that I lost my corned beef. It's the fact that I've never complained about my life being samey and unadventurous in all the years that it has, but the one time I try to brave something new, the cork just won't pop. I can't help but wonder if it's a sign from the gods to quit trying and just accept my fate. I let out a small humourless laugh through the tears before wiping my face and finishing making my tea.

The house is still and quiet but I'm not in the mood for watching TV. I miss grumpy Kieran barging through the door, hungry, as he always is. Like most teenagers, he spent much of his time in his room, but just knowing he was up there was a comfort. I could always make an excuse to pop in and see him, to offer him a drink or collect his dirty laundry and if he was ever out, I always knew he'd be coming back. Now the emptiness of the house is a feeling rather than a state and it's odd. But that doesn't mean I want Gary to stay; he needs to rebuild his own life. It's just something I'm going to have to get used to. No son, no Mum, no Gary. Just me.

The stillness thickens and prickles my skin. I'm sure it's emphasised by the sad deflated attempt at a celebration. Needing to busy myself, I have an idea.

Kieran's lifetime collection of junk is still cluttering up his room. It's all stuff he hadn't deemed important enough to take to university but apparently felt was fine to leave in my house. I decide I'm going to have a good sort-out. What's that saying? Clean house, clean mind? I shake my head – that doesn't sound right at all; I've always had a clean mind and no amount of mess in Kieran's room could change that.

My emergency stash of cardboard boxes from work come in handy once I've rebuilt them and filled them with Kieran's junk. Old school books, piles of posters kept under his bed, superhero figurines he hasn't played with in ten years and some board games that probably have most of the vital pieces missing.

My loft hatch is stiff, but the stick I keep for opening it still works if I really yank it, and the steps come down easily after that. *That's something at least.* I climb them, pulling the light cord when I reach the top. I clamber over the boxes I'd already stashed up there and feel a little bit of guilt at the fact I'm just as much of a hoarder as Kieran. I pick up a box to make some space and when the recognition of it registers, I have to sit down. For a moment, I just look at it.

After Mum died, I'd inherited this box. It contains all her little keepsakes: things that Gary would have never wanted in a million years. He was more interested in the sandwich toaster and the little retro DAB radio she had in the kitchen. I know what's in the box but I hadn't been able to bring myself to open it yet. I was too heartbroken and now I feel terrible because I'd forgotten all about it.

I cross my legs on the dusty boards and wipe the lid clean before lifting it. There's a photo of me and Gary lying on top, which was taken when I was about five and he was eight. I take in my plaited pigtails and brown corduroy dress and can vaguely remember the day. Gary is wearing brown velvet jeans and a red jumper and is looking at me with disdain. We'd been to a park and he'd pushed me over and I'd grazed my knee. He was angry because I'd snitched on him to Mum. God bless the Eighties.

My father had walked out about a year before that picture was taken and whilst I barely remember him, I do remember Mum's smile that year. It was always there, plastered on, oversized and exaggerated, but her eyes didn't crinkle in the corners. It wasn't until I got older I realised how hard it must have been to maintain that brave face for us and I wish we'd have behaved much better for her.

I continue to rummage. There is an old concert ticket for Boy George in the box, football match programmes from when she used to take Gary to watch Tottenham Hotspur, and my first pair of ballet slippers. Right at the bottom is an old wooden matchstick storage box that I don't remember ever seeing before. I pull it out and examine it curiously. It's quite intricate in its design, and I wonder why it hadn't been on display at home. It

291

was the kind of thing Mum would have loved to show off on her mantelpiece.

I take off the lid and inside the red-velvet-lined box is a stack of ancient-looking notelets, each one yellowed and fragile. My heart is beating in my eardrums with anticipation. They are certainly old enough to have been from my dad all those years ago. *Perhaps I'll finally discover where he's been for all those years.*

Hesitantly, I take out the top one and carefully unfold it. The date at the top strikes me hard: *1916.* I have to double-check it before reading on, confused.

7th February 1916

My dearest Elizabeth,

This is the farthest I've ever been from home, and I can tell you, France is almost as beautiful as the Home Counties. Perhaps one day, when the war is over, I can bring you and Rose here. The war is going to last much longer than we'd hoped, I'm afraid. Who knows how long we'll be knee-deep in muck for.

I hope Rose is looking after you. I know how you worry, but I'll be fine. We're working quite closely with the French and I've even been learning a little of the language. I'll teach you both when I get home.

Avec amour (I hope that's correct)

Yours,

Will

My eyes begin to burn a little and a ball forms in my throat. This is a letter to my great-grandmother from my great-grandfather. I remember my mum telling me the story of how her grandfather volunteered to fight in the First World War. He'd been killed in Belgium I think. Her mother, my grandmother, was five years old at the time and hadn't really remembered him, something I could always relate to. Naturally, my mother didn't know too much about him other than that he was twenty-four when he died.

Kieran bursts into my mind. He's not much different in age to what my great-grandfather had been. I try to imagine him going out to war. The thought of it twists and knots my insides, and I can't fathom how the mothers of the WWI soldiers felt, waving their sons off to war.

Of course, Kieran wouldn't have survived the boot-polishing stage, never mind the trench-digging and gunfire. I love him to bits, but he's a bone-idle little so-and-so, a trait that must be from his father's side. I couldn't imagine why a twenty-four-year-old man with a wife and daughter and his whole life ahead of him would want to go to the front line for the king's shilling. It was so brutal and horrific, but I suppose back then people did it for their country.

I read the letter again; the part about him wanting to take my grandmother and great-grandmother to France stands out. My grandma never even had a passport, never mind visiting France. That makes me feel sad – that one of the only surviving pieces of communication from her father said that he wanted her to see France, and she never went. Granted, there was another war soon after the first, but my grandmother lived until the late Eighties and still never made the trip.

I take out the next letter, which is addressed directly to my grandmother. The date is too faded to read but I can just about make out the intricate penmanship.

My dearest Rose,

I hope your mother is well. I miss you. I hear you've grown somewhat. You'll be as tall as me when I come home. When I return, I'll have many stories to share with you. As I write this, I'm on leave looking out on luscious green fields with red poppies and blue cornflowers growing. It's quite the picture

beneath the blue summer sky. You'll have to see this one day.
It's 'un lieu de beauté' as the French say. I've picked up a bit
of the language.

Some of my comrades have taken up poetry. It's not some-
thing I'm good at, but I'll send you a poem as soon as I get
the chance.

Take care, my darling.
Yours,
Daddy

The letter squeezes my chest. Something about the upbeat tone
suggests he really did think he'd return home – or he was putting
on a brave tone for his daughter. Hindsight paints a tragic picture
of a happy family destined for heartbreak.

There are a few more letters and, strangely, some are written
in French. I place them all back inside the box carefully and make
a note to ask someone to translate the others when I get a chance.

The letters play on my mind all evening. Knowing my grandma
never went to France in the end saddens me somewhat. I'm a lot
like she was: a homebody, unadventurous and happy in the safe
familiarity of where I've always lived. But it was her destiny to
travel to France, or at least it *should* have been, and that thought
is still weaving through my mind when Gary returns, partially
inebriated, from the pub.

'Have you been buying posh plonk?' he asks, picking up the
bottle of cava and inspecting it as he walks in.

'I … err … yes,' I say, no longer in the mood to celebrate.

'Two glasses, eh?'

I remain silent.

'One was for me, wasn't it?' he says with a small laugh. Like
it's so implausible that I'd have company round. 'You don't have
twenty quid I can borrow since you're splashing out on fizz, do
you? I've had a lot of outgoings this past fortnight and I need
something to tide me over until my next JSA payment.' He pops

the cork with ease and pours two glasses of fizz into large wine glasses since I don't own fancy flutes.

The hair on the back of my neck bristles and I take a deep breath to ensure what I say next comes out nonchalantly. The last thing I want is an argument. 'No news on the job front yet?'

He pauses, and his face reminds me of a Transformer as the different muscles pull together almost mechanically to arrange some kind of pained expression. ''Fraid not. They don't seem to be able to find anything to match my skills. Twenty years I worked as an engineer and I'm not going to throw away that kind of experience sweeping school corridors or stacking shelves. No offence.'

I'm far from offended, but I'm very close to cross. 'Well, maybe you'll have to.' I maintain an even tone. 'You're spending more than you have coming in and it's a vicious cycle. Jim said he'd offered you a few shifts so you might have to take him up on it, or I can see if there's anything going at my place if you like?'

'Cath, look, I'm waiting for the right job.' There's agitation in his tone. 'If I take up a few shifts with Jim, my JSA will stop and I'll be worse off.'

'You can work at my place while you're waiting for the *right job*. You could work full-time there.'

'Oh yeah.' He lets out a dry, humourless laugh. 'And get stuck there like *you* did because there's no time to look for anything better once you've been suckered in. What is it you've been there now? Eighteen years?'

His words sting and I glare at him. It's true. I was bright at school, did well in most of my GCSEs and even got my A levels in English Literature, history and media, but after falling pregnant I needed money for the bills and the shift patterns worked well for me with a baby. 'I think you've had too much to drink,' I say eventually, standing up to leave.

'Aren't you drinking your plonk?' he says, oblivious to how he's made me feel.

'You have it, it's warm anyway,' I say before storming out of my own kitchen. Hot tears well in my eyes. Not through sadness, but through embarrassment. Embarrassment that he feels he's better than me despite spending the last half a year in a parasitic state. Embarrassment for thinking he'd be pleased for me when I showed him what I had in the envelope. And embarrassment for not standing up for myself.

I hate how he makes me feel as if he thinks everything I've done is insignificant – but I've raised a child, I've always paid my way, and I've saved him from the streets. I may not have an engineering degree, but I like to think that being a good person counts for something. I know it's his circumstances making him so bitter, but it's still hard to take. He's a good person underneath and I'm sure he'll find himself again.

I just don't want to be in the crossfire.

It's time for him to leave.

Dear Reader,

I just wanted to say a huge thank you for taking the time to read *A Summer to Remember*. I visited Massachusetts a few years ago and after falling in love with that part of America, knew I had to set one of my books there. Provincetown in particular was a place that I really connected with because of its seamless blend of vibrancy and tranquillity. I really hope that comes through in the book because it is such a wonderful place.

If you've read any of my other books, you'll know that travel features in them all, from Scotland to Miami. I love swapping travel stories so do get in touch and let me hear your thoughts if you've ever visited any of the places mentioned in any of my books – you can find me on Facebook, Twitter and Instagram.

Reviews long and short, good and bad are incredibly valuable to authors. They let us know how we're doing, how we can improve and give us warm fuzzy feelings when people like our work. If you can spare a few minutes to leave one on your chosen retailer's website, I'd love to hear your feedback.

Finally, thank you again for your support in purchasing this book and, if you liked it, please check out my others.

Best Wishes,
Victoria Cooke

Dear Reader,

Thank you so much for taking the time to read this book – we hope you enjoyed it! If you did, we'd be so appreciative if you left a review.

Here at HQ Digital we are dedicated to publishing fiction that will keep you turning the pages into the early hours. We publish a variety of genres, from heartwarming romance, to thrilling crime and sweeping historical fiction.

To find out more about our books, enter competitions and discover exclusive content, please join our community of readers by following us at:

🐦 *@HQDigitalUK*

f *facebook.com/HQDigitalUK*

Are you a budding writer? We're also looking for authors to join the HQ Digital family! Please submit your manuscript to:

HQDigital@harpercollins.co.uk.

Hope to hear from you soon!

ONE PLACE. MANY STORIES